GW00728040

SKELETON ISLAND

GLADYS MITCHELL

Skeleton Island

SEVERN HOUSE PUBLISHERS

This 1985 edition from SEVERN HOUSE PUBLISHERS LTD of
4 Brook Street, London W1Y 1AA
First published in Great Britain 1967 by Michael Joseph Ltd

Copyright © 1967 by Gladys Mitchell

British Library Cataloguing in Publication Data

Mitchell, Gladys
  Skeleton island.
  I. Title
  823'.912[F]   PR6025.I832

  ISBN 0-7278-1188-6

Printed and bound in Great Britain by
Butler & Tanner Ltd, Frome and London

*This story is dedicated,
with very much love,
to my brother
Reginald
and his wife
Elizabeth*

CONTENTS

The title and quotations
are taken from
Treasure Island
by Robert Louis Stevenson

CHAPTER ONE

Wrong-Angled Triangle

'Keeping nothing back but the bearings of the island.'

So-called, since in all but the wettest and wildest weather it was connected with the mainland by a causeway built high on a wide bank of shingle, the island presented itself to two of the travellers as outlandish. It was an enormous outcrop of limestone rock which, in past ages, had been in truth an island until the flung-up pebbles had piled themselves into an isthmus which joined it to the rest of the coast. It rose steeply from the causeway to a height of five hundred feet and then fell gradually away to a waste land of naked crags at its southernmost point. Past these the sea swirled madly, even in the calmest weather, and the boiling waters were marked on old maps as *The Race*.

The car climbed slowly round the hairpin bends until it reached the highest point of the island. Then its owner said to its driver, a boy of nineteen:

'Pull up a minute, Colin. One gets a good view from here.' The speaker was a middle-aged, ineffectual man named Howard Spalding. The boy was his son by his first marriage. The other person in the car was Howard's second wife. The vantage point he had selected offered the wide, unlovely prospect of a stony, almost treeless land. Northward, the direction from which the car had come, lay the mighty bank of shingle against whose intractable menace unwary ships could beat themselves to death in winter storms. To the east was the splendid curve of the principal bay. Away to the west the cliffs fell sheer to the sea, their face as cleanly perpendicular as the drop of a plummet line.

The car pulled up on a verge of grass bounded by a freestone wall. The man got out, unslung the binoculars he carried and rested his elbows on the wall to rake the landscape through

9

the lenses. The boy remained at the wheel and turned his head to address the woman who was on the back seat of the car.

'Want to get out and look at the view?' he asked. She shook her head.

'By the time we've been here a year I'll have seen enough of it,' she said.

'God, yes!' He turned his head again and stared moodily out through the windscreen. 'By the time we've been here a year! Why couldn't he let me go up this autumn? I'm perfectly fit again now. And where are we going to live? I'm not having you pig it in some beastly insanitary cottage. And what on earth shall we *do* here?' He continued to glower upon the uninviting prospect ahead.

The time of year was early March. Except for a few sad crocuses there had been nothing of colour in the front gardens of the stone-built houses of the only town on the island. Once clear of it, disused quarries, and quarries still in production, had formed the features of a bleak, grey, windswept landscape. The sky itself was grey, and a tumbling, sullen sea had broken, snarling and foam-flecked, on the western side of the causeway over which they had passed to reach the island.

'I don't know what's in his mind. I never do,' the woman said. 'We must be prepared to make the best of whatever it is.'

'It's all very well for *him*! He's got his bird-watching and his book to write. But what on earth is there in it for *me*?'

The woman made no reply. She wound down her window and looked at the unfriendly countryside and then at her husband's narrow shoulders and the grizzled back of his head. He put the binoculars into their leather case and came back to the car.

'Better be moving,' he said. 'There's plenty to do. When we've unshipped the gear, Colin and I have to take the car to the garage and then walk back. Not much fun if we have to do it after dark.'

'Well, you were the one who wanted to stop off and look at the view,' his son said sharply. He let in the clutch and the car moved forward down the slope. 'Why are we going this way? I looked at the map and there's nothing south of all this except a few cottages and a couple of lighthouses. Why two, anyway?'

'Ah,' said his father, 'that's where my big surprise comes in! Just wait until you know what it is!' His childishness never failed to irritate his son.

'Oh, for heavens' sake!' he exclaimed. 'We're not children going to bed on Christmas Eve!'

'I only hope you're not going to land me with an impossible job,' said the woman.

'An impossible job? How do you mean, my dear?'

'Well, you paid off Minna and the char – not that they'd have come to a place like this! – so what do we do for servants? Can you get in some local people? Have you made any arrangements?'

'Arrangements?' He was genuinely surprised. 'I don't think we'll need any help. You'll see what I mean when we get there, and, after all, there are three of us. It will do Colin all the good in the world to hew wood and draw water for a bit. Build him up. Strengthen those muscles of his. He's no end flabby after all those weeks in hospital.'

'Thank you,' said Colin bitterly. The road which, although well-surfaced, all along had been narrow, now became narrower still and, for the first time, in need of repair. Colin slowed down. His stepmother leaned forward.

'You surely haven't rented one of those tiny cottages?' she demanded. 'You *know* we must have three bedrooms.' (She had not shared a room with her husband since the second year of their marriage.)

'A fisherman's cottage? Why, of course not, my dear. The fact is, I've rented a lighthouse.' He was too single-minded and self-centred to be able to interpret correctly the silence of incredulity which followed on this announcement. 'You see, the first lighthouse, the one you see nearer to us, was put up in 1789, or so I'm told – and it was discarded years ago as being out of date, so they built a modern one further out on the Point. Somebody bought the old one and now lets it, furnished, to visitors. I know you're going to fall in love with it, Fiona. Think of the sheer romance of seeing nothing but sea and sky!'

'But – all those stairs!' said his wife, her dire dismay adequately indicated by her tone. Her husband, genuinely astonished by her lack of rapture, exclaimed:

Skeleton Island

'All those stairs? Bless my soul, little woman, the stairs are no problem! The lighthouse isn't built on a sea-girt rock. It's on land, and there are modern living-quarters at ground level. You can't see much of them from here because of the high stone wall, but it's just an ordinary bungalow, that's all, and, as I tell you, it's fully furnished.'

'I suppose it's been empty all the winter and the beds will need airing before we can sleep on them tonight,' said Fiona, by no means mollified by hearing of the amenities of the place. Colin said nothing at all, but his actions spoke for him as he pulled up the car with a vicious jerk and a squeal from the brakes, at a door in a white-washed wall. He got out and the others followed.

'So this is it,' he said, gazing up at the lighthouse tower. 'Well, it's a good thing some of it is on the ground floor. You won't catch me climbing that thing.'

'No, of course not. I intend to do my bird-watching from the gallery and shall be glad to be undisturbed. Besides, with your poor head for heights, you certainly mustn't venture. We don't want a repetition of the scene we had with you on the fortifications at Dubrovnik. I really thought we should never get you down that outdoor staircase,' said his father, chuckling. Colin looked murderous, and Fiona said quickly:

'Never mind about that staircase, Howard. There's no need to be so superior. It terrified *me* – let alone people with no head for heights. You should never have started Colin off by daring him to climb it. People can't possibly help having no head for heights. It's like claustrophobia or having a horror of cats. It's . . .'

'Oh, for *Pete's* sake!' interjected Colin, restrained from using a stronger protest only by the fact that it would have been directed at the woman with whom he was violently in love. 'Let's get inside and know the worst, can't we?'

The inside was clean, well-cared-for and adequately furnished. The living-quarters consisted of two double and two single bedrooms, a living-room and a large square kitchen. Gas was laid on, since the lighthouse lantern had been lighted, when gas was first introduced, by a gas mantle behind a highly magnifying glass screen. There was no bathroom, but there was a zinc bath hanging from a hook on the scullery wall, and a gas water-heater of fair dimensions had been fixed above the sink.

'Well, we had better be off, if we're to get back here before it gets dark,' said Howard, when he and his son had unloaded the car. 'There is a gas fire in every room and the gas cooker in the kitchen, so I think you'll be all right while we're gone, my dear. Rustle up a meal from our stores. We shall be the best part of a couple of hours, I expect.'

'Why, how far is it?' asked Colin.

'Oh, a matter of four or five miles,' said his father, in an off-hand tone.

'Four or five *miles?* Do you mean we've got to walk all that way every time we want to use the car.'

'We shan't be using the car. When we choose to go out we shall go on foot. I am putting the car away in one of the lock-ups at that hotel we passed a mile or so this side of the town. All arrangements are made. I have only to get the car there and ask for the key to the garage.' He sounded, as usual, self-satisfied.

'Do you mean to say that we're going to be *marooned* on this beastly island?' Colin demanded.

'We should use the car in a case of emergency, of course,' said his father weakly. Colin detected the change of tone.

'Well, I'm not coming with you. I don't fancy walking five miles after driving the car all day,' he said sharply.

'Please yourself, my boy. I thought you might like to stretch your legs and get the lie of the land, but I shall quite enjoy the walk back by myself. Tonight I shall climb to the gallery, if the sky is clear, and study the stars. There is always something worth while if one takes the trouble to find it.'

'Rebuke noted and digested,' said Colin to his stepmother when his father had gone out to the car. 'What do *you* think?'

'I think he's very patient with you,' she replied. 'Go and put on the gas fires, and then you can help me air the bedding. We shall have to chance the mattresses, except yours. Whatever happens, you mustn't catch another cold, darling.'

'Oh, do stop making an invalid of me! Come here! I'll soon show you whether I'm flabby or not!' He stepped up to her masterfully and took her in a clumsy, powerful, inexperienced embrace.

'Oh, Colin, stop being silly!' she said, not attempting to struggle. 'You really are quite fatiguing. Do grow up. Go and light those gas fires, and use your muscles by spreading out the blankets and things. I don't want to start our new life by getting a cold in the head, any more than I want you to. And Howard with a cold in the head is completely disgusting, as you know.'

'If he's going to spend his time on the lighthouse gallery, he'll have a perpetual cold in the head,' said Colin, dropping his arms and kicking the rug. 'Oh, Fiona, we could have such fun by ourselves! You don't realise how deadly it's going to be here. Why won't you let me love you? I'm younger and stronger than he is, even if I *am* afraid to climb up a flight of stairs.'

'He *has* got your goat,' said Fiona, offering neither resistance nor submission to another clumsy and smothering embrace. 'You're still such a baby, you know, Colin. You think you've only got to scream loud and long enough, and you'll get what you want.' Colin dropped his arms to his sides again, then caught her as she lost her balance.

'Damn you, Fiona!' he said. 'I shall have you in the end, whatever you think! You're going to be *mine*, I tell you!' He turned on his heel, a gesture rendered void dramatically as he caught his foot in the rug and had to stagger in order to keep on his feet. She watched him go, a tall, thin boy who needed a haircut and who had not shaved since early morning. She rubbed her cheek, half amused and half touched by the calf-like nature of his love-making.

'The gas fires and the bedding!' she called after him. 'And don't put things near enough to scorch!'

CHAPTER TWO

Change of Air

'Then there followed a great to-do.'

Some sixty miles from the island the scene was vastly different. There were snowdrops and crocuses out in the Stone House garden in Hampshire. In the woods nearby the catkins already hung golden with pollen from the hazels. Blackthorn was out, and so were the almond trees at the gate. The first bright green was on the hawthorns. The ash was still in resolute black bud, but the elms were heavy with flowers.

Laura Gavin was seated in the Stone House parlour. With her was her friend Alice Boorman, who was spending the week-end with her. It was Sunday. Alice was due to be driven back to Norwich. Laura was to take her there, stay the night and return in her own time on Monday.

'I hate all and every one of Mrs Croc's beastly relations,' grumbled Laura. 'A whole six weeks she's going to be away. What on earth shall I do with myself at this time of year?'

'Pop over to Paris or the south of France, or somewhere. You can afford it, can't you? Paris is lovely in the spring.'

'Yes, I know, but this is just the term when frightful prep. schools start an epidemic, so I must be on hand in case they send Hamish home. He never catches anything, so they might just as well keep him, but they won't.'

'You ought to be thankful he's so healthy.'

'Well, of course I am. I want something to do, that's all. Dame Beatrice hasn't left me any work. We finished the final draft of her last book and sent it off before she went.'

'What is it? Anything useful to me at school?'

'I shouldn't think so. It's called *Abnormal Behaviour Patterns in a Multi-Racial Society*. It's a sort of prophecy about what would happen to our brains in a generation or two if all

15

races were completely integrated. Terrifying stuff – what I understood of it.'

'Well, I think that sounds interesting. Look here, if you're really at a loose end, why don't you move into the Kensington house to be near your husband for a bit?'

'I shouldn't be near him. He's been called to an Interpol jamboree in Switzerland and, even if I could leave England, he wouldn't want me around.'

'But he won't be over there long.'

'Won't he, just! They're going all over Europe to catch up on one another's methods. You forget that he's an Assistant Commissioner now. I think they have to keep finding him things to do.'

'Well, why not get yourself a job?'

'I've got a job.'

'Yes, but you say you can't get on with it at present, and you know Dame Beatrice doesn't care what you do, so long as you're happy and don't actually break your neck.'

'Well, what sort of a job could I get?'

'Teach on Supply.'

'What, a fortnight in a school here, and three weeks in a school there – boys, girls, infants, the lot? No, thanks! I should go off my head.'

'Well, look, I'll leave the *Times Ed.* here for you. I've finished with this week's number. Come on. We'd better get cracking. I've got some indoor athletics stuff to tabulate before I go in tomorrow morning.'

'Do it here, and I'll type it out for you. Then you can stay for lunch.'

'No, I want to get back before dark. Besides, I haven't got it all here. Anyway, the school secretary will type it. I want her to roll off some copies for the teams.'

'All right. I'll get Henri to put us up a picnic lunch and some coffee, then. That will save time on the road. We can cook when we get to your flat.'

Back at the Stone House on the following evening, Laura ate the delicious dinner which the solicitous Henri sent in by his wife Celestine, and, disconsolate because she missed her employer, her mentor and friend of long standing, Laura picked up the paper which Alice had left behind and turned her attention to the advertisements.

'Not that I'll apply to teach,' she said under her breath.

'Madame?' said Celestine, who was clearing the table.

'Oh, nothing,' said Laura. 'I was only talking to myself.'

'The resort of the lonely and sad at heart,' said Celestine, with the easy sentimentality of the French.

'You reduce me to tears!' said Laura. Left to herself, she turned over the vast number of pages, skipping through the lists of advertised teaching posts.

Wanted for the summer term ...

Wanted for next September ...

Applications to the undersigned ...

Apply by letter to the headmaster, giving references.

Attach copies of recent testimonials.

No testimonials, apply etc. etc.

If willing to assist with games ...

Ability to teach Russian to G.C.E. 'O' level a recommendation.

State subsidiary subject.

An interest in out-of-school activities ...

At last she came upon an entry which she read a second time. Then she put the paper aside and took up a book, but it failed to absorb her, and very soon she picked up the paper again, re-read the short advertisement, dropped the paper on to the floor and went to the telephone.

'Would you mind if I took a temporary job while you're away? ... No, only until Easter. You won't be back before the end of April? ... Righto, then, I'll apply. Of course, I may not get it ... Yes, I'll let you know as soon as I know myself. Anyway, it must be all right. The *Times Ed.* wouldn't take it otherwise ... Fine, thanks, but bored stiff ... All right. Mind you do the same. Don't overstay your welcome, because I can do with you here. Goodbye.'

Howard Spalding drove cautiously. He was a menace on main roads because he invariably chose to use the middle lane, even when the inside lane was free of traffic and on a Clearway. Blasphemous drivers either had to crawl behind him, pull out into the fast lane in front of other blasphemous drivers, or move dangerously into the slow lane with their fingers metaphorically crossed as they passed him on the near side, praying that he would not change his mind and swerve suddenly leftwards into them.

On the narrow roads of the island he held no threat. He still drove slowly, but there was nothing coming behind him from the rocky, desolate Point, neither did he meet any other vehicle all the way to the hotel. He was thinking of nothing in particular – certainly not of the lukewarm welcome given by his wife and son to their new surroundings. His limited mind, in fact, was relaxed and content. He was the more surprised, therefore, when, turning off the road to drive in at the hotel gates, he found these closed against him. They were of wrought iron, and on the curving drive which led up to the front door, and on the lawn beside it, some small boys were kicking a tennis ball about and uttering the shrill cries common to their species.

Howard got out of the car and tried the gates. They were locked. He signalled, and attracted attention. A child wearing a prefect's badge came up.

'Good afternoon, sir. Do you want to come in? I'll get Mr Skelton. We're not allowed to unlock the gates ourselves. Excuse me just a minute, sir.' He ran off and disappeared into the building. Howard was not left very long to wonder what all this might portend. The boy reappeared, accompanied by a man in the casual clothing of the younger members of his profession – flannel trousers, a pullover, and a sports jacket.

'Hullo,' said he, with an informality in keeping with his attire. 'Are you a parent? The Man's rather busy just now.'

'No,' said Howard, 'I am not a parent. I have merely rented one of the lock-up garages. I presume I may put my car in it?'

'Oh, I say! I'm afraid they're all taken, you know.'

'Taken? But I've paid for Number Five – a year's rent in advance.'

'Oh, dash it, what bad luck! Somebody must have slipped up.'

'I don't understand. I was told the hotel would be closed until the Easter week-end, with just a caretaker in charge. I was to apply to him for the key.'

'Oh, I say! The whole place has been let to the school, you know. I think you'd better talk to the Man, although he'll have my blood for interrupting him, I expect. Could you give me your name?'

'Howard Spalding. I'm staying at the disused lighthouse down at the Point.'

'Right. I won't be a moment.' He returned with an older man who was wearing a severe dark suit and an unidentifiable Old School tie. The gates were unlocked and Howard was admitted on to the gravel. 'This is Mr Noble, the senior master. I'll leave you both to it,' said the young man blithely. He took himself off. Mr Noble looked at his retreating back, sighed in a resigned manner, and asked what he could do for the visitor. Howard explained all over again, in a peevish voice, about the lock-up.

'Yes, I see,' said Mr Noble. 'Yes, yes, I see. Very difficult. I don't know how to advise you for the best.'

'But I don't need advice!' burst out Howard. 'I only need a garage for my car.'

'You see, they're all taken.'

'Then somebody will have to move out of Number Five. I've got a receipt! I've rented a lock-up! Look here.' He produced a piece of the hotel notepaper.

'Yes,' said Mr Noble, handing it back. 'Yes, quite. Well, I can't disturb the headmaster at present. Perhaps you'd care to come in and wait? I'll put you in Matron's room. I expect you would like a cup of tea.'

Laura had obtained the post she had seen advertised. She now welcomed Howard into her sanctum with simulated warmth. She disliked weedy, narrow-shouldered men, and Howard was indubitably weedy and narrow-shouldered. She also disliked peevish voices, and there was no denying that Howard's utterance was peevish. For his part, finding her fine, large form, frank gaze and undoubted comeliness reassuring, Howard accepted tea and a currant bun and told her his troubles, confining these to the inexplicable misappropriation of his garage, since he did not know, at the time, that he had worse troubles to come.

'Well,' said Laura, when she had heard the tale and had

poured him out a third cup of tea, 'the point is, you see, that most of the Staff have cars, and it's just as well to lock them away from the boys.'

'Yes, but what Staff and what boys? That's what I want to know. I understood that the hotel was closed from the end of October until Easter, but now it's turned into a school.'

'It seems that the real school buildings, down in Kent, caught fire, and there was so much damage that the headmaster either had to send all the boys home or find somewhere else for them to go until the repairs were complete. He found this hotel, and here we are. The real matron has been left behind to keep an eye on things in Kent. She's the headmaster's wife, as it happens, and luckily the headmaster's house, a detached building out in the grounds, escaped the fire. I'm here in a temporary capacity – that's to say, until Easter – and, believe me, you haven't seen life until you've been a temporary, inexperienced matron in a prep. school.'

'But what am I going to do about my car?' asked Howard, shelving her problems in favour of his own.

'Cut your losses (except that the headmaster will have to pay back your rent) and find another garage. That would be my insignificant but practical contribution to the discussion.'

'But why *should* I, Mrs Gavin? *Why should I?* After all, I was first in the field. Besides, I'm not sure there *is* another garage.'

At this point there was an interruption in the form of a knock on the door. Laura called out, and a boy appeared.

'Oh, *no!* Not you *again*, Michael!' cried Laura.

'Oh, no, Mrs Gavin, thanks awfully. Not me again. I've only come on a message. Mr Eastleigh says he can see Mr Spalding now, and is sorry to have kept him waiting. Would you care to come along with me, sir?'

Laura's room had been the hotel manager's sitting-room and she had been allotted the pleasant bedroom which went with it. The headmaster's study was what had been the hotel writing-room. It had proved adequate for its present purpose, as it had two bookcases in which unreadable matter had been kept for the benefit of weatherbound or moribund visitors, and which now served as display shelves for a selection of school textbooks. The headmaster gave Howard a chair, faced him across a large desk and offered him a cigarette which he declined.

'Well, now,' said Mr Eastleigh, 'I understand that we are faced with a small matter requiring adjustment. Could you just apprise me of the facts, quite briefly?'

For the fourth time since his arrival, Howard outlined the situation as he saw it. 'So, as I have the prior claim, I demand my rights,' he concluded, in the blustering tones of the insecure man.

'Yes, yes, I see,' said Mr Eastleigh. 'Oh, I do so much agree that you have the prior claim.'

'Oh, well, that's all right, then,' said Howard, with great relief. 'I'll just put my car in straight away.'

'I'm afraid not, you know.'

'Not? I don't see any reason against it, and, as I face a long walk home, I shall be glad to get the car put away at once. I presume that you have the keys of the lock-ups in your possession?'

'Only the one for my own car. Various members of Staff have the others.'

'Well, if you'll send for the key to Number Five . . .'

'I'm afraid it's not as simple as that, you know. You see,' he went on, cutting short an interruption from Howard, 'I could let you have a key to the lock-up, yes. Nothing easier. Heathers could garage in the outhouse. There is nothing but Mrs Gavin's car in there. The trouble is that I cannot allow unauthorised persons unrestricted access to the school premises.'

'But I'm *not* an unauthorised person,' protested Howard, waving his receipt. 'I'm authorised by the management of the hotel to be on these premises.'

'Ah, but these premises are now school property. Suppose, in getting out your car or in putting it back, you were to run over one of my boys? You will say you wouldn't run over one of my boys, but that would only prove to me that you don't know boys.'

'Of course I know boys! I've a son of my own.'

'Have you, indeed?'

'Why, yes. A boy of nineteen. I've watched him grow up from babyhood. Of course I know boys.'

'Nineteen,' said the headmaster thoughtfully. 'Public school, of course?'

'Naturally. Rendlesford.'

'Now at University?'

'Unfortunately, not yet. He had a severe illness last year, and, although the doctors have pronounced him perfectly fit, I thought it advisable to give him another year in which to build himself up. I've taken that disused lighthouse on the Point, where he can be quiet and take things easily. He is a highly intelligent boy, and I don't want him to overdo it yet. I hope he'll get a First when he does go up.'

His customary enthusiasm for his son's gifts had caused him to forget, for the moment, his own wrongs, and he was about to return to these when the headmaster asked:

'Could he teach French, and, possibly, a little German?'

'*Teach* them? I suppose he could, if he had to, and Russian, too. But his sights are set on the Foreign Office, not on teaching.'

'Ah, yes, that is not the point. You see,' said Mr Eastleigh, with that suspect blandness with which headmasters attempt to conceal their wiles, 'it has just occurred to me that we could resolve your temporary difficulty about the lock-up if your son were to become, *pro tem.*, – merely *pro tem.*, of course – a member of my Staff. There could be no possible reason for me to deny access to the premises to a member of Staff or his relatives, could there? Such a veto on my part would be ridiculous.'

'So is your suggestion,' said Howard, in weak anger, getting up to go. 'I am quite sure that my son would never consider such a proposition. It is no solution at all!'

'It is the only one which I am prepared to consider,' said the headmaster, in deceptively gentle tones. 'Believe me, Mr Spalding, I do sympathise with you. I should be extremely put out if I found myself in circumstances similar to yours. I admit it freely. But what can I do? I have my boys and their parents to think of. Just supposing you ran a boy down! I do beg of you to consider my proposal. Please talk it over with your son. The island offers little scope to a young man of his age, and he might be very glad of something definite to do. I would pay him a more than adequate salary, needless to say, and I would certainly undertake not to overwork him, if he's been ill. You see, if I could get a replacement, I could send back my senior master to look after six Common Entrance boys, whom we thought it better, for the sake of their work, to leave behind in Kent. I have engaged tutors for them, and they have been given quarters in my own house, but I should be better pleased if they were under Noble's eye.'

'Damn Noble's eye!' muttered Howard. Aloud he said, 'My son would never consider becoming an usher. You will hear from my solicitors. I will wish you good afternoon, and I warn you that an action will lie. I have right on my side. Besides, I shall use my car so seldom that there could be no foreseeable danger to your boys.'

The gates were unlocked for him again, and he drove off at what, for him, was a reckless pace, blind with frustration and fury. He flung himself into the living-room of the lighthouse much earlier than he had been expected, to find his wife lying on the sofa, Colin on his knees with his arms clasped tightly round her as he blubbered emotionally into her neck, and a smell of burning coming from the scorched blankets in front of the gas fires in the bedrooms.

CHAPTER THREE

Fish Out of Water

'It was about nine miles long and five across, shaped, you might say, like a fat dragon standing up, and had two fine, land-locked harbours, and a hill in the centre part ...'

It was Fiona who realised first that her husband had come back. Colin, in his muffled position and overcome by his frantic weeping, had not even heard him come in.

'Get up, Colin!' she said. 'Stop playing about. Your father's here.'

'Something's burning!' said Howard. He rushed to inspect the bedrooms. By the time he came back to the living-room Colin's head was under the kitchen tap and Fiona was setting the table for supper.

'I suppose we left the blankets too near the fire,' she said, before her husband could speak. 'Did you have a good walk, dear?'

Howard could not bring himself to reply. The defeat he felt he had suffered at the hands of the headmaster, the discovery of the scorched blankets (which, unfortunately, would have to be replaced before he gave up his tenancy) and the (to his mind) ridiculous scene he had just witnessed, took away, for the time being, his powers of speech. Her conception of the enormity of these happenings being in the reverse order of importance – indeed, she was, so far, unaware of the futility of his attempt to garage the car – Fiona brought in the cold viands which were to constitute the supper and called upon Colin to come to the table. He refused, and tore along the passage to his room.

'I think the long day has been a bit too much for him,' said Fiona, diplomatically. 'He's been crying, poor boy. He must still be very weak from his illness. You mustn't blame him.'

'*Crying?* A boy of nineteen?'

24

'He's so disappointed he isn't going to College this autumn. He's been unburdening himself to me.'

'What babyish nonsense! You shouldn't encourage him, my dear. I know he's been seriously ill, but he isn't a little boy now, and I don't know what people would think, if they saw him slopping all over you like that.'

'I know. I was just putting my feet up for a bit, after I'd done the salad and things, when he began to talk, and then he went all to pieces. It's really a little bit worrying, and I'm awfully sorry about the bedding, but he was in such a state, poor boy, that I simply didn't think about anything else. How was it you got back so early?'

She wondered, as soon as she put this question, whether, under the circumstances, it had been wise to do so, but she was immediately reassured. Her husband, between mouthfuls of ham, tongue, hard-boiled eggs and salad, gave her a graphic, bitter and sarcastic account of his reception by the headmaster.

'But I'll put my solicitors on to him! I told him I should, and I certainly shall,' he concluded.

'I don't blame you,' said his wife, his misinterpretation of the scene he had witnessed causing her to feel so much thankfulness that she spoke with unusual warmth. 'I should think so, indeed! The idea! You could have him up for breach of contract, couldn't you?'

'Well,' said Howard, pushing aside his empty plate and helping himself to cheese, 'I don't know about *him*. I am inclined to think it ought to be the hotel manager. *He's* the real culprit, I fancy, for letting the hotel over my head. But I'll put Kempson on to it tomorrow. He'll know the best thing to do. Isn't Colin going to eat any supper? I'd better go and bring him along.'

'He won't hurt, dear. He's probably better off in bed. He had a good lunch on the way down. He won't starve. I think I'll soon go to bed myself. I'll leave the washing-up until the morning. The gas stove works all right. Shall I make some coffee, or will you have another glass of wine?'

'We'd better see about making up the beds. I'll look in on Colin and just see how he is. I don't care about this outbreak when I thought he was getting so much stronger. Besides, I can't have him getting maudlin over *you*! It's most annoying.'

'I wouldn't worry him, Howard. He's probably bundled some bedclothes round himself and gone bang off to sleep. He's just tired out, I think.'

'Perhaps you're right. But I think we ought to do the washing-up before we go to bed. It's a bad start to begin by putting off the chores until the morning. When we've done it, you'd better toddle along. I shall go up to the gallery on top of the light-house tower and get some air before I turn in, I think. The stars should be out by now, and the night is clear.'

'I'll do the washing-up, and make the beds, then. Don't stay up there too long and get cold. The nights are still rather chilly.'

She gave him five minutes by the clock, and then went along to Colin's room. He had the light on, and was lying flat on his back staring up at the ceiling.

'Oh, hallo,' he said, when she sat on the end of the bed. He heaved himself on to his elbow. 'I'm sorry I made such a ghastly fool of myself. What does he – did he say anything about it?'

'No, it's quite all right. That's what I came to tell you. Good night. Sleep well – darling.'

He sat bolt upright at that, and stretched out his arms to her, but she was gone, and, not knowing where his father was, he dared not follow her. She returned to the kitchen, cleared the table, washed-up plates, cutlery and glasses and went to bed. Her husband was inadequate, she was bored by her marriage, she was not yet thirty years old, she was beautiful, healthy, discontented and unfulfilled – but Colin was not the answer, and she did not know any gamekeepers. She reviewed the scene on the sofa with a distaste which amounted to disgust. That it had been largely her own fault she knew, and that did not make her thoughts and her yearnings any easier to bear.

By the morning Howard, who had gone to bed after having spent a quietly rapturous hour on the gallery of the lighthouse looking through his telescope at the stars (for the windy night, though cold, had been beautifully clear), got up to breakfast in a very different frame of mind from that in which he had re-turned from the school. To prove how high his spirits had risen, he took a cold 'in-and-out' in the zinc bath, but, unfortunately, came to breakfast with blue hands and chattering teeth.

Colin, who had to be called twice, came to table in a vile temper and, having listened with curling lip to his father's boasting about having taken 'an exhilarating cold tub, a thing you ought to do, my boy; nothing like it for giving you an appetite,' told Howard that he didn't want pneumonia on top of everything else. He added, in an offensive tone, that middle-aged men should not play the fool with their circulations. He then ate three rashers of bacon and two eggs and took himself off for a look at 'this frightful place you've brought us to', while his father and stepmother did the washing-up.

Laura Gavin, five miles away, was not faced with the task of washing-up (fortunately, in her case, as this would have involved dealing with plates and cutlery for eighty boys, eight men, the junior boys' form mistress and herself), but she did face a domestic crisis of another sort. The school had occupied its present temporary quarters for a fortnight, but already the bird (to quote Laura's report to Mr Eastleigh) was flapping its wings over the kitchen quarters. She had gone along, having, from the first, ignored Mr Noble's *fiat* that he should act as intermediary between members of Staff and the headmaster, to report disaffection among the servants.

'The maids complain that there's nothing to do here on their afternoons off,' she explained to Mr Eastleigh. 'They say the place gives them the willies. I'm afraid we'll lose the lot of them unless they're sweetened up in some way or other.'

'Yes,' said Mr Eastleigh, who had not built up a successful and highly remunerative business by blinding himself to what went on below stairs as well as in the Staff Common Room. 'Yes, I know. How do you think it would work if I laid on a taxi to take them over to the mainland once a week?'

'Twice a week,' said Laura. 'By that,' she added hastily, 'I mean there would have to be two parties. Cook and the kitchenmaid (who's her niece, so Cook won't feel she's demeaning herself by sharing a taxi with her underling), and one of the parlourmaids and one of the housemaids can go on Tuesdays, and the other parlourmaid and the other two housemaids and the sewing woman can go on Thursdays. The taxi wouldn't take more than four at a time, anyway.'

'I'll see about it. But there's another thing, Mrs Gavin.' He paused and, with his elbows on his desk, studied his beautifully-manicured fingers.

'Say on,' advised Laura briskly. 'I expect you think I'm a lousy housekeeper. Want me to hand in my cards?'

'Dear me, no! I think you have settled in admirably, quite admirably.'

'I don't like that "quite", you know. It qualifies the adverb to the adverb's disadvantage, don't you think?'

'Really, really! I intended no adverse comment at all, Mrs Gavin. Quite (I beg your pardon!) actually, the reverse. What I want is some advice from you.'

('Blimey! What comes now?' thought Laura). There was another pause, an expectant one from her, an indecisive one from the headmaster.

'If it's about Mr Heathers,' said Laura, prompting him, 'I agree he's a wretched little object, unworthy (at present) of the respect and admiration of the boys, but I've found out he can play the saxophone. That ought to be some help to him. Mr Pocock makes a very fair vocalist and can play the guitar, and Mr Skelton could be taught the drums if you put it to him in your own inimitable way. You know, employ the boss's half-nelson. He's got a lovely wrist action and, being the P.E. panjandrum, he has a very nice sense of rhythm and plenty of follow-through. Why shouldn't we popularise poor old Erica by running a pop group? It would go down big with the boys.'

'Erica? Oh, – Heathers! Well, really!' said the headmaster. He began to laugh. 'A pop group to popularise Heathers? You certainly have a creative mind, Mrs Gavin.'

'Leonardo da Vinci's little sister,' said Laura modestly. 'But what did you want to see me about, if not that? I have the laundry to check.'

'Miss Beverley wants to leave. I have had her here in tears. Most disconcerting.'

'Her love-life's gone wrong, that's what.'

'Her *love-life*?'

'Yes. She and young Ferrars have parted brass-rags. He smacked one of her little boys and she's handed him the mitten.'

The headmaster, dismayed, realised that his knowledge of what went on among the Staff was not as comprehensive as he had supposed. 'Well, what am I to do about it?' he asked plaintively. 'She's under contract to stay at least until the end of the term, but, of course, I don't want to keep her if she really wants to go.'

'So you want me to find out whether she *does* really want to go. Is that it?'

'Well,' said the headmaster gratefully, 'you know how it is. With no other lady available, my wife, owing to unfortunate circumstances, not being with us . . .'

'In the country of the blind, the one-eyed man is king? Right, then. I'll sort her out. Not that you wouldn't be just as well off without her. You'd get far more work out of young Ferrars if she weren't here, you know. There's a lot of good in that boy, but she doesn't give him a chance. Between ourselves, she's quite a nasty little bit of work. I wouldn't put much past her.'

'You really think I should take her at her word, then?'

'Well, she's only doing this job for pin-money. She won't be on the streets if you sling her out.'

'Well, really!' said the headmaster. He began to laugh again. 'You seem to know a great deal more about the Staff than I do myself.'

'Ah, well, you know, we who live between the soup and the savoury get to know the smell of the stuffing,' said Laura.

While she was having this heart-to-heart talk with her new employer, Howard was having a serious conversation with his son. Summoned to the presence as soon as he came back from a half-hour stroll which convinced him that the island was an ante-chamber to hell, Colin felt the qualms of a little boy conscious of sin when his father put his head out of the living-room doorway and told him to come in, as he desired to speak to him. The peremptory tone which frightened his son was the result of extreme nervousness on Howard's part, but Colin's guilty conscience did not allow him to see that.

The truth, although he himself did not realise it, was that Howard had been psychologically affected by the physical reaction he had suffered as a result of his cold bath. Even his breakfast had not really warmed him, and it was not until he had sat crouched over the gas fire for some minutes that he could trust his numbed fingers not to drop the crockery when he dried it. It no longer seemed a good or even a possible thing to throw Mr Eastleigh to the lawyers. Suppose Eastleigh really had a case? Suppose Howard summoned him, and not only lost the suit but was admonished by the Bench for selfishly putting his own convenience before the safety and perhaps the lives of little boys? Howard's *morale*, in fact, was at such a low ebb that he was almost at the point of allowing the whole business to slide, and purchasing a waterproof cover for the car, when he gave a second thought and then some deep consideration to Mr Eastleigh's suggestion concerning Colin.

Had he but known it, he could hardly have chosen a better moment to put the headmaster's offer before his son. Colin, avoiding the fishermen's cottages and the modern lighthouse in case he might encounter a fellow-being, had struck out westwards across the point of the island and then had turned south to gain the cliffs. He dared not approach too near the edge, but from where he stood he had seen the fury of the Race and the long, exposed strata of the limestone which reached out below the cliff-level and into the sea. He had stood there, contemplating suicide, and wondering what Fiona would feel when his battered body was left at low tide among the cruel rocks, until, with a shudder at the thought of his own agonising demise, and a passing query as to whether he had the right to deprive the world of a potentially great man, he had walked across to a disused quarry, gazed at it with loathing and horror, paused while he recited to the seabirds some of the more despairing lyrics of A. E. Housman, and then, in a mood of blackest depression, had returned to the disused lighthouse, only to be met by the voice of doom requesting his attendance in the living-room.

'Oh, *God!*' muttered Colin. '*Now* what's he going to say?'

Laura's impression of the island was vastly different from that of Colin. For one thing, the very fact that it was called an island – although, geographically speaking, it was only when the winter gales were at their worst that the title was logically justifiable – prejudiced her in its favour. Then, again, she had

chosen of her own freewill to spend her time on it, whereas
Colin had been given no choice in the matter, but had been
obliged to give way to his father's (he considered) selfish whim.
Apart from other considerations, its uncompromising bleak-
ness and bareness, its quarries and its vertical limestone cliffs
repelled and disquieted him, but these were features which
stimulated and interested Laura.

Except for one tiny cove, where low tide displayed a small
arc of sand and a stretch of pebbles, the island appeared to
have no beaches, and she had been intrigued, on her walks
abroad, to notice that on top of the comparatively low cliffs
which lay about halfway between the cove and the Point,
derricks had been rigged so that small boats could be lowered
into the water.

The tackle consisted of three stout wooden posts, one of
which was perpendicular. The others were joined to it by iron
grapplings and slanted away from it at an angle of forty-five
degrees. Two large iron cogwheels, one of which was furnished
with a handle, were fixed to the upright post, and a fourth
enormous pole, acting as a crane, was rigged with tackle from
which a wire rope could be attached to the centre thwart of
the boat which was to be launched and drop it, at the end of
the plumb-line thus formed, into the deep water at the foot of
the cliff.

There were other points, too, which pleased Laura. The hotel
(temporarily Mr Eastleigh's school) was set in the most
attractive part of the island. The view from its upper windows
was not that of the turbulent Race, or even that of the strangely
symmetrical blocks of limestone which formed the cliffs. Behind the hotel, on the seaward side, the heights were covered
in trees and the prospect was mostly of the wide and beautiful
bay which curved from the eastward coast of the island to the
mainland and then along the sandy shore of the nearest seaside
town, whose broad, firm beach and white-washed houses and
hotels could be made out, with the aid of field-glasses, from
the upstairs windows of the school.

What was more, Laura's job, although (as she expressed it
in a letter to Dame Beatrice Lestrange Bradley, who employed
her, in the normal course of events, as secretary) not exactly

her particular cup of tea, had its compensations. For one thing, her sole responsibility was to run the domestic side of the school. She was not responsible for administration, discipline, class teaching or financial matters, and was, in most respects, a law unto herself. The headmaster allowed her the free use of her time. So long as meals and the masters' morning coffee were not delayed, so long as the boys were laundered, mended and first-aided, so long as supplies of food and fuel were maintained, she might occupy herself as she wished.

She found, by the end of her first week, that this dispensation was modified by the boys' demands and wishes. None of them was more than twelve, and twenty of them were only between seven and eight years old. As the only woman on the strength (except for Miss Beverley, who was the junior form mistress, and the servants) she found herself in the rôle of foster-mother, confidante, advisory bureau and conniver at immorality.

'I say, Mrs Gavin, aren't you glad Peters burnt the school down?'

'Oh, I say, I didn't, you know!'

'Well, it wasn't really his fault, Mrs Gavin. It was really Mr Ferrars. He was new last term, and wanted to help us with the bonfire and the guy, so, as Peters is a prefect and has to encourage new masters, he thought he'd better let him.'

'We really ought to have taken his I.Q. before we trusted him with fireworks,' said the squarely-built Peters, whom Laura had already noticed as a man of few but trenchant words.

'So we were all sent home early for Christmas – well, *jolly* early, as a matter of fact – and some of our people blenched a bit at having us for double the usual time, so I suppose Mr Eastleigh had to do something about it, because the school won't be ready again for years and years.'

'Probably never,' said Peters.

'Everybody was fearfully pleased with Mr Ferrars, though, so you won't say a word about it, will you? We made him an hon. member of the Illya Kuryakin Society, but, of course, he doesn't know, because it's such a secret society that none of the members know who they are except Peters and me. He's Solo and I'm Illya. As a matter of fact . . .'

'No, you're not to tell her! You know our rules!' inter-polated the stolid Peters. Laura gathered that she herself had qualified for hon. membership of the Illya Kuryakin Society, and was gratified but somewhat alarmed. Knowing something of the mentality of small boys, she could not help wondering how long the full membership of the Illya Kuryakin Society would be allowed to remain ignorant of the honour which had been thrust upon it, and what the harvest would be when the members were apprised of their good fortune and called upon to participate in some frightful act of sabotage or mayhem. She had clear recollections of the hair-raising exploits de-manded of Nicholas Blake's Nigel Strangeways when he be-came a candidate for membership of a school secret society while employed in investigating a case of murder.

She also found herself the unwilling Delphic Oracle of Miss Beverley. This young woman was twenty years old and the spoilt child of parents whose sole object, where she was con-cerned, was to get her safely and satisfactorily married. She had given up the London School of Economics, she told Laura, to go on the stage, but the stage, to her chagrin and astonish-ment, had not seen its way to employing her talents. She had then worked for an unspecified but (Laura gathered) a com-paratively short time as housekeeper and model to an artist, but he, alas, had a mistress of whom he was fond and to whom he was faithful, so, becoming tired of washing beer-mugs and glasses and of being sent round the corner, in the middle of studio parties, to obtain fresh supplies of the various invitations to conviviality, she had quit, after smacking the face of the mistress and being punched in the eye by the artist.

After this, she told Laura, she had 'simply mucked about at home' until she had seen the advertisement for her present post. Having 'played up' the London School of Economics to Mr Eastleigh, and 'played down' subsequent adventures, she had obtained the post of junior mistress and had been amusing herself by trying to seduce junior master Ferrars. This had now proved abortive, Ferrars (most unreasonably) taking more thought for keeping his job than of ministering to her ego, so what, she demanded, should she do? Laura's suggestion of a melodramatic leap from the cliff-top (which, she averred, would make Mr Ferrars think a bit) was not well received.

'Oh, I couldn't do *that!*' squeaked the young lady. 'I am to come in for Uncle Mally's ten thousand a year when I'm twenty-five. But Ronald isn't playing fair. There's a girl in that beastly seaside town. I'm absolutely certain he keeps standing me up for her. He's just a Casanova, and I've had enough of it.'

Laura had several favourite walks. She took these by her-self whenever she could, but on Saturdays and Sundays she was invariably compelled to suffer an escort of two or three little boys who missed their mothers and had need of more mature female society than that provided by Miss Beverley. She, in any case, had stated in unequivocal terms that she saw quite enough of them in class without wanting them hanging on to her skirts during her free time. With this attitude Laura could sympathise. She would have felt the same way herself. The only difference was that, with her, the feeling would have remained unspoken.

Her favourite walk was by a narrow path, just outside the hotel grounds, which led to the broken, romantic cliffs over-looking the bay. This path was out of bounds to the boys be-cause the crumbling cliffs were temptingly climbable. Moreover, the path also led to a ruined castle in such a dangerous state of disrepair that it had been fenced off, and warning notices had been posted at salient points. As it was easily visible from the hotel grounds, Mr Eastleigh had not only warned the school at its first assembly in its new home that instant ex-pulsion would follow any attempt to break bounds, but had followed this up by putting a formidable permanent notice on the games board, the one notice board which every boy was certain to look at.

The path led to the cliff-top and then meandered southwards past the castle. From there, in bends and windings, it went down to the little cove, the only one on the island. The beach was stony and uninviting, but there were boulders on which one could sit, and at low tide there was the small arc of sand which Laura had already noticed. A powerful swimmer, she had made enquiries of the man left by the hotel proprietor to look after the hotel's interests, and had learned that the cove offered safe bathing and was much favoured by summer visitors for that reason.

So far, the grey sky reflected in the grey sea, coupled with the strong winds of early March, had not tempted her into the water, but she had promised herself a swim on the first fine, boyless day that offered. Boyless because their habit of attaching themselves to her on her walks, although endearing, was also inconvenient. She could not take boys down to the cove unless the headmaster lifted his ban, a move she did not think likely, and she felt that it would be cruel to let the boys see her following a course which was forbidden to them, particularly if she was carrying swimming things.

One Wednesday afternoon, a few days after Howard had had his interview with the headmaster, she decided that the day promised fairly enough for a dip. She was Spartan where cold water was concerned. A well-nourished body, a perfect circulation and a powerful free-style in swimming combined to make her impervious to temperatures which would have given lesser mortals cramp or even heart failure, and she had tossed off her clothes and was in the water when she became aware that her privacy was being invaded. Turning the last bend in the cliff path was young man.

'Damn!' said Laura, disgustedly. 'Wonder how long he's going to stay?' She turned and threshed out to sea. The tide had turned and was setting strongly shorewards, so it would be easy enough to swim in again when she was ready. When she turned back, the youth was still there, his hands in his overcoat pockets and a long scarf wound about his throat.

CHAPTER FOUR

The New Swim

'A belt of fog had lifted almost simultaneously with the rising of the moon.'

Laura seldom had difficulty in making up her mind, and none at all on this occasion. When she was ready, she swam in and addressed the young man.

'You'll have to look the other way. I'm coming out,' she said.

'Why, are you naked?' asked the youth.

'Yes, of course. That is, I shall be, in a minute.'

'Oh, righto. I'll go away, if you like.'

'That doesn't matter. I'll have one more good burst to get really warm, and when I swim in again you don't look. Right?'

'Right.'

When she was wrapped in a bath sheet and was drying her hair with a towel, he said, without turning his head:

'If I took off my overcoat and shut my eyes, I could hold it out as a wind-shield. Any good?'

'Yes, thank you very much. That would be grand. But you needn't shut your eyes at present. I'm perfectly decent. I'll tell you when.'

Colin took in beautiful arms, fine hands and a frank and handsome countenance with a good-tempered mouth and a determined chin. Without embarrassment The Woman (for so he thought of Laura, in excited but respectful capitals) dried her shoulders and beautiful bosom and then her long legs.

'Lift up that coat a bit higher and duck your head,' she said. Colin obeyed. 'All right now. I'm dressed. And thanks a lot for the overcoat,' she added, a few minutes later. 'I've only got my feet to dry.' He put on the overcoat, glad of its warmth, and sat down on a boulder adjacent to the one on which she had perched herself.

36

'I really ought to have carried you over those stones,' he said, noting with concern that one of her feet was bleeding slightly. Laura chuckled.

'I should have been some handful!' she said, noting his thinness and something fine-drawn about him. 'Remember Denis and Anne in *Crome Yellow?*'

'You're like her in other ways, too, I wouldn't wonder.' He did not attempt to keep the warmth out of his voice.

'You flatter me. Besides, I'm active and energetic. Even the name's not the same.'

'I'm Colin Spalding.'

'Laura Gavin.'

'Mrs, I see.' He indicated her wedding-ring.

'Since more years than I care to count. I have a boy of ten, who, at present, thank goodness, is at school. Do you mind if we walk about for a bit?'

'Oh, yes, you ought not to sit still after your swim, not in this weather. How you can do it beats me. My father is always urging cold baths, but I simply can't face them, even in front of the kitchen fire, which is how we have to take our baths at present.' He got up and held out his hands to help her to her feet. 'We've taken that disused lighthouse at the other end of the island. I don't suppose you've been as far as that, have you?'

'Oh, yes, I have. How jolly to live in a lighthouse! I suppose you can see the mainland from the top, and lots of ships and so forth?'

'I've not been to the top. I can't stand heights. I don't mind this path, because it's nowhere near the edge of the cliff, and it's on such a gradual slope. Could we go just a bit slower, though? Otherwise you'd better go on without me. I'm not all that long out of hospital, and I haven't got back into mid-season form just yet.'

Laura, whose Amazonian stride and hill-woman's muscles had been making nothing of the upward slope, not only slowed but stopped.

'No harm in looking at the view,' she said kindly. 'I wonder how decrepit that castle really is? I've a private bet with myself that one of these days, headmaster's threats notwithstanding, one of our hopefuls is going to chance his luck in there. Nothing on earth would have kept me out of it when I was a kid.'

'Did you say headmaster?' asked Colin, with sudden interest. 'Do you mean you teach at the school?'

'No. I'm the matron.'

'Good Lord! You must have been sent from heaven!'

'Undoubtedly. But why the rapture?'

'Because you've made up my mind for me.' They walked on and took the path which led past the hotel. 'This is where I push in and ask the headmaster for an interview. Would you mind telling me his name? My father did mention it, but I've forgotten what he called him.'

'Mr Eastleigh. Are you coming on to the Staff?'

'Well, I *wasn't*, but now I jolly well *am*, if he'll have me. Do you tuck the boys up at night?'

'Some of them.'

'And the masters?'

'Not so far as I've gone. I don't think my husband would like it.'

'I shall be the exception that proves the rule, I trust. Well, I'll push in, before the native hue of resolution, *etcetera* – in other words, before I get cold feet. I hope yours are quite warm?'

'Perfectly warm, thank you.'

'Next time I must kneel before you and request the privilege of drying them. Goodbye for now. When next we meet, it may be as fellow-workers in the vineyard.' He had not been so happy or felt so light-hearted since his twelfth birthday. It was with a jauntiness to which he had long been a stranger that he walked up the gravel drive and rang the front-door bell of the school.

'Well, I'm delighted, my boy, delighted!' said Howard, when his son came back in the late afternoon and gave the news. 'I'm sure you'll enjoy it. I expect it will come a little strange just at first, you know. You must allow for that. But, once you've settled down, you'll do splendidly, splendidly, I'm sure.'

'I suppose it's the best thing, Colin,' said Fiona, when

Howard had gone up to study the stars that night, 'but it's going to be dull here without you.'

'I'll be home every Friday night to Monday morning except for my duty week-ends, and they only come one in four, so not to worry.'

'You're suspiciously keen on this business, aren't you? Are there any women on the Staff?'

'You're jealous!' cried Colin, delighted. 'As a matter of fact, there *is* one rather callow little schoolmarm, but I understand she's leaving the place pretty soon after I get there. Apart from her, there are no females except the matron and the servants.'

'The matron? Oh, I shouldn't count *her*,' said Fiona, lightly.

'That's where you're wrong,' thought Colin; but he decided that any mention of Venus rising from the waves might be indiscreet at this juncture. He added: 'I wonder whether you remember a chap I was at school with? He was on that Mediterranean cruise with us when you and my father teamed up. Fellow named Ferrars – no end of a blood at school. Was in the Sixth when I was a new boy. You *must* remember him.'

'Ronald Ferrars? Oh, yes, I remember him,' said Fiona.

'Well, he's on the Staff of the school. Mind if I bring him over?'

'I thought you didn't like him much. That business of climbing the mast, you know. You told him you had no head for heights and he was – well – not very nice to you about it.'

'Oh, that's old history. You liked him, didn't you?'

'Oh, he was all right,' said Fiona, with a sudden vivid and not unpleasant memory of moonlight nights on the boat deck after Howard had gone to bed and Colin, then aged sixteen, had preferred a quiet, solitary swim in the warm, indoor pool to any other form of night life. 'Bring him along, by all means, if you want to.'

'Well, he knows the ropes at the school and can probably give me lots of pointers, so that I don't put my foot in it with the headmaster or get to loggerheads with the boys – all that sort of thing, if you see what I mean.'

'Well, see what your father says, but I'm sure he'll be pleased. He's delighted that you've taken the job, you know.'

'Yes, well, it settles the hoo-ha about the car, but I think I

shall like the job, anyway. By the way, I may have to send
Ferrars by himself. Do you think you'll recognise him again?'

'I don't know. But why will he have to come by himself?'

'He may not have to, but I don't expect he and I will be given
the same afternoons off. I believe there's a rota and so forth.
You'll be nice to him, won't you, Fiona? It may make a lot of
difference to me if I can jolly him along a bit.'

'Are you nervous about the job, Colin?'

'Well, yes, I suppose so. I wasn't all that popular at school,
and I don't know how I'll get on with the boys and masters
unless I've got a friend at court. I mean, I *expect* I'll be all
right, but with Ferrars behind me – I mean, he was such a blood
at school . . .'

Laura, meanwhile, had been in conference with the headmaster since tea.

'Now I don't want you to think that what I may be going to
say is intended as anything in the nature of a reflection upon
your handling of your responsibilities,' was Mr Eastleigh's
opening remark. 'Far from it. I am delighted with the way
you've dealt with matters.'

Laura waited. Mr Eastleigh rearranged the positions of the
perpetual calendar, his pen-tray and the silver cigarette box on
his desk.

'You're giving me the push?' asked Laura, to help him out.
'Don't mind saying so, if you are.' He looked up, and, leaving
his juggling, put his fingertips together.

'Good heavens, no!' he said firmly. 'No, no, no! Nothing
like that! Far from it. No. The point *is*, Mrs Gavin, I am wondering whether, as a great personal favour to me, you would
consider a change of job here.'

'Anything but the cooking,' said Laura cheerfully.

'Well, with Miss Beverley going and Mr Spalding coming,
I have the opportunity to make some changes, one of which
intimately concerns myself. In short, I shall be sending the
senior master, Mr Noble, back to Kent to look after the
Common Entrance boys and also to keep an eye on the repairs to the school and make certain that the building is in a
fit state for use next term, and this means that, if you agree,

(and *only* if you agree) I could bring my wife here to act as housekeeper and matron, while you . . .' He paused again.

'While I take on Miss Beverley's job with the youngest boys, do you mean? I see.' She did not sound particularly enthusiastic.

'It would not necessarily be the *youngest* boys, Mrs Gavin. That would be up to you. As a matter of fact – I speak in confidence, of course – I am not too happy about Mr Heathers' handling of his form. There are only twelve of them, but they seem to give him a good deal of trouble. I thought I would put them to Mr Robson, who will soon have them back in shape, and give Mr Heathers the small Sevens and Eights (although there are twenty of them he ought to be able to manage if I look in now and again and frighten them a bit), then I could give you Mr Robson's Elevens, a very nice set of boys and well in hand. Now please don't decide in a hurry. It will be a big change for you, and, of course, you won't get quite the same kind of freedom as you're having as matron. Just go away and think it over.'

'There's no need for that,' said Laura. 'I like Mr Robson's Elevens and I'll willingly take them on. Have you a spare copy of their time-table? What subjects am I supposed to take, and with what forms? I think it's a marvellous idea to have Mrs Eastleigh with you. She'll soon bring back the roses to your cheeks.'

'Noble will cope better with the Common Entrance boys than the tutors do, and chivvy the workmen far more success-fully than my wife can, I'm sure,' said the headmaster, the roses coming to his cheeks in the form of a pleased flush. 'Well, I'm infinitely obliged, Mrs Gavin. Your salary will remain the same, of course, and, as the only woman member of Staff, you need have no extraneous or supervisory duties, so you should get a fair amount of free time, one way and another, more, I dare say, than you enjoy as matron. If you do not always care to use the Staffroom, I am sure my wife will be only too happy to accommodate you in the matron's dayroom, where, of course, you will feel at home. I'm sure you'll like her.' He smiled rather charmingly. '*I* do.'

'I say, Mrs Gavin,' said Peters, looking in at the matron's room at break on the following morning to have a fresh dressing put on a gravel-rash knee, 'the Man told us in Assembly that Miss Beverley's leaving. We shall organise a whip-round to buy her a present, of course, so do you think you could get it for us? Scent, or a box of chocolates, or a handbag, or some handkerchiefs, or something. Prancer suggested some stockings, which sounded wizard, but the prefects wondered whether boys ought to give a lady stockings. What do you think?'

'I think stockings would be very nice indeed, and quite all right for boys to give. I know she takes fives in shoes, so there wouldn't be any difficulty about getting the right size. I wonder how much money you're likely to collect?'

'The prefects are going to dun everybody for sixpence. That comes to two pounds. Will that be enough, do you think?'

'Plenty. I can get two pairs of very nice stockings for that, really good ones, at nineteen and elevenpence a pair, or four pairs at nine and eleven. Which would you prefer?'

'Can we leave it to you?'

'In that case, I should make it the four pairs. The nine and eleven are really very good, and it would make a more important-looking present. I'll get the shop to throw in a fancy box and spend the odd fourpence on ribbon tie it up. How would that be?'

'Can you get ribbon for fourpence?' asked the practical Peters.

'I expect so,' Laura answered easily. 'Leave it all to me.'

'Right. Thanks awfully, Mrs Gavin.' (She had vetoed the word 'matron' from the beginning.) 'Oh, dash it, there's the bell. I'll have to go. We've got Mr Pocock next period, and he simply froths at the mouth if anybody comes late to his lesson. Is it true we're having a new master?'

'Yes, quite true. He's only just come out of hospital, though, so, if the prefects *could* use a bit of influence . . .'

'Yes, of course. But I hope, if we encourage him, he won't burn the hotel down like Mr Ferrars did the school. I like it here. When do you think you could do the shopping for us?'

'I'm free from half-past two onwards,' said Laura, 'so I'll go this afternoon.'

'Oh, but we haven't collected the money yet, Mrs Gavin.'

'That's all right. You can pay me when you get it all in. It's early closing on the mainland tomorrow, so it won't be any use for me to go then.'

At twenty minutes to three she drove out through the hotel gates, locked them behind her – thus obeying one of Mr Eastleigh's very few inflexible rules for the Staff – and drove southwards towards the causeway and the mainland. At about a mile from the school she was passing through the first of the ugly, stone-built villages. On the far side of it the road began to descend, fairly gradually at first, and then, when she reached the second and larger village, dignified on the island by the title of The Town, she had to embark upon that series of sweeps and bends which took the road sharply and, at some stages, almost precipitously down to the causeway.

As the car descended, a wonderful panorama opened up. On one side lay the glorious arc of an almost semi-circular bay. On the other was the enormous bank of shingle, fifty to sixty feet high and two hundred yards across, which carried the causeway. This bank of shingle also swept round in an arc, but its grandeur lay not so much in its size and shape as in its menace. The grey sea snarled and snatched at it, for ever adding pebbles to the millions which made it into the crustacean monster that it was, and for ever, when the wind changed to the north, dragging away the tons of pebbles from its edge, as a beast of prey will tear and drag at the inanimate carcass of its kill.

At the mainland end of the causeway the scene changed. The road still ran fairly steeply downhill, but substantial houses with gardens and garages, trees, fences and flowering shrubs gave a general urbanisation to the scene and blotted out bay and shingle-beach until, as the car turned the bend at the foot of a steep little hill, Laura could see below her the mainland town and its inner harbour. She drove over a bridge and along some narrow streets until she came out upon the handsome promenade, with its hotels and seaside shelters, its firm and beautiful sands, its Jubilee clock and its statues of George the Third and Queen Victoria.

Here she left the car in a public car park and walked back to the narrow streets in search of the shops. It did not take her long to purchase the stockings and then, mindful that the prejudices of small boys involve an unalterable conviction that women must be given perfume – this in as ornate a container as the available cash will stretch to – she bought a small flask to place among the stockings, added wrapping paper in brilliant blue and gold, a couple of yards of white satin ribbon and a vulgar but spectacular pink silk rose.

'And if that doesn't satisfy them, I have misread my own son's prejudices and embryo eroticism,' she confided to the shop assistant who had helped her to choose the pink rose.

'Perfectly, madam,' said the shop assistant, adding to the girl on the next counter, when Laura had gone, 'Funny, her buying that rose. You'd have said the best quality and no nonsense about her.'

Laura walked back towards where she had left the car, and, as she came in sight of the sea, she looked at her watch. She had plenty of time to spare before she had need to return to the school. She changed her mind about retrieving the car, turned about, and made for the inner harbour.

In it, pleasure craft of all kinds, including two squat, old-fashioned paddle-steamers, were laid up until the boating season began. The inner harbour was the mouth of the river and was crossed by two road-bridges. Laura rested her arms on that parapet of the bridge which was nearer to the car, and studied the assembled craft. Among them a particularly fine, large boat stood out. She left the road bridge and strolled along the water-side street which bounded the inner harbour on its eastern side. She wanted to take a closer look at the cruiser and to find out its name.

This, she discovered, was *Pronax*. The boat was a thirty-five foot diesel cruiser with a centre wheelhouse. It was Thorny-croft built and was capable of sleeping at least four people. It was moored with its fenders touching the harbour wall, and there was nobody on board. Laura stood, hands in coat pockets, staring at the boat and speculating upon its probable cost, when a big young man halted beside her and said:

'Pretty, isn't she?'

'Very,' said Laura. 'She's a lovely little job.'

'Twin B.M.C. Commander diesels, and a fibre-glass hull and,

down below, wax-finished solid teak and Formica panelling.
You seem keen on boats. Like to come aboard and look her
over?'

'Very much.' They went aboard and the owner showed Laura
round. *Pronax* was a roomy boat with a well-equipped galley
and plenty of storage space. Propped up at the back of the
bottle shelf in the tiny dinette was a badly-focused snapshot
of two young men. One was obviously her present escort. The
other ... She picked up the snapshot and said:

'Well, what a small world! So you're a friend of Ronald
Ferrars!'

The young man took it from her, glanced at it carelessly, and
said:

'I'm not, so far as I know. That's a friend of mine named
Bunting. He's got a tenth share in this boat, but we don't see
much of him these days. I think he's pursuing some girl. It's
rather a hobby of his.' They returned to the roomy cockpit. 'By
the way, this boat's on charter, if you and your friends would
ever like a trip.'

'I'll remember that,' said Laura, an idea beginning to take
shape in her mind. 'How much would you want if one hired
her?'

'All depends. Anyway, here's my business card. If you think
any more about it, let me know. Wrong time of year at present,
of course, but any time you're passing...'

Laura drove back with her purchases and put the car away.
She was about to go into school when she ran into Colin, who
was looking extremely pleased with life.

'Hullo,' he said. 'Had a nice afternoon?'

'I've been on a secret mission,' said Laura. She showed him
her purchases, but did not mention her visit to the *Pronax*.
She was still mystified by the uncanny resemblance that Ferrars
bore to the part-owner Bunting.

'Very jolly,' said Colin, referring to the purchases. 'In my
time we never went further than cheap scent or a box of
chocolates. Talking of secret missions, I'm feeling a bit that
way myself, as a matter of fact. I've just been having a little
chat with the boss. You know that out-of-school activities
thing?'

There was a permanent notice on the games board. After Colin had added his name to it, it read:

Dramatic Society, M. R. Grange
Choir, L. T. Robson
Stamp Club, S. G. Pocock
Art Club, P. B. Skelton
Archaeological Society, R. J. Ferrars
Natural History Society, D. K. Heathers
Russian Circle, C. J. L. Spalding

From half-past one until half-past two on Wednesdays, boys were expected to attend the meetings of one of the first four clubs. After that, their time was their own, provided that they were engaged upon an approved hobby or were out on an archaeological or a nature expedition. Mr Heathers (Erica to the school) had suggested a geological society, but since this, under his leadership, was bound to end up as a series of cliff-climbing exploits, the headmaster had killed the suggestion at birth. He was not too happy about the Natural History Society, but told himself that he could not veto everything.

When the magic words *Russian Circle* went up on the board, there was immediate excitement and a considerable amount of moaning, especially from the choir. Mr Robson was a very able musician. He was also a martinet. He tested the voice of every new boy and selected or rejected it accordingly, but, once you were chosen, there was no argument, you belonged, body, voice and soul, to the choir.

'Old Bloodybones will never let us off choir practice to learn Russian,' said one disappointed chorister to another.

'Let's go and ask the Man about it,' suggested his friend. This was entirely in order. Mr Eastleigh had few of the attributes of Caesar, being essentially kindly and well-disposed, although these characteristics had to be heavily disguised at time; but he could be appealed to, and the appellants were certain of a patient hearing.

'You see, sir, if my parents knew I had the opportunity of learning Russian, and couldn't take it because I'm in the choir, sir, they'd be very disappointed, sir, so could I be excused the choir, sir, and learn Russian, sir?'

'Not without Mr Robson's consent, Mannering. You must go and put it to him.'

'It wouldn't be any good, I'm afraid, sir.'

'No, I don't really think it would,' agreed the Man, with a slight smile. After the tenth choir member and six of the art club had convassed his views – the dramatic society and the stamp club consisted of devotees rather than of run-of-the-mill members – Mr Eastleigh, deciding that Russian would look rather well on the school prospectus, sent for Colin.

'I think, Mr Spalding,' he said, 'that we will dispense with the Russian Circle. Perhaps, instead, you would assist Mr Heathers with the Natural History Society. I think you told me that you had no head for heights. This will put a useful check on the boys,'

'You don't think the Russian Circle a good idea, sir?' asked Colin, flushing with disappointment and chagrin.

'I think the *teaching* of Russian such a good idea that I propose to time-table it, my dear fellow. You will give every form three periods a week in place of the French and German lessons I have put you down for.'

Colin walked on air. His habit of writing love poems to Fiona was a waste of time, he decided. Henceforth all his leisure would be devoted to a further study of the Russian language. He explained all this to Laura, omitting, however, to mention his abandonment of his Muse.

CHAPTER FIVE

The Rented Lighthouse

'... very little company, the more was the pity.'
'I was very uneasy and alarmed, as you may fancy...'

Laura had not been required to give up her room and take that vacated by Miss Beverley. All that happened was that Mrs Eastleigh, reunited with her husband, moved into the suite consisting of bedroom, connecting sitting-room and private bathroom allotted to himself from the beginning by the headmaster, and Mr Grange moved into Mr Noble's vacant room, which was better than his own. Colin was given Mr Grange's room. He was sorry, in a way. It faced south and commanded a view of the lighthouse and made him think too much about Fiona and what he thought of as his disloyalty to her now that he was in love with Laura.

It was at the end of his second week at the school that he invited Laura to go home with him for the week-end. He gave the reason with only part of the truth, for he nursed his new passion in secret, he thought, telling himself that she could never be his; that his love was doomed to be 'the desire of the moth for the star, of the night for the morrow'. However, hoping against hope, he said:

'I say, I wish you'd come to the lighthouse this week-end. You'd make the place tolerable.'

'Tolerable for whom?' asked Laura, although she was sufficiently well acquainted with the unabateable egoism and unconscious selfishness of very young men to know the answer before he gave it.

'Why, for me, of course,' said Colin, surprised. 'Although, naturally,' he added, 'it will be a good thing for Fiona, I dare say, to have another woman about the place. Shall we use your car or mine?'

48

'Does Mrs Spalding know you've invited me?'

'Yes, of course, and my father, too. They'll like to have you. They know it was your doing that I took this job. Will you come?'

'I'd love to see the lighthouse.'

'That's settled, then. I can take you on Friday, after school, and we can come back together on Monday morning.'

'Oh, no, I'm not going to let your people in for having to sleep me. If it's all right with Mrs Spalding, I'll come on Saturday to lunch or tea, whichever your parents suggest.'

Colin looked disappointed.

'That won't be much,' he said.

'I expect it will be quite enough for your stepmother,' said Laura. 'It's all right to have an extra person to meals; it's quite another thing to have to find them a bed and give them breakfast next morning.'

Colin knew that the only possible arrangement, as his stepmother had pointed out, would be that Laura should have his room, and that he himself would be obliged to sleep on the settee in the living-room, so he agreed that perhaps she knew best, and added that she would find his father dull.

Upon arrival she was given sherry by Howard, then shown over the bungalow by Fiona. Lunch, out of tins, which made a change from school meals, (and also, although not such a welcome one, from the French cooking of her employer's chef), was followed by a visit to the lighthouse tower. Fiona declined to join in climbing the stairs which led up to the lantern room and the gallery, and Colin, with his accepted abhorrence of heights, did not suggest himself as a member of the expedition.

Laura, always observant, noted with interest the glance which Fiona gave him, and the slight petulant frown which accompanied it, when he said that he would go for a walk. She announced that tea would be at half-past four, and that, meanwhile, she was going to put her feet up for an hour, after Colin had helped with the washing up. The couples parted at the base of the tower, and Laura soon realised what Colin had meant when he represented his father as being dull. The tower although neither as high nor as streamlined as the new light house some nine hundred yards away to the south-west of it, was high enough to make talking a thankless process on the winding iron staircase as it went on and on, and up and up. It was lighted here and there by rectangular windows of double thickness, but, as all the living-quarters were at ground level, there were no rooms in the tower itself except storage spaces. Even the lamp room, so-called, was not a room in the accepted sense, but an inside balcony surrounding the magnifying glass of the light.

There was a door from the lamp room to the gallery which surrounded it, and this Howard opened and, having difficulty in getting his breath back after the climb up the stairs, he did not speak, but signed to Laura to step out into the air. This she did, to meet a tearing south-west wind which threatened to blow the hair off her head.

'Let's get round to the lee side!' bellowed Howard, finding breath enough to yell these words into her ear. He led the way, and, with the bulk of the lamp room between her and the wind, Laura gazed at the view with considerable interest and with much less discomfort than she had experienced on emerging from the lamp room.

The view consisted mostly of sea, for on this side the lighthouse overlooked the huge bay which the island helped to shelter. As she looked about her, however, she realised that from the gallery not only the bay but a distant view of the school came into her orbit. There was no mistaking it, for a misguided architect of the nineteenth century had chosen to give it the appearance of an American film producer's idea of a castle. The entrance doors were beneath a massive tower, and lesser towers, abominably pinnacled, formed the wings of the building, and these, together with the entrance tower, now provided classrooms, dormitories, staffrooms and the headmaster's private suite.

'You get a good view of the school from here,' she said. Howard handed over the glasses through which he had been watching the Channel Islands boat cutting her way towards port.

'A splendid view,' he agreed. 'Alter the focus if it doesn't suit you. There is independent adjustment on both eyepieces. Of course, I don't bother much about looking at the scenery.

I am a bird-watcher and an astronomer – the latter in only a
very small way, of course. Birds are my major interest. I am
hoping for great things in the course of my tenancy here.'

Then it began. Having begun, it went on and on and on, until
it seemed to Laura that time stood still and there was nothing
left in the world but Howard and his flat, bleating, one-toned,
middle-aged voice telling her about birds, and other birds and
more birds. Laura was not prepared to go as far as Bertie
Wooster's friend Mr Corcoran, whom birds bored stiff except
when broiled and in the society of a cold bottle, but by the
time she had been standing on the lighthouse gallery for the best
part of an hour and a half, she could understand Corky's
feelings.

There was no doubt that Howard Spalding had made a close
study of his subject. He told Laura, early on in his monologue,
that the island, with its entire lack of what he called beaches,
was a dead end so far as waders were concerned, but of other
seabirds he gave full details and a faithful account.

'I have listed no fewer than eighteen species which I con-
fidently expect to observe before we leave here next Easter,'
he told her. He proceeded to enumerate them, supplying a considerable amount of information about each one. He began
with the Manx shearwater and concluded with the Sandwich
tern. Between these he regaled Laura with accounts of the
life-cycle, breeding habits, migrations and *habitat* of Cory's
and the sooty shearwater, the fulmar and the cormorant, the
Pomarine skua, the great black-backed, the lesser black-backed,
the Mediterranean and the little gull, and, as well as describing
the Sandwich variety, he enlarged upon the history of the
whiskered, the gull-billed and the Caspian tern.

Even this was not sufficient. Leaving the seabirds, he went
on to speak of the hobby, the peregrine and the red-footed
falcon. These also he hoped to study, although not from his
perch on the lighthouse. They would have to be stalked and
watched from vantage points inland. He took her round to the
windward side of the lighthouse again, to indicate these vantage
points.

Laura, cold, dispirited and experiencing the helpless anger
of the irretrievably trapped, coupled with a bitter dislike of

the trapper, suddenly noticed something much more interesting to her than her host's interminable discourse. This was the sight of Colin leaving the bungalow by a door in the white-washed wall which protected the windows of the living-quarters of the lighthouse, and slinking – there was no other word for it – round the corner so that, almost immediately, he was hidden from view. So he had *not* been for a walk, she thought. Surely it had not taken him more than an hour and a half to wash up the dishes which had been used at lunch, and, anyway, why this obvious anxiety to be undetected leaving the lighthouse?

Howard continued his natural history lecture. He had led the way round to the lee side again, so that she could hear him. He had dealt with the hobby and the peregrine, and was now embarked upon the red-footed falcon.

'Known to ornithologists as *Falco vespertinus*,' he stated, 'it is actually not unlike the hobby, but cannot be mistaken for it by the expert, as it is a more delicately built bird. Its colour-ing is similar to that of the hobby, of course, but its general habits make it distinguishable, for whereas the hobby, like the peregrine, will swoop on its prey (a small bird, for example) while the latter is in the air – albeit the hobby, as I pointed out, is also fond of insects, which the peregrine will not touch – the red-footed falcon, or *Falco vespertinus*, not only eats insects but is also interested in frogs, lizards and small mammals. Of course, the peregrine will also eat small mammals – it has been known to take larger ones, such as the rabbit – but, as you see, there need be no confusion in identifying the species.'

'Yes, I see that,' said Laura, with an effort.

'*Falco vespertinus* – its name, again, renders it individuality, since peregrine is known as *Falco peregrinus*, as you would expect, and hobby is *Falco subbuteo* (two b's) – *vespertinus*, as I was about to say, is rare, of course, being seen occasionally in eastern and southern England, but almost never, I believe, in the rest of the British Isles. It is a crepuscular bird and I do not expect to see it hunting – that is, if I am fortunate enough to see it at all – May is the likeliest month – until late in the evening.'

Laura had almost ceased to listen. She had spotted Colin again. He had left the vicinity of the lighthouse and had begun

to run. More often than not he was out of sight, for the terrain
around the lighthouse consisted of humps and bumps from the
digging out of quarries, and there were holes of considerable
size where workings had been begun and then abandoned. In
addition, considerable cover was provided by the naturally uneven surface of the island.

At last, just when Laura had decided that she must put a
stop to Howard's eloquence by pleading that she was feeling
very cold – this was true enough – she had squinted down her
nose and decided that it had turned an improbable shade of
pale mauve – Howard himself suggested that perhaps they ought
to return to the living-quarters.

'If Colin has gone out, and we are up here, I am afraid my
wife may be lonely,' he said apologetically. 'In any case, I ought
not to monopolise our guest the whole of the time.'

Laura said nothing. They were almost at the door to the lamp
room. She opened it and led the way down the stairs. There
was a gas fire in the living-room. Thankfully she went straight
over to it and crouched down.

'Good gracious, Howard!' said Fiona, coming in from the
kitchen. 'You've never kept Mrs Gavin out on that windy little
ledge all this time, have you?'

'I got carried away, my dear.'

'Pity it isn't true in actual fact,' said his wife, sourly. 'What
can you have found to look at all this time? You've been gone
for nearly two hours! I do think it's too bad of you. Mrs Gavin
must be frozen!'

'I'm sorry, my dear. I was telling Mrs Gavin about the birds
which will visit the island later on. Come to think of it, I am
a trifle chilly myself.' He moved towards the gas fire. Laura
moved aside to make him room. 'How long has Colin been
gone?'

Fiona shot a quick glance at Laura.

'Gone? Oh, I don't know. He left me all the washing-up to
do, I know that much. I wanted to ask him such a lot about the
school. I didn't get a chance to talk to him last week-end, because those frightful friends of yours were here.'

'I thought you liked the Kempsons. I only asked them because I thought you'd be glad of some company apart from my

own, and Ronald Ferrars never comes at week-ends. Arthur Kempson—'

'Oh, *he's* all right, I suppose, but you took him off directly after lunch, just as you did Mrs Gavin today, and *I* got stuck with the awful wife. I have always detested that woman. She talked about her idiotic Yoga the whole time. Colin nearly went mad, and so did I.'

'What did we go mad about?' asked Colin, choosing this moment to reappear.

'Oh, nothing, really,' said his stepmother. 'Come and help me get the tea. You cut thinner bread and butter than I do.'

Colin made a small-boy grimace at Laura, and followed Fiona into the kitchen.

'How does he make out at the school?' asked Howard, seating himself.

'Pretty well,' Laura replied. 'The boys think it's marvellous to learn Russian. They all want to join the cast of U.N.C.L.E. or go into the Foreign Office or something.'

'That's what I have in mind for Colin himself when he's finished his time at Oxford. He seems to have a real gift for languages. It seems a great pity that he has to miss a year because of that nervous breakdown. He's very highly strung, I'm afraid. Clever boys so often are, and Colin is a very clever boy.'

Laura did not contradict either of these statements, although she disagreed with both. She did not believe that very clever boys were particularly subject to nervous breakdowns. She regarded them as a lazy lot, on the whole, who could be trusted neither to worry about their work nor to burn the candle at both ends. In her view, it was the run-of-the-mill students who overworked and suffered from anxiety neuroses. As for Colin's being a *very* clever boy, he had shown no particular signs of possessing supernormal brain-power, so far as she was aware. He was, in fact, rather childish in many respects.

'They're very quiet out there,' said Howard, when Laura offered no comment on Colin's cleverness. 'I wonder whether they need any help? Colin doesn't like helping with the chores. I hope he hasn't said anything unkind to Fiona. Usually they hit it off pretty well together, although Colin gets very moody at times.' He raised his voice. 'Anything I can do to help in there?'

There was no reply for a moment, but Laura, whose hearing was acute, thought she heard a slight scuffling sound, followed by short but urgent muttering. Then the answer came from Fiona.

'Good heavens, no! We shan't be long. How does Mrs Gavin like her tea?'

'Just as it comes,' said Laura, knowing that this was how she would get it, anyway. She had yet to meet the hostess who paid any attention whatsoever to the preferences of guests in this respect.

'We cash in on the deliveries to the other lighthouse,' said Fiona, appearing with the tray, followed by Colin, who carried a cakestand, 'but their butcher comes only twice a week, on Tuesdays and Saturday afternoons, and I haven't a fridge. Oh, that will be the boy now.'

'Have you got to know the people in the other lighthouse?' Laura asked Howard, when his wife had gone out to deal with the butcher's boy.

'I think Fiona has,' he replied. 'There are three keepers, two of them married. Of course, they have their duties, and the two married ones have children, I believe. We ought to invite them over, I suppose, but I have my book to write and Fiona dislikes young children. All the same, she needs the society of other women. I wish we could suggest that the women take it in turn to look after the babies. Then one or even two of them could come here and keep my wife company. I spend so much time either writing or studying or on the lighthouse gallery that I'm afraid she has a dull time with me.'

'Not half so dull as when you're gassing about your beastly herring-gulls and things,' said Colin. 'I expect you bored Mrs Gavin stiff.'

'Not at all. But I was nearly *frozen* stiff,' said Laura, laughing quite convincingly and speaking the only half of the truth which was socially acceptable. 'It's amazingly breezy up there.'

'More than it is down here, then,' said Colin morosely. 'I never knew such a pest-house.'

'Did you have a good walk?' asked his father.

'If you call it that. By the way, I shan't be over next Saturday. I'm going to Bournemouth.'

'Bournemouth? I thought you detested seaside resorts.'

'They're putting on *Uncle Vanya*. A party of us are going to see it. Incidentally, there's a spare ticket. I suppose you wouldn't care to come?' It was safe enough to make the offer. He knew quite well that his father would not accept it.

'It's very kind of you to invite me, my boy,' said Howard, in noticeably cold tones, 'but I could hardly leave your mother here alone. The performance will be in the evening, I suppose?'

'Yes. Seven-thirty.'

'What's at seven-thirty?' asked Fiona, coming into the room again.

'My dear, Colin and his friends are going to Bournemouth next Saturday to see a play. He has a spare ticket and has very kindly offered it to me, but, of course, I can't leave you here alone. I should not be back, very likely, until the early hours of the morning.'

Fiona looked out of the window at the white-washed wall and shuddered.

'No, I couldn't be here alone,' she said. 'I really couldn't stand it. It's so lonely, and the wind makes such a noise.'

'Well, look here,' said Colin, as though inspired, 'why shouldn't *you* have the ticket? It seems a pity to waste it. I'll pick you up here at ten o'clock on Saturday morning. We're going to have lunch in Bournemouth, and then some of the blokes will watch football, and then we'll go on to the show. You could have a push round the shops in the afternoon, and meet us for tea, and so forth. Then I could run you back here, and stay over Sunday, as usual. How's that for an idea, do you think?' He gave her another of the glances which had passed between them before.

'I'd simply love it,' said Fiona. 'Would you mind *very* much, Howard? I'm dying to see some shops and a civilised town.'

'It will do you the world of good,' said Howard, after an embarrassingly long pause, 'and, of course, I shall enjoy a day on my own. My dear, give Mrs Gavin another cup of tea. Mrs Gavin, another slice of cake? Are you proposing, by the way, to make one of the party next Saturday?'

'Chekov isn't my cup of tea,' said Laura. It was the first she had heard of the expedition. Colin's eloquent gaze implored her not to mention the fact that he had invented it on the spur of the moment. 'Oh, Lord! Not Rattenbury and Stoner!' she thought. It was a dismaying idea.

What was equally dismaying was a row which flared up between father and son as Laura was preparing to leave. It was half-past six. The sun had set and a misty dusk enveloped the island. Howard had gone outside to look at the sky, and came back to report that he should do no star-gazing that evening. He added that, in any case, he and Colin would escort Laura back to the school.

'It will only need one of us to do that,' said Colin. 'You go, and I'll stay here and keep Fiona company.'

'I wish you would not refer to your mother as Fiona.'

'Why on earth not? She's nearer my age than yours, and she's *not* my mother. Don't be a fool!'

'I suppose,' said his father, in tones which trembled, 'I have asked for that. Perhaps I *have* been a fool. Exactly how far did your walk take you today? And how long did you stay out?'

Colin stared at his father, and then began to bluster.

'What on earth do you mean? What are you accusing me of? Where has your little mind wandered to?'

'Oh, Colin! Oh, Howard!' cried Fiona. 'Remember we have a guest!'

'Who is now going to take herself off,' said Laura, loudly and cheerfully.

'I shall drive with you,' said Howard. 'Colin, you will follow us in my car, and we will drive back together. I should like an opportunity to talk to you, man to man.'

'Oh, and what about Fiona? Is she to be left here alone?'

'You have your choice. Either do as I say, or drive to the school in Mrs Gavin's car and *walk* back. It will do you good to take a little *real* exercise instead of philandering here in the kitchen and *pretending* to go for long walks. Do you think I could not see you from the gallery of the tower? Did you suppose that I was unaware of the time at which you left the house this afternoon?'

'Really, Howard!' protested his wife. 'After all, there was a good deal of washing-up to be done.'

'With which, on your own admission, he did not help you!'

'I am afraid I *must* be going,' said Laura. 'I promised to play chess this evening. And, really, I don't need an escort. It is only a few miles, and my headlamps are in perfect working order.'

'I'm coming with you,' said Colin, his face puckered dolefully as though he was going to cry. 'And I shan't come back, Father, do you hear? If Mrs Gavin will give me a lift, you can jolly well keep your own car here and bring it back to the school when you jolly well like!'

'Mrs Gavin will *not* give you a lift,' said Laura coolly. 'I'll see you in school on Monday morning.'

'I'm very sorry,' said Howard miserably, when he had seen her into her car. 'The boy is at a difficult stage, I'm afraid. He doesn't mean any harm, but he makes himself a nuisance to my wife. I've watched it going on for some time, and I must put a stop to it. It isn't fair on Fiona, this kind of calf-love. To begin with, I was immensely glad and relieved that he seemed to take to her so readily, but this adolescent devotion is beginning to be rather trying.'

'Yes, but it's a phase they all go through,' said Laura, keeping to a casual tone. 'One comfort, it soon passes over when they meet the real person. I expect your wife has been very kind to him, and this is his way of expressing his gratitude. Young men are like that, aren't they?'

'Oh, well,' said Howard, in a tone of relief, 'I hope you are right. I hate being at odds with the boy, and, of course, he isn't really fit yet after his illness.'

Colin came out to them.

'I am sorry, Father,' he said. 'I did get gassing in the kitchen about school and so forth, and I didn't go for much of a walk. No – er – no hard feelings, I hope?'

'Of course not, my boy,' said Howard, making his tone much too brisk. 'Now, about seeing Mrs Gavin home . . .'

'Oh, nonsense, Mr Spalding!' said Laura, in definite and vigorous protest. 'Goodbye, and thank you *very* much for having me, and for giving me such an interesting talk about birds. Goodbye, Colin! Be seeing you!'

She let in the clutch and bowled away northwards, thankful that the unpleasant episode was over, but wondering how often it was likely to be repeated. She made a private resolve that she would never again accept an invitation to visit the lighthouse, but reflected that, after having been the witness of such a scene between father and son, it was unlikely that either of them would want to see her there.

CHAPTER SIX

News from Nowhere

... had seen a little lugger in what we called Kit's Hole.'

'... when they got down to the Hole the lugger was already under way, though still close in.'

It was Laura's custom to write twice a week to Dame Beatrice, of whose relatives' various addresses she had taken note. She missed the company of her employer, and the letters were a way of keeping in touch, although the correspondence was inclined to be one-sided, since Dame Beatrice seldom replied except by laconic postcard.

A funny thing happened on the way to the bathroom (wrote Laura, on the day following her visit to the disused lighthouse). I have to climb a flight of stairs from my room in order to gain access to the tubbery and on these stairs I pass a tall, narrow window which overlooks the cove where I swam. You can't see the shore of the cove, but only the end of the Point and a fair amount of salt water, because forward from the cove the next landfall is one of the Channel Islands, I don't know which, but I think it is Guernsey.

Well, I always pause at this window and take a butchers at the view. This morning, as usual, I was up at the crack of dawn, because I share this particular bathroom with Mr Grange and Mr Skelton, and they (although just and Godfearing persons, and men of good repute) are apt, like all too many of their sex, to leave the bathroom not at all as they would wish to find it. It is my habit, therefore, to make sure I get first dip, which means a scum-free bath, unsplashed walls and a dry bath-mat and surrounding floor.

Well, as I paused at this window, I noticed a boat coming in. Nothing odd in that, you may say. A cove is a cove is a cove. Yes, I know. I also know that a boat can lie not so very far off shore at this particular cove, and still be in five fathoms – which is, by interpretation, thirty feet – of water. It all sounds perfectly reasonable, and it would be, if the time had been, say, ten-thirty instead of six-thirty in the morning, and if the month had been May instead of mid-March.

I was sufficiently intrigued to go back to my room and get my binoculars. These I trained on the vessel and noted that it was a powerful motor-yacht and carried two small boats. I estimated its length as being at least eighty-five feet. There were a couple of men on deck, and one of them was having a good look through a telescope at the cove, the cliffs and, ultimately, the school. As we have among the boys a small kid who is the son of the present president of Querigua Montes, I thought it well to apprise the Man of the boat's presence in our waters, as all the Staff have been briefed that there is always a chance that small Manoel may have to withstand attempts to kidnap him, and that, if one of these attempts came off, it might involve the school in an international incident.

After breakfast, however, the boat had gone, and Mr Eastleigh, noting this, dealt with me kindly, but decided, I think, that I was the usual (in his opinion) jittery female and must be told not to panic. However, he thanked me for my zeal and asked after you. He knows you by sight because he's attended some of your public lectures.

Yesterday I went to lunch and tea with young Spalding's people. They have taken over the disused lighthouse I told you about. Spalding's father is about fifty, I should think. He's keen on seabirds and is writing a book about them. He manages, in conversation, to make them seem remarkably dull. I nearly froze to death up on the lighthouse gallery while he held forth about, among other of our feathered friends, the Manx shearwater. It breeds on turfy, rocky islands, (which calls this one to mind), and apparently it is but a visitor hereabouts, and actually nests further north and west, as well as in south-west Europe and the Scillies. The Manx shearwater we get is not, as, in your ignorance, you may have supposed, *Procellaria puffinus puffinus*, but rather *Procellaria puffinus mauritanicus*, which breeds in the Balearics and comes to see us from August to October.

I had to put up with this sort of thing from two-thirty until nearly half-past four, standing on the lighthouse gallery in the bracing air and a Force 8 gale, and went down to tea more dead than alive. The only item of interest during the whole of this martyrdom was the spectacle of young Spalding – now, by his request, known to me as Colin – have *not* reciprocated by inviting him to call me Laura – sneaking out of the house after I had been up on the gallery for what seemed about a fortnight, and pretending, when he came back, that he'd been for a long walk. I *think* he's pursuing Mrs Spalding – a row between father and son indicated this. Fiona by name, she is about thirty and his father's second wife, but no doubt she has ways and means of choking Colin off, since, dull though her life most probably is, his antics can scarcely do more than come under the heading of light entertainment, if that. He is a callow, conceited, schoolboyish youth with no head for heights and a distressing tendency to quote Neitzsche in the original German. This surely can't endear him to *any* woman, particularly if she understands German, Neitzsche being fundamentally unsound as regards our sex.

Fun and games this afternoon (wrote Laura, three days later). Mr Ferrars, known to his intimates, i.e. Colin and Mr Heathers, as Ronnie, and to our sweet but unimaginative lads as the Ferret (hopeless description!), has gone out and got himself posted as missing. He is the only person, except for the headmaster, the games master and Mr Grange, who isn't in charge of a form, so he has been told to help Mr Heathers, yclept Erica – a most apposite name, as the innocent young gent has a certain chubby girlish charm about him – with the Sevens and Eights. I have only ten boys in my form, so they are put in with Mr Pocock's lot for games and I get the afternoons free, as I am considered too delicately nurtured and, I rather think, too bone-headed to take any part in the coaching. I offered to do Mr Eastleigh's typing, but he prefers to keep his secrets to himself.

Well, apparently Heathers and Ferrars think it's a complete waste of time for two of them to watch twenty extremely well-behaved little boys kicking a ball about and pulling one another down into the mud, so they take on the job in turn, and it happened to be Ferrars' day off.

Nobody saw him go, and he gave no indication of his plans, but, when they get time off, most of the masters make a bee-line for the mainland except for Heathers, who teaches geography and is a bit of a geologist. Tea-time came, and no sign of Ferrars, but this impressed nobody, because, except for the master in charge, there is no rule that any of the Staff need turn up for tea, although most of us do, at this time of year, because there's nothing much else to tempt one, and, anyway, we are all supposed to sit in with our own forms at Prep., which lasts from six until seven.

It has become the custom, however (for we are a matey lot in our Staffroom), to put some of the forms together for Prep. so as to give freedom and a bit of leisure to the deserving. Thus Mr Pocock and I take it in turn at doing the chore with our combined groups (although Mr Eastleigh did tell me that I could count Prep. as an extraneous duty and so dodge it, if I liked), and Robson and Skelton also have an arrangement. Old Mr Grange, who counts as Senior Master now that Mr Noble has been sent back to Kent, insists on taking his turn, although he hasn't a form. Grange is known (inevitably, I suppose) as Mariana, and is popular because he produces the annual school play, and so all the little Thespians suck up to him like mad in order to be considered for chief parts. All small boys think they can act Sir Laurence Olivier's head off. It's only in adolescence that they retreat into their shells and shy away from making a public appearance. I shall never forget how utterly insufferable Hamish was, the year before last, when chosen to play Mr Toad in *Toad of Toad Hall*, but that's by the way.

To resume my narrative: nobody bothered, or even thought about it, when Ferrars didn't show up for tea, but when he was still absent at five minutes to six Heathers became plaintive. It looked, you see, as though he would have to take prep. until Ferrars got back, and that was breaking a gentleman's agree-ment, this being that whichever one of the partners takes games, the other takes prep. and puts the form to bed.

I wasn't 'on' that evening, so I went to my room and lay on

the bed and re-read *Thank You, Jeeves* until I heard the bell that ends prep. Then I went down to the day-room, where the lads get milk and biscuits, and helped Mrs Eastleigh to supervise this Lucullan feast. After it, the custom is for us to assemble for night prayers and then begin to put the lads to kip. The youngest kick off at seven-thirty and the others at quarter-hour intervals until we have interred the oldest ones, the twelves. After that, the rest of the night is our own, and we go to bed as soon as we like, except for the master who is on night rounds at ten o'clock.

When, at seven-thirty, Ferrars still was not with us, and Heathers, naturally enough, became restive, because now, in addition to taking them for games and prep., he had to put his babes to bed. I felt sufficiently sorry for him to act as stand-in, an offer which he accepted with becoming gratitude. Skelton always puts my Elevens to bed. He's the games man. Well, my method, on such occasions, is simple but effective. All in bed by the appointed time – a story. Failure in this respect – no story. Some obtain the same effect by flourishing a threatening hairbrush, others by denying to the undeserving a seat at the Saturday film-show in the dining-room, but I. find that my way works like a charm with the Sevens and Eights. The occasion I am describing was no exception, and by a quarter past eight I had done my rounds and was in the Staff common-room ready and willing to play chess with Mr Grange, who is an expert. Fortunately I've learnt enough from you to be able to give him some sort of a game, although I'm in nothing like his class.

It's pretty quiet in a men's common-room. They don't knit and gossip, as women do, but concentrate on cross-words, or the daily papers (which come from the mainland and don't reach us until near enough lunch-time) or play bridge, chess, draughts, or occupy themselves in just plain reading or even in marking exercise books, although this is pretty rare and is considered anti-social. All, then, was no gas and an absence of gaiters, when the holy calm was shattered by Heathers. I don't think anybody had noticed, up to that time, that he wasn't among us, but now he came bursting in, wild-eyed and in-coherent, asking what on earth should he do? The Man had sent him to get Ferrars, who was wanted on the telephone, and no Ferrars was on the premises.

'Do you mean he's still out?' asked Pocock. This, it transpired, was what Heathers did mean. 'Well, answer it yourself,' advised Pocock. 'I expect Ferrars has had a breakdown in his car. No need to get in a flap. There's no law to say that he's got to be in by nine o'clock.'

'But he didn't take his car. He only went for a walk,' bleated poor little Erica. 'He must have met with an accident.'

'All right,' said Skelton. 'Do as Pocock says, and go and answer the 'phone. The call is probably from Ferrars himself. The Man thought the caller said '*for* Ferrars, instead of *from* Ferrars, I expect.'

It didn't turn out to be that. I didn't think it would. Mr Eastleigh isn't the man to muck up a telephone message. He always insists on answering the 'phone himself, incidentally, before he hands over the receiver. I suppose most of the calls are for him, anyway, but, if they do happen to be for the Staff, I suppose he likes to keep his finger on the pulse, as it were.

Heathers came back after a few minutes and again asked us what he ought to do. The call was from some girl who wanted to know why Ferrars had stood her up. Apparently he'd promised to meet her for a drink at the pub at the mainland end of the causeway, and hadn't shown up. She was feeling more than a bit shirty about it, Heathers said.

'And so am I,' went on Heathers, legitimately aggrieved. 'It means that the blighter intended all along to shove prep. off on to me, and get me to put the chaps to bed.'

'Odd,' said Grange. 'Who *is* this girl?'

'I've no idea,' said Heathers. 'I didn't even know there *was* a girl. I thought it was that Miss Beverley. I suppose that's where he got to on Saturday and Sunday, only he took his car then. Really, he *is* the limit. I call it a lousy way to go on.'

'Well,' said Grange, 'I'll give him – what's the time now? – a quarter past nine? – say I give him until ten. If he's not back by then, I suppose I'll have to let the Man know.' Lock-up's at ten, except on Saturdays, you see, so that fixed zero hour.

'I think you ought to let him know at once,' said Pocock. 'Suppose the young idiot has tumbled into one of the quarries?

It would be easy enough, you know. A chap of his age doesn't stand girls up without a pretty good reason. *I* should say he's hurt himself or something.'

'Perhaps you're right,' said Grange, and Robson and Skelton backed up the idea, so off went Mariana to the boss and laid the depositions before him. Mr Eastleigh came back to the common-room with him and asked whether anybody had the least idea which way Ferrars would have taken, but nobody had. Then Colin had a bright thought.

'It's possible my father may have seen him,' he said. He explained about his parent's capers on the lighthouse gallery. 'Unfortunately, the lighthouse isn't on the 'phone,' he added, looking hopefully at the headmaster.

'It is not *like* Mr Ferrars to absent himself in this way,' said the Man, 'without a word to anyone. You are all free agents, apart from your obvious commitments, of course, so he had a right to do as he pleased, but I sincerely hope that nothing untoward has happened to him. I should be happier if he had taken his car. That would only mean that it had broken down. A car accident, as such, would have been reported to us by this time. I do not care for the thought that he has been wandering about on foot after dark, with all these quarries around. I think, therefore, that it would be a good plan for you to contact your father, Mr Spalding, if you think he can help us in any way. You had better take someone with you.'

'I'll go,' I said. 'In *my* car,' I added, having seen something of Colin's driving. So off we pushed, and landed up at the lighthouse in a reasonably short time. Colin, of course, had a key, but he also had the sense to give a shout, announcing himself, as soon as we got inside the lighthouse door. It was as well that I'd gone with him, as his father was up on the gallery studying the stars, and Colin, of course, won't go up there, so I had to. I soon located Mr Spalding and told him why we were there. He went all jittery on me – scared about something, I should say – and talked much too fast.

'Oh, dear!' he said. 'No, I've seen nothing of him since a week ago, when he came to take tea with us, as usual. I've seen nothing in particular all day, except a powerful vessel which crept in under the cliffs and made for the cove. She came at about two o'clock and dropped anchor, and a boat put off, but I lost sight of it, as I cannot see the shore of the cove from here, and then, of course, the sea-mist rolled in and one couldn't see anything. I went down to have my tea, and did not come up again until after dark, as I wished to study the night sky. By that time the boat – the large one – must have gone, since I saw no riding-lights.'

'Well, I'm sorry to have bothered you,' I said. 'We thought there was just a chance that you'd spotted Mr Ferrars and could tell us which way he might have gone.'

Anyway, to go on with my story, we went back to school to find the place in a nice state of excitement. For the first time I learned that there is a prison on the island. What is more, one of the prisoners had escaped. The warders had been to see Mr Eastleigh to warn him not to let the boys wander about tomorrow, as, although the escaped man is not considered dangerous, there is always such a thing as taking a chance.

One dislikes being fanciful, but I couldn't help wondering whether the boat which I'd spotted on the Sunday morning and which, according to Mr Spalding, had shown up again on Tuesday afternoon, had anything to do with the escape. These things seem to be planned by master minds with all the resources of the American Marines nowadays.

Mr Eastleigh had to make up his mind what to do, and it didn't take him long. He assembled us in the common-room and told us that no volunteers would be allowed to go and look for Ferrars. With a possibly desperate criminal on the loose, he could not risk letting any of the garrison leave the house. The boys must be guarded, and anybody trying to make a forced entry – 'the man will be in need of money and a change of clothes, most likely' – must be choked off. We saw his point, of course. What was more, I don't think anybody was very keen to go out and shout for Ferrars, with a desperado probably lurking in one of the quarries, so there we all were, ready to repel boarders, and much preferring to meet the escaped convict, if we had to, on our own ground, rather than in the open country.

This, of course, was all very well, but I couldn't help thinking of the wretched young Ferrars lying helpless in one of the quarries with a broken leg or something. However, it was obviously out of the question to go and look for him that night, especially as we had no idea in which direction to begin the search, and, in any case, I'm usually prepared to concede that orders are orders, and to fall in with the wishes of my commanding officer. You must have noticed this. So nobody complained.

I tried to work it out as I lay in bed. (We wage slaves keep early hours, and I had hit the hay at about ten-forty-five.) If Ferrars had arranged to meet the girl for a drink, he couldn't have planned to get to the *rendezvous* until, at the earliest, six p.m. I don't know exactly when he left the school, but he would have had a fair amount of time to fill in before meeting the girl at the pub.

Well, it all seemed so improbable, especially as he didn't even take his car. The time of year was the very early spring, the weather was on the chilly side and it was just the sort of day when a sea-mist comes up and blots out everything, and that was exactly what had happened. I took a bet with myself that he'd got caught in the mist and perhaps fallen into one of the quarries or even over the cliff. This thought had me worried, and I decided that, in the morning, something would have to be done about him.

Then another idea came to me. If Ferrars' only plan was to meet this girl, he surely would have taken his car. He's the last person to go for long, lonely walks. It seemed to me that he must have been up to something. I thought and thought, but nothing came, so at last I got up and looked out of my window. There was nothing to be seen except the stars. The mist had cleared later in the afternoon, and now there was a lovely clear night, although there was no moon. I was prompted to go up the stairs to that window I told you about, and look towards the cove where I had seen that big boat, but there was nothing there at all, so far as I could see – no riding-lights, I mean – so I gave up and went back to bed. More news (if any) tomorrow. By the way, it was news to me that Ferrars sometimes takes tea at the Spaldings' lighthouse on his afternoons off. Do you think Mrs Spalding is the attraction? He can hardly go there to be lectured on our feathered friends by Howard – or can he? And do you think he was making for the lighthouse and is carrying on what used to be known as an intrigue? It might account for his not taking the car, mightn't it? – not to advertise his presence, you know.

However, he could hardly be staying the night there, so, as he hadn't met the girl, I thought he might still have met with an accident after he left the lighthouse.

CHAPTER SEVEN

Second Childhood

'I now felt for the first time the joy of exploration.'
'... the general colouring was uniform and sad.'

Breakfast duty, like tea duty, was on a rota. Laura woke from a short and troubled sleep just as dawn broke and, feeling unrefreshed, got up immediately and decided to go for her walk, telling herself that the headmaster's orders applied only to the hours of darkness.

She had descended the stairs and was about to let herself out by the side door when another thought came to her. She might as well find out whether Ferrars had returned from his wanderings. The Staff had been given the single rooms in the hotel, the doubles having been turned into dormitories for either three or four boys or used as classrooms. The dining-room had been retained as such, and the largest lounge did duty as the school assembly hall. The bar had become the woodwork centre and the long, narrow sun-parlour was in service as a gymnasium, although no apparatus could be used there except the balancing forms, the horse and the buck.

The official notice board in the common-room held not only the school time-table and the Staff duty rota, but the masters' room numbers. She consulted it, and discovered that Ferrars occupied bedroom thirty-six on the second floor. She went upstairs again, and cautiously tried the door. All the keys, by the headmaster's orders, were kept in the locks and on the outside, since the doors, as in other hotels, were self-locking, and there had been unnecessary and irritating occasions, during the first week, when masters had locked themselves out and had been obliged to trouble the headmaster for a second key which was kept in the hotel office.

The door of room thirty-six opened soundlessly, and Laura

70

stood in the doorway and listened. There was no sound in the room, the curtains had not been closed, and soon, even in the faint light of the very early morning, she could see that the narrow bed was unoccupied. She closed the door again and, this time, left the building, carrying the stout ashplant which accompanied her on long walks, and slinging on a pair of binoculars.

It was just after six o'clock. If Ferrars had decided upon tramping the island before meeting the girl, there were only two routes he would be likely to have taken. These roads formed, roughly, the letter Y in reverse. That is to say, there was only one road from the end of the causeway to the hotel and a mile beyond it, and then it forked, one way, that to the left, leading to Spalding's lighthouse and out to the new lighthouse on the Point, the other, that to the right, going out to the quarries and the few arable fields beyond them. After that it led towards the high, relentlessly perpendicular, grass-covered cliffs which formed the west coast.

There were only two villages on the island, for the chief place, at the end of the causeway, was properly called a town. It was ugly, compact, and grey-walled with nothing of the dignity and beauty of Cotswold towns, but was far more reminiscent of the mining villages of Durham or South Wales. It had several mean-looking shops and a couple of public houses, a church built in the mid-nineteenth century and a Baptist chapel. There was also one cinema and this concluded the amenities.

The two villages were placed one at the junction of the stem of the letter Y and the other half-way along its western arm. These villages housed the quarrymen and fishermen. The town, presumably, was the supply depôt of the island and had been built, no doubt, to form a useful link with the mainland. Somewhere behind and to the east of it lay the prison. Laura's cove was about half-way between the prison and Spalding's lighthouse.

Laura's instinct inclined her to take the path to the cove. About two-thirds of the way down the long, winding slope which led to the shore, a narrower path, trodden by feet and not made by hands, led away to the broken cliffs. The cove itself was empty, except for its boulders. There was no boat lying off-shore and no sign of any human being. She took the path. It was rough and uneven, but it meandered, mostly down-hill, and skirted the edge of a quarry which must have been abandoned early in its history, for it was nowhere very deep, and the quarrymen had not even troubled to cart away some of the excavated stone, but had left it lying untidily, some on the lip of the asymmetrical hole and some in rough heaps in its depths. Grass and bushes had grown up, but not so thickly that she was unable to see that there was no sign of Ferrars.

She walked on. The path broadened and narrowed in illogical fashion and was never straight for more than a dozen to twenty yards at a time. Now it ascended and wound inland for a bit, now it dipped to a shallow little valley and at one point it came out upon low cliffs. Laura went to the edge of these and looked about her long and earnestly, but there was nothing except the sea, and, a long way off to her left, on the arc of the bay, a faint suggestion of the buildings of the main-land seaside resort from which her car had brought her to the island.

She went back to the path and followed its windings until it dipped between gorse bushes, rose to a little knoll and suddenly came to an end on the edge of a precipitous drop. On the other side of this she could see, in the distance, a rectangular menace of dark grey stone which she took to be the prison. There was no obvious way of crossing the dangerous inlet, so she turned back and made her way towards the cove.

To her right, but some distance ahead, she could see the ancient castle. Nothing was left of it but a tumble-down gate-house and a small, rectangular keep. It occurred to her that Ferrars might have decided, in spite of the warning notices, to climb over the fence which barred it from the public and take a look inside. If he had done so, anything might have hap-pened to him, for the warning notices were grim.

Laura stood still and looked about her. On the far side of the cove a very steep path seemed to lead to the grounds of the hotel. She did not believe that this could really be the case, for she had explored these fully and there was no trace of any path which might lead down to the cove. However, she thought it worthwhile to find out where the steep path went, so she descended to the cove, picked her way among the boulders and began to mount the headland.

As she had supposed, the path skirted but did not lead to the hotel grounds. It brought her out high above the cove and in view of the rented lighthouse. It stood startlingly white against a gloomy, early-morning sky which promised rain. The sea, now that she had turned her back on the bay, where, owing to the long breakwaters which enclosed the harbour, the water always seemed comparatively calm, was becoming ruffled as the wind got up.

To the right, on the landward side, there were trees and bushes on the slope from the hotel to the cliff top. It was almost the only wooded area on the island. She made her way towards it, downhill at first and then in a fairly steep climb with no path to act as guide. Sometimes she stopped and shouted for Ferrars, and then listened, but, apart from some startled birds, there was no response. She had forgotten the escaped convict.

She reached the hotel boundaries, where some glass-fronted observation châlets had been erected, and an iron fence, grimly spiked at the top, barred off the private grounds from the rest of the hillside. She did not think that even the biggest and boldest boys would attempt to scale it. Apart from the spikes themselves, she did not think that the space between them would accommodate the width of a shoe. For her there was nothing for it, so far as she could see, but to scramble down to the cove and return by the way she had come.

It was easy enough to find a way down and to regain the original path. The cove itself looked desolate and unwelcoming, and the wind, which had risen higher by this time, blew in, cold and damp, from the sea. When she had passed the tremendous limestone cliff on which the castle stood and from which it seemed to be growing, she found herself on a pleasant little grassy plateau. Here she saw that there was a means of approach to the castle by way of some fencing which had been broken away. She looked at her watch again and decided that there was still time for exploration before she needed to return to get ready for breakfast. There was just a possibility that Ferrars was lying there injured and helpless.

Beyond the broken fence was an area of rough pasture, gorse bushes and blackthorn, but there was a well-defined trackway across it which led to a bridge and the castle. The bridge, however, was strongly barricaded off with barbed wire. It spanned a lower archway between two enormous out-croppings of the rock on which the castle was built, and at the end of it, distant perhaps a score of yards, was the shell of the gatehouse.

She studied the set-up for perhaps as long as five minutes, and then made up her mind. It was possible, she thought, to squeeze past one end of the barbed-ware barrier where a bit of the hillside had either crumbled away or had been forcibly dislodged by adventurous local youths, so she laid her ash-plant on the ground, and, exercising due caution, particularly in not looking down, for the rock-strewn ground, at this point, was some forty feet below her, she worked her way round and was soon on the bridge. The gatehouse was no more than an open archway and was partially barred off by a notice-board of formidable size which announced, in thick black letters a foot high: *Danger. Keep Out. Falling Masonry.*

'If that's all,' said Laura, aloud, 'I may as well take a chance.' She drew her ashplant between two uprights of the fencing, but, before she ventured all the way in, she took the precaution of gazing through the gatehouse arch into the small courtyard of the keep in an attempt to determine whether the masonry had sustained any recent damage. Her survey was reassuring, particularly as the ruined keep was open to the sky. The notice, she concluded, was directed against those who wanted to climb about on the walls. There seemed no danger so long as she remained away from these, and under the open sky, but, before going any further, she stood in the middle of the courtyard and called on Ferrars to answer. There was no reply, so she ducked under a narrow, round-headed archway and entered the keep.

It was in such a ruinous state that she thought at first it offered no points of interest, but then she saw, in one of the angles, a spiral stair. She went over to it. It was on the seaward side of the keep and seemed in fairly good repair. She stood at the foot of it and called again, but nothing except the booming reverberations of her own voice, as it went echoing down a winding passageway, came back to her.

Laura had the average person's instinct for exploration, and newel staircases had for her an almost morbid fascination, so much so that her employer, who was psychiatric consultant to the Home Office, had waxed facetious upon the subject and had spoken, tongue in cheek, of retrogressions and conditioned reflexes, references to which the non-suggestible Laura was accustomed to respond with rude hoots of laughter.

She paused, however, on the brink of this particular newel stair. It occurred to her that perhaps, in the interests of her husband and her young son, it might be as well if she refrained from getting herself knocked out by a fall of stone from the roof. She called again, but there was no answer. She laid her stick on the ground, ascended five steps, one hand on the newel post for support, stopped and listened. Then she called Ferrars' name for the third time before she turned carefully round on the narrow stair and went back to the outer air.

Something white was blowing about the interior of the roof-less keep. She followed it and snatched it up just as a gust was about to blow it into the courtyard. It was a handkerchief, a man's handkerchief, freshly laundered (by the look of it) and bearing the embroidered initial R. Ferrars' first name was Ronald. She called out again and again, but still received no answer, so at last she tucked the handkerchief into her pocket and turned back towards the hotel.

CHAPTER EIGHT

Manoel is Missing

'It was not very long after this that there occurred the first
of the mysterious events . . .'

Laura had squeezed cautiously past the end of the barbed
wire and negotiated the slight cliff-fall, and was fairly back on
the track which led to the broken fencing and the lane, when
she remembered her faithful ashplant. She also remembered
something else: somewhere on the island, unless he had
managed to elude the police cordon or been captured or had
managed to escape by boat, there was the convict lurking about,
and he was, she had to infer, a desperate man. It occurred to
Laura that there might have been another cause for thankfulness
in her having exercised caution in exploring the castle, apart
from the risk of falling masonry.

However, the stick was a favourite one, so she went back for
it. She remembered exactly where she had laid it down and
she re-entered the forbidden territory, cautiously, as before, in
the confident expectation of picking up the ashplant and re-
turning to the hotel with it. To her chagrin, surprise and alarm,
it was no longer there. There seemed only one interpretation
to be put upon this. Somebody else must be in the keep – and
who more likely than the convict to seize the chance of arming
himself with a lightweight but still formidable weapon? It was
not a pleasant thought.

Laura was the last person to panic, but it seemed the height
of foolishness to stand upon the order of her going. She went
at once, and, as soon as she was outside the barbed-wire barrier,
she ran until she reached the gates of the hotel. The time was
twenty minutes to eight. She took the stairs in great bounds and
made for the headmaster's sitting-room. She knocked loudly.
Mr Eastleigh himself opened the door.

'Quick!' said Laura. 'I think Mr Ferrars is in the ruined

castle. I need help and some rope or perhaps a stretcher. Can we organise something at once? I think the escaped convict may be there, too.'

'Breakfast will be ready in twenty minutes,' said the headmaster, calmly. 'We are not going to chase about after Ferrars or the convict just now. I am not pleased with Ferrars, and if you have been searching for him on your own, Mrs Gavin, without telling anyone what you were doing, I consider you have been very foolish and irresponsible. You know there is this escaped convict about. Go and get yourself tidy. You look dishevelled.'

Laura took herself off with outer meekness and inward fury. She felt about ten years old. On the stairs she met Skelton, the games master.

'Good morning,' he said. 'What's up? You look wind-swept.'

'Oh, shut up!' she said. 'I've just had that from the Man. I say, Ferrars isn't back, and I think the convict is hiding in the castle ruins and Ferrars may be there too. I want to organise a search party, but Mr Eastleigh won't hear of it. He ticked me off. Why shouldn't we look for Ferrars?'

'Job for the police now, not us. You don't mean you've been cruising around on your own?' He looked at her sternly.

'Why shouldn't I? Anyway, I'd forgotten about the convict. I was only thinking of Ferrars.'

'He's a young ass. As for you . . .'

'Oh, all *right!*' said Laura crossly. She went to her room and presented herself at the headmaster's table some fifteen minutes later, tidy and self-possessed, although inwardly she was still fuming.

'I have given the police your message about Ferrars,' said Mr Eastleigh. 'I had already reported his absence from the school.' He smiled at her. 'Now have your breakfast and then you can tell us what you've been up to. No, not a word until you have got to the toast and marmalade stage.' He laughed at her indignant expression. 'I am really very angry with you,' he added.

'Why, what has Mrs Gavin done?' asked his wife, coming into the room.

'I have forbidden her to mention it until we have eaten some, at least, of our breakfast. Sometimes I think my Staff need bear-

leaders, but we will say no more about it until the proper time.'
He laughed again at Laura's scowling face and passed her a
plate of ham and eggs. 'Now, then,' he said encouragingly, a
little later on, 'come along, Mrs Gavin. Out with it. What makes
you think that the convict and perhaps Ferrars are in those
ruins?'

Laura gave an account of her walk.

'But you might have been set upon and killed!' exclaimed
Mrs Eastleigh. 'What on earth should we have said to your
husband?'

'I don't believe I should be killed all that easily,' argued
Laura. 'Besides, I don't think the convict was armed. He took
my ashplant. At least, somebody did. It was a bit odd about
the handkerchief, though.'

'Have you got it?'

'Yes, I brought it down with me.' She produced it from her
handbag.

'Oh, yes, that belongs to Ronald Ferrars,' said Mrs Eastleigh.
'I know it from the laundry mark. What is so odd about it?'

'Well, it wasn't there when I went just a few steps up the
newel stair, and it *was* there when I came down again.'

'Oh, it blew in from somewhere. There always seems to be
a wind blowing on this island. He might have dropped it anywhere and at any time,' said the headmaster.

'Yes, I suppose so,' agreed Laura, but she spoke doubtfully.
Before more could be said upon the subject there came a knock
on the door.

'Oh, dear!' said Mrs Eastleigh, getting up. 'Can't we even
have breakfast in peace?'

'Sit down, my dear. I'll see to it,' said her husband. 'It may
be a message from the police.' He went to the door, partly
closed it behind him and re-entered, looking perturbed.

'What is it?' asked his wife. He shook his head, finished his
cup of coffee without sitting down again, and went out of the
room.

'I wonder whether they've found Ferrars, and he's met with
an accident or been clobbered by the convict?' said Laura.
'Well, I'd better go and get ready for Assembly, I suppose. I
might as well show up. I'm teaching, first period.'

Assembly, which took the form of a short service consisting of hymn and prayers, followed by any notices which Mr Eastleigh chose to give out, was, ordinarily, a noisy, haphazard sort of affair until the headmaster entered. It was Mr Grange's business to see that the boys were in some sort of order and were seated crosslegged on the floor, then he sent a prefect to Mr Eastleigh. Upon receipt of the message, the headmaster, followed by the rest of the Staff, came in, and the boys stopped their cheerful chattering and stood up.

On this occasion, however, Laura, from her place in the official queue, could hear nothing except Mr Grange's voice. It sounded solemn and doom-laden and was falling into the kind of hush which she associated with the major crises of her own schooldays, crises in which she had often taken a distinguished although not an enviable part.

'What's blowing up?' she muttered to Skelton, who was standing immediately behind her.

'Rumours, so far,' he muttered back. 'Manoel's missing.'

'Oh, *gosh!*' There was no time for more. The prefect appeared in the doorway and there were the usual exchanges.

'Mr Grange's compliments, sir, and the boys are in the hall.'

'My compliments and thanks to Mr Grange. We will attend him.'

The little procession entered the large lounge, and the assembled boys, with shining morning faces and wearing the mid-week clean shirts, stood up and stood still.

'Good morning, School.'

'Good morning, sir.'

'Hymn number twenty-five, part three, omitting the second stanza. *Glory to thee, who safe hast kept and hast refreshed me while I slept.* Thank you, Mr Grange.'

For some reason, Mr Grange always played the hymn, although Mr Robson was the music master. Perhaps Robson had a soul above hymns, Laura thought, as she joined in the singing. She enjoyed the Assembly hymns. Her own contralto voice, the headmaster's and Mr Skelton's bass, Mr Robson's, Colin's and Mr Heathers' tenor and the robust, untrained but powerful baritone of Mr Pocock, easily contained the boys' immature, light and airy trebles. Mrs Eastleigh did not attend

Assembly, and Ferrars, when he was present, mouthed the words (for the look of the thing) but did not sing, as he was tone-deaf.

Prayers were restricted to one read by the headmaster, the Lord's prayer recited in unison, then the headmaster's Latin benediction. After that, the school raised its head and waited with receptive ears for the notices. The one thing Mr Eastleigh had always set his face against was any admonishing of the school or of individual boys at Assembly. He held that such use of the occasion, however convenient it might be in some respects, cancelled out any aesthetic or moral good the short service might have done. The notices were a different matter.

On this particular morning there could be no doubt that his hearers were ready, even breathlessly anxious, to hear what their headmaster had to say.

'*Amen,*' said Mr Eastleigh. 'Be seated. No doubt most of you know already what I am going to tell you. A boy in the Nines, Manoel de Roseda y Lambre, is missing from school. I wish to see the boys who share his dormitory. Any other boy who thinks he has something useful to impart will wait in the entrance vestibule immediately after this Assembly. The head boy will take down names and forms, and see that the masters concerned are apprised of the fact that these informants may be a little late in coming to class. Thank you, Mr Grange.' He retired, followed by the Staff, and reassembled them outside the door. 'Set your classes some written work,' he said, 'and come to my study when I send. I will see whether the boys can tell me anything, and then I must have a word with you all. Mr Heathers, who has the first period free, will look after Mrs Gavin's boys. I want you to go to my room, Mrs Gavin, if you will be so good. I believe you write shorthand. I shall need a *verbatim* account of what is said, to pass on to the police. Of course, they will probably want to do their own questioning as well, but I should prefer to have something ready for them.'

The masters dispersed to collect their books from the common-room, Laura went to the headmaster's study (once the writing-room and library of the hotel), and the boys, dismissed, form by form, by Mr Grange, assisted by the prefects, came out into the entrance hall talking and buzzing excitedly.

When the tumult and the shouting had died, Mr Eastleigh, who had been called to the telephone, reappeared to find some thirty small boys collected in the entrance vestibule.

'The dormitory boys first,' he said. '*And,*' he added, looking at the assembled herd, 'I trust, for his own sake, that no boy is here to waste his own and my time.' Accepting this plain hint, a dozen boys who had been hoping to get out of first lesson melted unobtrusively away. The boys who had shared a dormitory with the missing child followed the headmaster to his study.

Where they found me (wrote Laura) looking all business-like with notebook and ball-point. I was wishing my shorthand was as good as old Kitty's, but I reflected that one can't have everything, and that Mr Eastleigh was lucky to have anybody on the Staff who could write in shorthand at all.

We have eighty boys here. Twenty of them are the seven and eight-year-olds and they are bedded down in rooms for four. The rest of the school, being bigger chaps, are in threes, so the whole school occupies twenty-five of the forty doubles, the rest having been turned into classrooms, day-rooms, the masters' library, our own bedrooms and so forth. What I mean is that, as the kid who's missing is all of nine years old, he was in a three-room, so there were only two room-mates for the Man to question.

He had them up in front of his table as though they were defaulters on parade and asked them why they hadn't gone to him the night before, instead of waiting until the morning to tell him that Manoel was missing. The explanation was simple enough and, with small boys, entirely credible. It seems they'd been playing hide-and-seek with Colin for about three-quarters of an hour between tea and prep., and that Pocock, who is a bit of a martinet, had found them unsettled and noisy at the beginning of prep, and had forbidden any boy to utter so much as a single word.

They said they had tried to tell him that Manoel was not in the room, but were threatened with annihilation if they did more than actually breathe, so, of course, they gave it up. After prep. came milk and biscuits and, naturally, they couldn't be expected to pass up on those. Then it was time for bed, and the two corridor prefects had come along to switch the lights off and had asked where the Spanish kid was, and they had tried to explain, but the prefects had told them to dry up, and heaven help the Spanish kid if he wasn't back in five minutes, because Mr Pocock was on duty and in a beastly bad temper at that, and was threatening chastisement to anybody found out of bed.

So there (concluded Laura) the defence rested its case. The Man was a bit terse with the kids, but admitted to me, after he had thrown them out, that they could hardly have been expected, in the face of the opposition they had received, to do more than they had done. One trouble is that little Manoel isn't all that popular, so nobody, not even his room-mates, I suppose, were prepared to risk being smacked by Mr Pocock if he caught them snooping round the house after lights-out.

Well, the rest of the kids could add nothing helpful. All we got was the dope about the game of hide-and-seek. The two corridor prefects admitted that Gateson and Comrie had told them that the Spanish boy was missing, but they 'hadn't really listened, sir, because, the Spanish boy being a foreigner, they didn't think Mr Pocock would be down on him, sir, if he found him roaming about, and we had nine other dorms. to do along our corridor, sir'. They were very sorry if they'd done the wrong thing. Well, that's all there was to be obtained from them, so the Man sent them round the school to tell the Staff there would be a common-room meeting in twenty minutes' time and to ask Mr Spalding to be good enough to repair to the headmaster's study forthwith.

Colin arrived, looking scared, and immediately began to express himself to the effect that Manoel had certainly been present during the game of hide-and-seek, because he had noticed particularly how excited the boy had seemed.

'Just one moment, Mr Spalding,' said the Man. 'I think we shall get on faster, and also obtain a clearer picture, if I do the questioning and you confine yourself to answering me. I am expecting the police at any moment, but I should like to hear your story before they come.'

'But I haven't *got* a story,' says Colin, appalled. 'All I know is . . .'

'Yes. Now, tell me, what gave rise to this game of hide-and-seek? What made you think of it?'

'I'd been telling my table at tea about the smugglers who used this island as a base, sir, and it all arose from that. They divided into two groups, smugglers and excise officers, and the thing turned into a form of hide-and-seek, with the excise men trying to find the smugglers, that's all.'

'And how long did the game go on?'

'I couldn't say. Not more than about half an hour, I imagine. It took a little time to get it organised, and I know that the bell went for prep. before all the smugglers were rounded up, so we couldn't have gone on all that long.'

'And de Roseda was one of those who joined in the game, I take it?'

'Yes, he was. It was understood and agreed that nobody was to leave the house, of course.'

'I wonder whether he understood that?'

'His English is quite good. I don't see why he shouldn't have understood.'

'Oh, well, thank you, Mr. Spalding. You might ask Mr Pocock to spare me a minute.' When Colin had gone, the Man told me that he was going to ask Mr Pocock how it had come about that he hadn't noticed Manoel was not present at prep., so it might be as well if I made myself scarce and went and sat in the common-room ready for the meeting. As Pocock is one of the senior masters, I could well understand that Mr Eastleigh wouldn't want to bawl him out in front of me, so I retired as requested and have no idea of the actual words which passed between them.

The common-room meeting itself came to nothing. Nobody had any fresh information or suggestion, either about Manoel or Ferrars, and I think Mr Eastleigh was about to call it off when he had to answer the telephone. He came back after nearly ten minutes to say that the convict had been picked up, but had contrived to change his clothes since his escape, and that the police wanted to know whether the clothes the convict had got hold of belonged to anybody at the school. Upon this, the gentlemen ushers were sent to their rooms to give their wardrobes the once-over and report any losses, and the caretaker

was told to ring the bell for an early break and Mrs Eastleigh
was requested to see that Cook sent the mid-morning coffee up
to the common-room half an hour earlier than usual. When the
men had gone to their rooms to carry out their inventories, the
Man told me that my misguided expedition of the early morning was not to be held against me. Acting on my information,
the convict had been found in a little hidey-hole at the top of
that newel stair which I had not had the nerve to go up.

CHAPTER NINE

Dea Ex Machina

'A full moon was beginning to rise and peered redly
through the upper edges of the fog...'

Laura, as she had informed Dame Beatrice in earlier letters,
was not overworked. The only mornings when she had no free
time were the Fridays, but she had all the afternoon games
periods to herself, and, apart from teaching history, which
occupied twelve periods each week, her sole responsibility was
to take small groups of what the headmaster tactfully referred
to as 'the less able boys' for extra English. This, in effect,
amounted to attempting to teach them to spell – an unrewarding
task, since the ability to spell correctly is inborn, not taught.
At least, that was Laura's opinion and it is fair to state that the
majority of 'the less able' agreed with her, and exerted themselves more to please her than because they thought any other
good would come of their efforts.

'As you pointed out last week in history lesson, Mrs Gavin,'
said Chorley, a tall, handsome, serious boy in her own form,
'in the fifteenth century nobody bothered about spelling. You
told us that the same man might spell the same word three
different ways in a single paragraph. So what does spelling
matter?'

'It's a question of ethics,' said Laura. 'You know the
difference between right and wrong, don't you?'

'You told the Tens that it was one of the hallmarks of a
gentleman to arrive punctually at lessons.'

'To spell correctly is also ethical, as any American will tell
you,' Laura responded. 'I note that in your last essay, you,
although living in the twentieth and not the fifteenth century,
also contrived to spell the same word in three different ways
in the same paragraph. "Weight for age" is correct; "wait for

age" would be acceptable in some contexts, perhaps, but not in this one; "wate for age" is just plain wrong.'

'I thought I'd try them all, and leave you to pick the one you liked best.'

'You should go far as a politician, Chorley.'

'Thank you, Mrs Gavin. What "wait" would it be when Mr Eastleigh says, "Wait outside my door"?'

'The middle one. Oh, dear! You haven't got to, have you?'

'I'm afraid so, yes.'

'What have you done?'

'I wrote on walls.'

'*You?*'

'Well, it's so odd that Mr Ferrars should be missing at the same time as that little squirt de Whatname. I didn't write anything rude. I only wrote, *Who burnt down the school and why?* I don't quite know how I was rumbled, because none of the masters saw me do it. All the Extra English boys, above the Nines, were rounded up and asked to write the sentence, and I was dropped on.'

'How did you spell "burnt"?'

'Oh, b-r-u-n-t, of course. Isn't that right?'

'And "school"?'

'Er – let's see – er – s-h-c-o-l-e, I think.'

'Enough said. The headmaster sent for all the exercise books. It was a fair cop, laddie. When do you go along to receive your just reward?'

'This afternoon, in break. I expect I'll be kept in from games, too. The Man doesn't care for people to write on walls. The last chap who did it was expelled, but I believe he did some – well, some drawings. They were all cleaned off before any of us had the chance to get a squint at them, so I don't know what they were like.'

Laura dismissed the lad and, as soon as morning school was over, she went to the headmaster's office and said that she thought Chorley might have presented her with a valuable clue to the disappearances of Ferrars and Manoel.

'Chorley,' said Mr Eastleigh, 'has surprised me. He is a most reputable boy. I propose to admonish him and deprive him of his afternoon's games. I am not in favour of caning young

innocent boys. All the same, I will not have them writing on
walls, however innocuous their sentiments and comments. But
what is this clue you speak of?'

'I learnt some time ago that it was Mr Ferrars who set fire
to the school in Kent.'

'*Ferrars?*'

'Yes. How much do you actually know about him, Headmaster?'

'*Know* about him? Why, what should I know? I was glad to
get him. There are not so many science graduates who are willing
to teach in preparatory schools. Most of them go into industry,
I believe. He seems a capable young man and the boys like him.'

'That's all very fine, but consider the facts. You claim he is
a science man. Wouldn't you think he could be trusted to let
off a few fireworks, then, without producing the San Francisco
conflagration?'

'You mean that Ferrars *deliberately* set fire to my school?'

'Well, it looks uncommonly like it to me,' said Laura
bluntly. 'If so, it means he wanted to get out of the place. I
can't suggest a reason, unless, of course, he's kidnapped Manoel,
a deed which could be more easily carried out from here, with
all this sea around us, than from your school in Kent. What do
you say about that?'

'But Ferrars could not have known that we would be coming
to this island. Besides – Ferrars a kidnapper and an in-
cendiarist? I can't believe it, you know. You mean that Ferrars
– but he is a Rendlesford and Cambridge man...' His voice
tailed off. He ruminated. 'I suppose you couldn't peruade Dame
Beatrice to cut short her holiday and come along and look into
things for me, could you?' he asked at last. 'This disappearance
of the child de Roseda y Lambre – what sticklers the Spaniards
are for the family tree! – is no good to the school at all. We
have several ambassadors' sons here, as I suppose you know,
and once it becomes generally known that it is possible for them
to disappear – to be kidnapped or what-have-you – I might as
well sell up if I can find a purchaser. And that won't be very
easy, either. Think of the publicity! As it is, we are in the hands
of the police. It is only a matter of time before the public press
gets hold of the thing, and then the fat will be in the fire with a

vengeance. But Ferrars—' He shook his head.

'You must admit it's more than coincidence that he and Manoel have disappeared at the same time,' said Laura.

'I say, Mrs Gavin,' said Chorley, meeting her as the boys came in from games, 'it was quite all right. The Man jawed me a bit and made me promise not to write any more words on walls – he said it was only Fascists and Commies and Ban the Bombs who did that sort of thing nowadays – and then he asked me what I'd meant. I said I hadn't really meant anything, so then he told me to tell the truth, because, with the Spanish kid and Mr Ferrars missing, it was too serious for trying to shield people, so I told him about Mr Ferrars and the fireworks, and he sent me out to games. If I hadn't been in your form – I mean, none of the *masters* would have got away with it with Mr Eastleigh – I am sure I'd have been tanned, if not expelled, so, what I mean . . .'

'Oh, go and have your tea!' said Laura. Since leaving the headmaster she had spoken on the telephone to Dame Beatrice, who was spending a few days with her sister-in-law, Lady Selina Lestrange. It was a duty visit which both parties might be glad to terminate, thought Laura. She did not care for Lady Selina, who, although she sometimes asked Dame Beatrice's advice with regard to the cadet branches of the family and their inexplicable activities – 'Peregrine has joined something he calls a pop group and is growing his hair' – disapproved of Laura's intelligent and witty employer, and was in awe of her undoubted and undisputed gifts.

As Laura had hoped, the telephone conversation was rewarding, and when tea was over she was able to go to the headmaster and inform him that Dame Beatrice would be with them on the afternoon of the following day.

'It is very good of her,' said Mr Eastleigh. 'I shall be most relieved to have her advice and help. As I think I may have told you, so far I have been able to keep the thing out of the newspapers, thanks largely to the fuss about the escaped prisoner, but now that he has been apprehended, the press will be hounding us at any moment. Incidentally, the police brought the clothes the man was wearing when he was captured, to see whether there was a tie-up with Ferrars.'

'There was, I suppose.'

'I do not know why you should suppose it.'

'I found Ferrars' handkerchief near where the man was captured.'

'Ah, yes, so you did. Well, you are quite right. The criminal was dressed in some of the clothes Ferrars was wearing when he left the school. By the way, the police have returned your ashplant. You will find it in the umbrella stand in the front vestibule.'

'Many thanks. An old friend of mine, that stick. Does that mean that Ferrars is in prison garb, then? Surely not, if he's gone off with Manoel.'

'I don't know what to think. You see, the odd thing is that the criminal was not only wearing Ferrars' suit and waterproof, but his underclothing as well, apart from his socks.'

'What does he say he did with his prison clothes?'

'He told the police where to find them.'

'And they did?'

'Yes.'

'Nothing missing?'

'Nothing, except his own socks, which, of course, he had on. All was carefully checked at the prison.'

'Well, Ferrars can hardly be going around with nothing on,' said Laura. 'It must mean that Ferrars is a complete bad hat and had a disguise stashed away somewhere. But I wonder how he got Manoel to go with him? It indicates that he must have sneaked back here and somehow or other enticed the kid away.'

'Surely somebody would have seen him, if that were so. I have already spoken to all the boys who played that game of hide-and-seek with Spalding, but I shall interview them again and question them even more closely. It does not seem as though anybody saw the boy after the game ended, but somebody *must* know something about his disappearance. Little boys of nine, even the sons of South American presidents, don't disappear into thin air.'

'Leaving not a wrack behind? No, you're right enough there,' said Laura. 'There must be a clue somewhere.'

The clue, if there was one, did not appear to be in the possession of the Nines. There were fourteen of them, counting the missing boy, and they were interviewed by the headmaster after he had seen Colin. Two captains had been chosen for the game of Smugglers and Excisemen, and the rules explained. These were that the smugglers were to have ten minutes in which to go into hiding, that nobody was to leave the building, that the kitchen regions were out of bounds. The game would be won by those individual smugglers who managed to get back to the formroom, where the game began, without being touched by an exciseman – spotting *without* touching not to be counted. At half-time the parties were to change sides.

Manoel had been a smuggler first. The game had been played in the half-light of the fading March day, and he, being an adroit and eel-like little boy, had been one of the first to get back to the formroom, where Colin was waiting to check the winners. After about a quarter of an hour, by Colin's calculations, everybody on the smugglers' side had either got back or been captured, and the sides changed over. The bell had been rung for Prep. before the game ended, and so Colin, who was not down to take Prep. that evening, had no idea that Manoel was not present at that imposition and curtailment of liberty.

Armed with this information, which Colin had given him twice, and whose two accounts of the game had not varied in any particular, the headmaster spoke to the group of nine-year-olds as a whole, and then, to their mingled terror and excitement, to each one individually. By the very nature of the game they had played, however, it was very difficult to discover which child had been the last to see Manoel. Both the 'smugglers' and the 'excisemen' had dispersed as soon as they got the word from Colin, and, after that, it was each for himself. The only point which seemed to be fixed was that Manoel had certainly been present up to the beginning of the second half of the game. After that, there was no certainty about it, except that he had not answered the bell for Prep. and had not gone along for his milk and biscuits later.

'I suppose,' said the headmaster to Colin, after he had dismissed the Nines, 'the boy cannot still be on the building?'

'How do you mean, sir?'

'Well, this is a very large and rather complicated house. I

am beginning to wonder whether he may have shut himself away in one of the attics, for example, or in one of the large cupboards, and been unable to get out again.'

'Well, there are two reasons against that, Headmaster. One is that he was on the seekers' side at the time, and so, far from wanting to hide, he would have been tailing the boys in the opposing team. The other is that, surely, if he *had* managed to get himself shut away somewhere, he'd have made enough noise to be heard long before this. Besides, we've searched the whole place.'

'All the same, I shall have the house thoroughly searched again,' said the headmaster to Laura, who was dining with him and his wife. 'Then, if we meet with no success, I suppose I must cable the boy's father and give the police *carte blanche*. So far, I have simply reported the boy and Ferrars as missing, but it now seems to me that there is nothing for it but a full-scale operation, beginning in the house itself. The police, of course, have not been in the school so far, except for my interviews with the Inspector, but, unless we find the boy at once, a full-scale enquiry, beginning with a police search of the premises, and police questioning of the boys, will have to come. Once it does, there is nothing to stop the boys writing all sorts of wild things in their Sunday letters home.' He sounded an extremely worried man.

'Oh, well, it isn't Sunday yet, so let's put a cheerful face on it. There's no knowing what Mrs Croc. will unearth, once she gets down to it, you know, and, if the worst comes to the worst, you will have to warn the boys that all their letters from now on will be censored,' said Laura.

'I do not run a police-state, Mrs Gavin.'

'Of course not. Sorry I spoke.'

'No, no. The suggestion is a most sensible one. I am not anxious to act on it, that is all. For one thing, I do not want the boys to think the situation graver than it is.'

'They could hardly think that, unless they suspect the poor little chap has been murdered.'

The headmaster shook his head, but did not look surprised or horrified.

'No, no,' he said. 'It's the money these people are after. His father is a millionaire, no less. He *bought* himself into power, or so it is said.'

'The whole thing might be political, then, as well as a kidnapping for money.'

'It might. There is no telling that, at present. I shall be glad when Dame Beatrice arrives. I have tremendous faith in her.'

Dame Beatrice turned up on the following day, having driven from her home in Hampshire – or, rather, having been driven, for her chauffeur was at the wheel of a car which the boys regarded with awe. She was given tea by the gratified headmaster, and was invited to address the assembled school. This she declined to do.

'I will speak to Mr Heathers and Mr Spalding,' she said, 'if they can be spared from their duties.'

Heathers and Colin had just finished tea and were shepherding boys out of the dining-room when they received the headmaster's message. Dame Beatrice had gathered very little from Laura's letters about their personal appearance, and found herself confronted by two young men of dissimilar aspect in that one was fair-haired, portly and wore glasses, the other was tallish and slim, with a pale face and dark hair.

'As you two are the youngest men on the Staff, apart from Mr Ferrars himself, I am assuming that you know more about him than the older masters are likely to do,' she said briskly. 'I have some slight evidence that he was responsible for the fire which has closed, temporarily, the school in Kent. You, Mr Spalding, would know nothing, at first hand, about that. Mr Heathers?'

'Burnt down the school?' The plump Heathers took off his glasses, polished them nervously on a spotless handkerchief and almost dropped them before he put them on again. 'I never heard that!'

'What was your own part in the Guy Fawkes festivities?'

'I took no part. I was born during a particularly noisy air-raid in 1942. Fireworks disturb me very much. I retired to my room and put in my ear-plugs and drew the curtains across the window. I was very nearly burnt to death.'

'Oh, come now!' protested Mr Eastleigh, who, by Dame Beatrice's request, was present at the interview.

'I did not hear the fire-bell – my ear-plugs, you see, Head-master, muffled every sound.'

'But your wing of the school was nowhere near the part which caught fire. The flames were got under control before they even reached the central hall.'

'Very well,' said the aggrieved Heathers. 'All the same, they might not have been, you know. I still think that I was in danger. I knew nothing about the fire until Mr Noble came and found me, and advised me to leave the building.'

'Did either of you know Mr Ferrars before he joined the Staff?' asked Dame Beatrice.

'Yes, *I* did,' said Colin. 'I didn't know he was here until after Mr Eastleigh appointed me, but then I found I'd been at school with him.'

'But you were not the same age, of course.'

'Oh, no. He was in the second year Sixth when I was a member of the Ticks' Union – er – when I was in my first term, I mean.'

'Apart from being in the second year Sixth Form, which, in itself, implies some degree of eminence, was he, so far as you remember, an outstanding boy?'

'I don't think so. He wasn't in the First Fifteen, or anything like that. I don't think he was terribly interested in games. Boats were more in his line.'

'Was yours a rowing school?'

'Oh, I don't mean those sort of boats. I mean yachts and motorboats, and even bigger stuff.'

'How do you know that? There were no facilities at your school for yachting, were there?'

'No, but I met him two years after he'd left school and was at Cambridge. My father had taken me on a Mediterranean cruise, and Ferrars was on it, too. I knew him, but, of course, he didn't know me from Adam. I wasn't even in his house at school. On the cruise he spotted my blazer and then he was rather decent to me – we used to swim and play deck tennis, and that sort of thing – until one day he told me he'd got per-mission to climb the mast and go out on to the crow's nest. You know what it's like on those big boats, I expect. The mast is of metal, and it's canted a bit, and you climb an iron ladder inside it. He asked me to come with him, and he thought I was just a common or garden pansy when I said I couldn't. I tried to explain I've got no head for heights, and that climbing anything gives me vertigo, but, of course, he thought I funked it. I suppose it *is* that, in a way. Still, he was pretty decent about it, and I was glad of that, as he sat at our table for meals.'

'You mentioned yachts and motor-boats.'

'Oh, yes. Well, even after this mast thing queered the pitch, he used to talk to me quite a bit at odd times. He didn't dance, and he didn't drink or play cards, so I expect he thought my society was preferable to none. Well, he told me his ambition was to take a five-ton boat round the world single-handed. He said he spent nearly all his holidays in boats, and he certainly did seem to know a lot about them. He said that, at school, he used to keep a small ketch in Chichester harbour – we were a Sussex school – and sneak away whenever he could and sail her. It was out of bounds, of course, but he said he was never caught, although he had some near squeaks once or twice. The only snag, he said, was that he had to be pretty careful about weather, in case he couldn't get back, but he was always lucky.'

'Yes, that's right,' said Heathers. 'Almost the first thing he said to me, when he knew we were coming here, was that he wondered whether there would be anywhere he could keep a boat.'

'And was there?' Dame Beatrice asked. Heathers shook his head.

'No,' he replied, 'not at this time of year. There's the bay, but it's not all that much sheltered, and the tides round here are tricky. Then there's the Race. You have to creep in almost under the cliffs, I believe, unless you stand right out to sea. But I don't know much about it, actually.'

'But you do know that Mr Ferrars did not keep a boat anywhere near here?'

'I can't say I *know*. We shared duties, you see – or split them, I should say – so we didn't go out together on our free afternoons.'

'Does either of you know of any special connection between Mr Ferrars and the missing boy?'

'He wasn't his form master. Ferrars didn't have a form,' said

Heathers. 'That's why he and I split the duties. He helped with my Sevens and Eights.'

'I'm sure there wasn't any special connection,' said Colin. 'The boy was in the Nines, and Ferrars took them for maths. and science, that's all.'

'Science has had to become botany and zoology,' put in the headmaster. 'There are no facilities for chemistry here.'

'Botany and zoology would suggest fieldwork,' said Dame Beatrice. 'Did the missing child have intimates?'

'Nobody in particular,' said Colin, 'so far as I know. He wasn't a popular boy, but I think he rubbed along all right with the others, although he seemed a bit friendless and solitary.'

'What about pocket money? Was he well supplied?'

'Pocket money is supervised. I attend to it myself,' said Mr Eastleigh. 'The amount is laid down and strictly controlled.'

'Postal orders, and so forth, in letters from home?'

'The post is opened in public. In any case, all post offices are automatically placed out of bounds. The boys write a weekly letter home and stamps are provided.'

'I should like to speak to the boys who shared Manoel's dormitory, and I think it would be better if you were not present, if you have no objection to my seeing them in private,' said Dame Beatrice.

'Please do just as you wish. I realise that they may talk more freely to you that way.'

'Then, if I might see them together?'

Two nervous little boys, inclined to assume a bland, poached-egg expression as a disguise of their real feelings, were shown in and told to sit down. Then the three men went out, closing the door behind them, and the children were left to be confronted by a small, black-haired, yellow-skinned old lady with claw-like hands and herpetological leer.

'Well,' she said, seating herself behind the headmaster's desk, 'so here we have . . .?'

'Please, Gateson, please, Dame Beatrice.'

'Please, Comrie, please, Dame Beatrice.'

'Spoken like men of principle and of decisive action. You shared a three-room with Manoel de Roseda y Lambre. What did you think of him?'

It was obviously an unexpected question. The children looked at one another. Then Gateson nodded to Comrie.

'You say.'

'Well,' said the North Briton, 'he wasn't everybody's money.'

'I see. Talking of that, did he seem to have more than the usual amount to spend?'

The boys exchanged glances again.

'The Man – Mr Eastleigh – is rather strict about that,' said Gateson, 'but – well – de Roseda told us once that he had an arrangement.'

'Indeed? With whom?'

'He wouldn't say. Anyway, we didn't really believe him.'

'Oh? Why was that?'

'He never seemed to spend more than anybody else.'

'Was he a generous boy?'

'Not to us, but we thought he gave a lot of his money to his church,' said Comrie.

'He was a Catholic, you see,' explained Gateson.

'He and two or three others used to be taken to their church every Sunday when we were at our proper school in Kent,' said Comrie.

'And here?'

'Manoel – de Roseda – told us there isn't a Catholic church on the island, and the nearest one on the mainland is in the town, and the town is out-of-bounds.'

'Even for Sunday services?'

'Well, I suppose one of the masters could have taken him, like they used to in Kent, but the other Catholics happen to be in the Common Entrance form, and didn't come here with us, so there was only de Roseda, and I suppose none of the masters wanted to give up Sunday morning just to take one boy to church. It meant about twenty miles there and back, I suppose.

'What about the rest of you?'

'Oh, we're all right, because the room here, where we have Assembly, is called Chapel on Sundays, and Mr Eastleigh takes it one week and a curate comes over the next week and takes it at half-past three, and has tea with Mr and Mrs Eastleigh afterwards. Mr Pocock fetches him in his car, and takes him back, and has dinner at an hotel on the mainland.'

'Well, we *think* he does. He has a drink, anyway,' put in Comrie.

'And how did de Roseda react to the changed conditions?'

'About coming here and not going to church?' asked Comrie. Dame Beatrice nodded.

'He used to cry every Sunday night,' said Gateson. 'I think he thought he'd go to hell if he couldn't go to church, you see.'

CHAPTER TEN

The Bird-Watcher's Wife

'...the hill bare and dark, the head bound with cliffs forty or fifty feet high, and fringed with great masses of fallen rock...Among the fallen rocks the breakers spouted and bellowed...'

'So there, for what it's worth, is an indication of how the boy could have been spirited away,' said Dame Beatrice to the headmaster. 'There need not have been any violent action. An arrangement that, at the first favourable opportunity, he would be taken to a Catholic church might cause him to commit himself to going off secretly with his abductor without noise and with perfect confidence. I only offer it as a suggestion, of course, but that is the way a kidnapping could have been carried out with the full consent and connivance of the child himself.'

'Dear me! He had been to me, of course, to ask whether he would be taken to Mass, and I was concerned for him and had committed myself to taking him every fourth Sunday to the Catholic church on the mainland, but I could not promise more, and, as it turned out, I could not manage even that, as, four weeks later, I had a visit from the chairman of the governors of the public school I keep in with. He came on the Saturday and stayed until after breakfast on the Monday morning, so I had to break my promise to Manoel, and, I am afraid, forgot all about it. I suppose I might have delegated the job to one of the younger men, but I always hesitate to impose on them, so I said nothing, and the boy has not been near me since to remind me of my promise.'

'He would hardly like to do so, perhaps.'

'I suppose not. Mind you, Dame Beatrice, I could easily understand a little chap of four or five years old being enticed away in this manner, but Manoel was turned nine. The police, in any case, are treating it as a case of a runaway boy, a truant

98

from school, although, as Ferrars is also missing, they are not prepared to rule out both kidnapping and also murder – the murder of Ferrars by the recaptured convict, I mean. It is significant that the man was wearing Ferrars' clothes, except, I understand, his pullover, shirt, socks and tie.'

'Remain,' said Laura, when she and Dame Beatrice were alone, 'some rather significant facts. *All* Ferrars' clothes, from the skin upwards, except for the socks, shirt, etc., were being worn by the criminal. You don't, surely, if you're on the run, stop to strip a dead man to the buff in order to get a change of outfit. Then there's the biggish boat which appeared in the cove here, and which I myself spotted from the landing window. Most important of all, it seems to me, nobody could have known beforehand that the school was going to land up in a spot where a kidnapping was so likely to come off. So how are you going to start?'

'By having a talk with your bird-watching acquaintance, Mr Howard Spalding,' said Dame Beatrice. 'He may have noticed something from his lighthouse gallery.'

'We tried him, you know, and he hadn't, but go ahead, and I wish you joy! Don't say I haven't warned you what he's like. You'll be lucky if you don't come away possessing beady eyes and a beak.'

'I already possess beady eyes and a beak,' said Dame Beatrice, pursing up her mouth in imitation of the latter, 'so entertain no fears on my behalf. I suppose you noticed one rather significant thing which young Mr Spalding mentioned when I interviewed him?'

'You mean that he'd been previously acquainted with Ferrars? But it seems he had no idea that Ferrars was on the Staff here. Even when he ran into him it doesn't seem to have made much impression.'

'Quite so. Ah, well, we must wait and see what my interview with the older Mr Spalding will produce. I should wish you to accompany me. You will form a valuable link. Have you any objection?'

'Anything you say. When do we go?'

'The sooner the better. The child must be traced. You say the lighthouse is not on the telephone?'

'No, it isn't.'

'All the better. We will take the household by surprise. Not a word to young Mr Colin. I will arrange with Mr Eastleigh for you to be released from all your duties whilst I am working on his behalf.'

'I *shall* be popular with the rest of the Staff,' said Laura, grinning. 'It means that some unfortunate blighter will have to take on my classes and lose his free periods, unless Mr Eastleigh looks after them himself.'

This, it turned out, was what the headmaster proposed to do. His method was to set the boys some written work, remain in the room until every child was busy, remark curtly that he expected silence and concentration, and then retire to his sanctum and get on with his own jobs. As he was held in considerable awe, this plan worked well for a couple of days, after which Old Adam resumed its healthful, uninhibited sway, as the headmaster had assumed would be the case. He was unperturbed and merely expressed to his wife the hope that Dame Beatrice would soon be able to dispense with Laura's services.

'You tell me,' said Dame Beatrice to Laura, 'of two facts which may be of considerable importance.' They were driving out of the hotel gateway. 'First, I have high hopes that Mr Spalding – I propose hereafter to refer to him as Mr Howard in order to distinguish him from his son, Mr Colin – that Mr Howard is not so intent upon his bird-watching as to be unaware of what there is to see on the island apart from birds and the stars.'

'That's right,' said Laura. 'In other words, if he didn't see Ferrars on the day F. disappeared, the inference is that Ferrars wasn't anywhere where he could be spotted from the lighthouse gallery. Howard seems to be alert to all shipping and was also well aware of Colin's sneaking movements outside the lighthouse after the love-making – or row, whichever it was – with his stepmother. That's one fact, all right. What's the other one?'

'That this young school-master, Mr Ferrars, who seems to have vanished at approximately the same time as the child Manoel, was known to the Spaldings before they came here.'

'Not all that well. Colin says Ferrars was a very big boy when he himself was a rather small one.'

'They were on a Mediterranean cruise together.'

'I don't see what you're getting at.'

'I understand from you that Colin thinks so, but, as one personable woman sitting in unbiased judgment on another, would you consider Mrs Spalding to be generally attractive to young men?'

'Oh, yes, of course. I can't think why she married a stick-in-the-mud like Howard. I should have thought she could have done ever so much better for herself.'

'Is Mr Howard a wealthy man, would you suppose?'

'I've never thought about it, but, now that I do, I shouldn't think he is anywhere near the bread-line. That's a Rover car, and, in these days, a Mediterranean cruise for three people isn't exactly cheap. Then, he's rented this lighthouse for a year, which means (as he's taken it fully furnished) that he must have a home somewhere else, one supposes. Colin is ex-public school and going to Oxford next year, Fiona is beautifully dressed, and her pearls, if I am any judge, are real and so are the diamonds and rubies in the coat-brooch she wears . . .'

'Then perhaps we have some explanation of an otherwise incongruous situation.'

'A pretty ordinary explanation, too. I wonder how long they've been married?'

'My experience suggests to me that it cannot be very long.'

'Oh? How do you deduce that?'

'Use your intelligence, child. If Colin had been brought up from childhood with this young woman, it is unlikely (although not, of course, impossible) that he would be violently in love with her now. He must have been, I would venture to say, not younger than fifteen or sixteen when the marriage took place.'

'I see. Yes, that sounds reasonable. She can't be more than thirty now, and Colin is nineteen, going on for twenty. To go back to what we were saying, you mean that, if Colin has fallen a victim to her charms, to employ the well-worn phrase, there's no reason why, on that Mediterranean cruise, Ferrars should not also have made a pass or two. Is that it?'

'We must not theorise too soon, or argue ahead of our data.'

'Where do you suppose Ferrars is, then? – hidden away in the linen cupboard?'

Dame Beatrice did not answer this frivolous question. She remarked instead:

'We come back to the fact that the convict was wearing Mr Ferrars' underclothes. That would seem to indicate that Mr Ferrars had discarded them.'

'Wanted to change his known image. You can't go about snitching wealthy parents' important offspring and still remain in the guise of an inoffensive young prep.-school master. He would naturally discard his undergarments because they would have laundry-marks, and so forth, by which he could be identified. I dare say that by this time he's wearing a walnut-stain make-up and sideburns. Another thing, remember, is the fact that Ferrars, although a science master, was the Guy Fawkes of that school in Kent. But for him, Mr Eastleigh would never have had to bring the boys to this island, with its many facilities for making a clean getaway by sea.'

'I have not observed these "many facilities". Point them out,' said Dame Beatrice.

'Where do you think Manoel is, then?'

'We may know more about that when I have talked with Mr Howard.'

'But it was after dark when Manoel disappeared. Howard couldn't have seen him leave the school. He hadn't even seen Ferrars by daylight.'

'I appreciate that, of course. Oh, well, we must find out what we can.'

'If you don't believe Manoel went off with Ferrars, who *did* take him away, then?'

'The police may be right, you know. This need not be a case of kidnapping. The child may have absconded.'

'To get to a Roman Catholic church?'

'There could be less likely reasons. He must have been bitterly disappointed when Mr Eastleigh not only broke his promise to him, but actually, on his own admission, forgot about it.'

'And you really think he may simply be A.W.O.L.? After all, the kid is only nine years old.'

'An irrational and adventurous age. I have in my files case-notes of several such incidents. In one, a mentally-retarded girl of nine left her school during the dinner-hour and, by imposing upon complete strangers, made her way from a London suburb to Waterloo station and from there to Poole, in Dorset. From Poole railway station she walked to a village twelve miles away to visit an aunt of whom she was fond. She was very soon traced, as it happened, because the aunt wrote to the parents to ask why they had sent Maisie without notice and without luggage.'

'Good gracious me! And people just paid her fare and saw her through?'

'Apparently. I had another case of a boy of the same age who drove away an unlocked car and took it to Harwich and stowed himself away on a cross-Channel steamer in order to get (as he thought) to America to become a cowboy. I could quote other instances, all within the age-group of eight to eleven years.'

'And, according to my spies, young Manoel was in unlawful (according to school rules) possession of a fair amount of money. Well, well! Where would he make for? The Channel Islands?'

'It is not possible to say, but the police can be trusted to find him if he has absconded, particularly as that appears to be their theory.'

'I wouldn't mind going to look for him myself. If he isn't found by the time term ends, I rather think I will, if you don't mind.'

'You are not likely to succeed where the police have failed.'

'Don't you believe it! I know this kid. Rum, self-contained little object, very secretive. If he's really on the run, I bet I can track him down before the police get so much as a smell of him.'

Dame Beatrice changed the subject.

'I wonder whether Mr Howard is up on his balcony?' she said.

This was not the case. They found Fiona in the living-quarters, partaking of mid-morning coffee and biscuits. Laura introduced Dame Beatrice, who came at once to the reason for the visit.

'Oh, dear!' said Fiona. She was pale and her eyes looked

heavy for want of sleep. 'Howard isn't here, and I don't think I can tell you anything which would be of any help. Do I understand that the boy was under the supervision of Colin when he disappeared from the school? Even so, that doesn't make Colin in any way responsible for what has happened to him, does it?' She spoke jerkily. It was easy to see that she was under extreme nervous tension.

'When may we expect to find your husband at home?' Dame Beatrice enquired.

'Goodness knows! He is off on one of his bird-watching expeditions. It might be days before he gets back. *Why* do you want to see him, did you say?'

'We wondered whether he saw anything of the boy from his position on the lighthouse gallery, that is all.'

'How *could* he see anything of him? It was dark when the boy left the school, wasn't it? Is my poor husband expected to have cat's eyes, or to operate a searchlight?'

'It is scarcely likely that the boy was able to leave the island that night if he was alone,' said Dame Beatrice, 'and the police theory at present is that he *was* alone, and has merely run away from school. They will hold to this opinion until it is disproved, but, no doubt, will also keep the possibility of a kidnapping in mind.'

'Well,' said Fiona, in dogged but weary tones, 'I would help if I could, but I can tell you nothing, and I am sure that, if my husband were here, he would say the same. We have seen nothing of the boy, nothing at all, so far as I know.'

'So far as you know?'

'Oh, there are several children belonging to the lighthouse keepers and the fishermen's cottages. I would not undertake to tell one child from another. In any case, the police must have combed the entire neighbourhood. I mean, they would do, wouldn't they, for anyone who's missing?'

'There happens to be another missing person,' said Dame Beatrice.

'*Another?*' There was no doubt of Fiona's nervousness now. Laura stared at her, knowing that she must have heard from Colin of Ferrars' absence from the school.

'I believe he was at public school with your son,' said Dame

Beatrice. 'I refer to a young man named Ferrars.'

'Oh, yes, but they hardly knew one another at school. There is a difference of four or five years in their ages. There's nothing to connect him with Colin,' said Fiona wildly.

'I understand, though, that they met on a Mediterranean cruise after Mr Ferrars had left school.'

'I can't see the point in all this,' said Fiona, with the pettish anger of the badly frightened. 'What has the cruise to do with Ronald's disappearance? Ten to one, he and that little boy have gone off together. I can't see how our previous acquaintance with Ronald – it was, in any case, very slight – can have anything to do with his disappearance or that of the child. They *must* have gone off together. Ronald was always very irresponsible, that I *can* tell you.'

'Has Mr Ferrars been to visit you since you have been here?'

'Yes, Colin brought him over when neither of them was on duty at school tea. It was a flying visit. They had to be back to take preparation and see the boys to bed.'

'Did you recognise Mr Ferrars again? I do not know how long it would be since you had seen him.'

'Oh, we went on the cruise when Colin was sixteen. It was, to be precise, our honeymoon, but we had to take Colin along.'

'So that would have been . . .?'

'Four years ago this next July,' said Fiona. 'I hardly recognised Ronnie when he called here. He had filled out and seemed a man, not the boy I remembered.'

'But you *did* recognise him?'

'Oh, not until Colin introduced him, and he mentioned things which had happened on the cruise, and remembered that Colin was afraid to climb up inside the mast with him.'

'I wonder,' said Dame Beatrice, changing the subject with some abruptness, 'whether, Mrs Spalding, you would be kind enough to allow me to climb to your gallery and find out how much of the island can be seen from the top of the lighthouse tower?'

'Why, certainly, if it will help in any way. What about you, Mrs Gavin? Will you go too?' Fiona's relief at the change of subject was obvious.

'Oh, I've been up before. I'll stay down here and keep you

company,' said Laura, who had received a signal from her employer. 'Don't stay up there too long in this wind,' she added, to Dame Beatrice.

'It's always windy in this place,' said Fiona, when the other had gone. 'I hate it here. I'll make some fresh coffee so that Dame Beatrice can have a hot drink when she comes down.'

'Good idea,' said Laura. 'Can I do anything to help?'

'No, I don't think so. I do hope she won't stay up there too long. A good thing Howard isn't with her. You know what he is when he starts talking.'

'Yes, I do. I nearly froze to death. Have you ever been up there?'

'Yes, I went up once on my own. It was after the police had been. I wanted to find out exactly what could be seen from that gallery.'

'A goodish bit, actually.'

'Yes, it was idiotic of Colin to think he could sneak away from this place like that without being spotted. I'm sorry you were let in for that idiotic row between him and Howard. It was quite ridiculous, anyway. Colin is a nuisance at times, but, of course, I never allow him to make love to me. I had it out with Howard afterwards and I think I made him see sense. Well, come on in to the kitchen and talk to me while I make this fresh lot of coffee.'

Up on the balcony Dame Beatrice scanned the surrounding countryside, walking slowly round the outside of the lamp room, sometimes into the tearing teeth of the wind, sometimes sheltered from it. The sea was a heaving mass of dirty, grey-green menace flecked with the foam of the Race. The hotel had the appearance of a child's toy fort. The great sweep of the bay moved gently, but there was no sign of the little cove in which Laura had swum; the cliffs hid it from view. A tramp steamer moved, a black shape not much bigger than a match-box, across the horizon, and a lightish wash showed where the waves were breaking on the sandy beach of the mainland watering-place, but of anything helpful in the search for the child there was no sign at all.

'Very nice,' she said, when she came down again. 'Thank you very much, Mrs Spalding.'

'I hope you've seen all that you wanted to,' said Fiona.

'What are the doors I passed as I went up and down?' Dame Beatrice enquired. 'There seemed to be a number of doors opening off landings on the staircase.'

'Doors? Oh, the tower is nothing but junk-rooms now. I believe they were the living-quarters when the lighthouse was in use as a dwelling for the keepers before this modern bungalow was added. I think that's what Howard told me. But, really, I hate this place so much that I'm afraid I wasn't interested.'

'So, under the lamp room itself,' went on Dame Beatrice, ignoring this last statement, 'there would have been sleeping quarters and somewhere where one could cook and eat meals, I suppose.'

'Oh, yes, there would be a bunk room and a galley, and so on, as you say.'

'And a store-room at the foot of the tower, no doubt. Have you been into these various rooms?'

'No. I have had no reason to.'

'So you have guessed at the junk? You have not seen it?'

'Oh, no. I couldn't care less about what's in the place. Howard told me the tower was filled with junk, and that's all I know.'

'Well,' said Laura, when they had drunk the coffee Fiona had prepared and were on their way back to the school, 'how many sea-birds have you spotted this morning?'

'None, child.'

'*None?* What did you find to do up there then? I take it there was no sign of Manoel? And what about Howard? How on earth did you manage to find out that he wouldn't be here?'

'I made no attempt to do anything of the kind.'

'I can't understand it – his trotting off like this, I mean.'

'Neither can I, unless . . .'

'Unless he *does* know something about those disappearances and is afraid of giving himself away, knowing that you are *She Who Makes Nets of Our Words and Uses Them to Ensnare Us?* So you think he's got a guilty secret, do you?'

'I think it might be interesting to obtain the full story of how the escaped convict spent his few hours of freedom. How did you get on with the nervous Mrs Spalding?'

'Oh, all right. We're not twin souls, of course, and I'm not much inclined to believe her when she says she does her best to hold off Colin. My ears and observations have led me to a different conclusion. Still, I suppose poor old Howard bores her silly, and Colin, of course, is at the stage of "Your eyes are lode-stars and your tongue's sweet air more tuneable than lark to shepherd's ear when wheat is green and hawthorn buds appear".'

'Dear me! You are well-versed in the language of the heart.'

'Not so that you'd notice, although Gavin (and I'd hate to remind him of it) did once tell me that "after that a star danced," and under it I was born. I thought it was very nice of him. That was before we were married, needless to say.'

'Mrs Spalding seemed over-anxious to underline the assertion that Mr Ferrars had visited the lighthouse on one occasion only, and that in company with Colin,' said Dame Beatrice.

'Far *too* over-anxious, in my opinion. Proof presumptive she was lying. In fact, we know she was. We know he came over there pretty often on his own, and I'm certain he spent that last afternoon there until he was due to meet the girl he'd dated up.'

'It is a long walk from the school to the lighthouse, and a longer one from the lighthouse to the mainland, where I understand he was to meet the girl,' said Dame Beatrice. 'One would have supposed a journey by car, but it seems that his automobile is still at the school.'

'All the more certain that he *did* go to the lighthouse to see Fiona,' said Laura. 'Howard might have heard the car, you see. I'd worked that one out some time ago.'

'You speak as one having authority,' commented Dame Beatrice, admiringly.

'One has sown one's wild oats,' admitted Laura, grinning.

CHAPTER ELEVEN

The Convict's Story

'... his wandering, guilty and hunted life.'

By virtue of her honorary position as consultant psychiatrist attached to the Home Office, Dame Beatrice's contacts were many. She found no difficulty, therefore, in getting in touch with the governor of the island prison and was invited to visit him for a report upon the experiences of the escaped prisoner.

The prison itself was a grim fortification built of the dark-grey island stone, but the governor's quarters were snug and comfortable and his sherry was delicious. He chatted on general topics at first and then said:

'You wanted some information about Marsh. I have a report here. It's not a transcript of his own words, but it has been carefully checked and, wherever possible, corroborated, so I think you'll find it's accurate, so far as it goes. Whether it will tell you what you want to know is a different matter. Anyway, for what it's worth, here it is. As it has to be retained here for our files, I'm afraid I can't have it taken out of the building, but you are welcome to stay here as long as you like to study it. I'll leave you in peace to make what you can of it. When you're through, just give me a buzz. I shall be in my office next door.'

'May I take notes?' Dame Beatrice asked.

'So far as I am concerned, you can copy out the thing as it stands, if that will help you. The Home Office has a draft of it, of course. There's nothing top secret about it.'

Rendered into official language, the report was short and stilted. It gave the convict's name, age and number, the nature of the offence for which he had been committed to this particular prison, his previous convictions and his medical report. Then followed the account of his escape and recapture.

He seemed to have been in and out of prison for the past

thirty-five years, and had been sentenced twice for house-breaking, and three times for burglary. There was no suggestion, however, that he had ever resorted to violence or made any attempt to resist arrest. This was his second attempt to escape. The first time he had been at large for nearly a fortnight. This last time he had been picked up in a matter of a few days.

He had made a bolt from a quarrying party as the result of a prearrangement, it was thought, with some of the others. He did not admit that there had been a conspiracy, but a fight had broken out and while the warders in charge of the party were settling it, he had downed tools and sneaked off. By the time the *fracas* was over and he was missed, he had managed to get clean away, the island topography affording plenty of cover.

His first concern was to effect a change of clothes and to procure food. His next was to reach the mainland before road blocks were set up and a police cordon thrown across the causeway which connected the island with the mainland.

At first his only plan was to put as great a distance between the prison and himself as he could, but by doing this he had to go south towards the Point instead of north towards the mainland, for the prison was only two miles from the end of the causeway and he saw no chance of being able to leave the island, by the only way out, until he had got rid of his prison garb.

While he had been taken, day after day, to the quarry – the blasting had been done by skilled quarrymen, not the prisoners – he had tried to make out the lie of the land and had decided that his best chance was to take full advantage of the broken country which lay between the quarry and the only woods he could see, and lie up in the latter until he could get, under cover of the darkness, to a house at which to procure a change of clothes.

The woods, as it happened, where those which clothed the hillside at the back of the school, and he had soon realised that they were no refuge for a hunted man when there were boys all over the place. Taking considerable risks, therefore, he had scrambled down part of the cliff and, more by luck than judgment, had come out upon some flat rocks which he traversed until he came to a place where it was possible to climb the cliffs again. From here he had seen the fishermen's cottages and, beyond them, the lighthouse.

By this time the short March day was beginning to close in, and he saw that, beyond the first lighthouse, there was another. He could not understand why there should be two, or why one should show no light from the lantern, whereas, from the other, the great light was already revolving and flashing.

Lighthouse keepers and fishermen, he argued, were likely to be rough, tough customers, unlikely to be argued or bullied into helping him. He supposed his best plan would be to lie up until the morning and then prospect for some house or cottage where there was nobody at home except a woman whose husband had gone off to work and so had left, it was to be hoped and expected, a Sunday suit behind him. The plan did not commend itself as being anywhere near ideal, and he was hungry, but it was the best he could think of, so he crawled away inland and went to ground in a disused quarry.

From his hiding-place he could see the top of the unlighted tower, and became aware that someone was up there. He could see a dark shape against the sky. Then, carried on the wind, which was blowing strongly in his direction, he heard a woman's voice call out:

'Are you going to be much longer? Your supper's nearly ready. I'm sick of being down here by myself!'

It was very cold in the quarry. That, and the mention of supper, gave him an idea. It was clear to him that, whatever its present purpose, the lighthouse was no longer functioning as such, for the beams and flashes further out on the Point indicated the true guide and warning to mariners. There was only one person – a man, presumably – on the tower he was watching, and, with any luck, only one person – a woman, judging by the voice – down below. There might be a chance to slip inside the place when the man came down for his supper, and an opportunity to steal some food when both had gone to bed. He also thought that, possibly, if he played it right, he might even get hold of a suit of clothes.

The warning of his escape had already been given, but he deduced that nobody would think that he had run southwards. They would concentrate all their energies in watching the approaches to the mainland. He reckoned that if he could only hide up for the better part of the night he could make his get-away at dawn if only he could exchange his prison garb for civilian clothes.

He crawled out of the quarry, which was muddy and damp, and cautiously approached the disused lighthouse. Then he crouched under the protection of the wall which enclosed the yard and waited and listened. At the end of about ten minutes he heard movement on the other side of the wall, and the woman's voice again raised in high and semi-hysterical tones.

'Do come down! I'm frightened! Supper's ready! Do you hear?'

There was a shout from above, but he could not make out the words. Shortly after this, a clattering sound indicated that somebody in heavy shoes was descending from the gallery and, as he could hear the sounds so clearly, he decided that the door at the foot of the tower must be open.

A light from an open door in the living-quarters showed him a gate in the wall, and a man's silhouette crossed this. There was an exclamation of relief from the woman, a slight noise as something fell, and a response in a peevish voice from the man, followed by a vexed exclamation, 'Oh, bother! I've dropped my torch!'

'Look for it in the morning,' said the woman. Then came the sound of a door being shut. The convict crept inside the gate-way and crouched and listened, and strained his eyes against the blackness to try to make out the door to the tower. Thinking he had located it, he went forward on hands and knees and suddenly put his hand on the torch which the man had dropped.

Hoping that the door to the tower was open, he switched on the torch, found that his supposition had been right, stood up and entered the tower. Still using the torch, he climbed half-a-dozen stone steps which mounted spirally, and tried a door on the right-hand side. It was locked. Cursing his luck, he went higher, and, twenty feet up, found another door. This he opened.

It led into a small, cramped, stone-floored room half-choked with junk of various kinds. By the light of the torch, he made out empty cardboard boxes and packing-cases, a roll of worn carpeting and various bales and bundles, old newspapers and the like. He unrolled the carpeting, thinking that it would make some sort of shakedown, and found inside it a complete set of clothes.

These items had been listed in red ink on the report Dame Beatrice was reading, and were as follows:

Items recovered from Marsh: One string vest, almost new
One singlet, ditto
One pair knee-length drawers
One pair brown brogue shoes
One pair grey flannel trousers
One tweed sports jacket
One belted raincoat.

It had also been noted that nothing had been found in the pockets of jacket or trousers, and there was a further note to the effect that the garments had been identified as the property of one Ronald Ferrars, a master at Castle Hotel School and now reported missing, and that they were being retained by the police.

The convict's story went on to say that he had changed into these clothes immediately and then, deciding that his luck was too good to last, had bundled up his own clothes, stolen out again, put down the torch more or less where he had found it, thrown his prison clothes into the quarry, and then had put as much ground as he could between himself and the lighthouse tower. He had kept to the road, had seen a light in a cottage, and, emboldened by acute hunger and his own changed appearance, had knocked at the door and told a story which got him food and a mug of cocoa, and directions as to the best way to get to the mainland. It was not yet eight o'clock at night, so his appearance had occasioned neither suspicion nor alarm, and his account of how he had fallen on rough ground and twisted his ankle was accepted without surprise. He was even given the address of a man with a motor-cycle and sidecar who would give him a lift as far as the town. The self-contained islanders of the small village obviously did not know either that a convict had escaped or that the island hotel had been taken over by the school. Fortified by the meal, unwilling to

risk discovery by asking for the lift, but sustained by that
particular brand of unthinking optimism which makes many
criminals what they are, he had set out northwards, but retained enough commonsense not to risk his luck a third time.
He walked and rested until morning. From the quarry in which
the prisoners worked he had often seen the ruined keep on the
cliff-top above the broken ground which eventually led down
to Laura's cove, and he decided to take shelter in it.

From daybreak onwards his story coincided with that of
Laura. As soon as dawn broke and the mist began to lift, he
had discovered, as she had, a dangerous but possible means of
circumventing the purpose of the barbed wire. He had gained
first the gatehouse, then the interior of the keep, and, lastly,
the little hidey-hole – probably the remains of a medieval
garde-robe – in which he had been found.

Just as he had decided to sneak out and try his luck, he had
heard Laura, but had not seen her. He did not realise that he
had lost the handkerchief, but he heard her go away. He had
climbed down into the courtyard and possessed himself of her
ashplant, but he thought, from the weight of the stick, that she
was a powerful man, so he decided to wait where he was until
the coast was clear. Then the prison working-party came into
the quarry below, and he dared not show himself. He had
proved an easy prey when his captors came along.

Dame Beatrice read the account very carefully twice. She
did not need to take any notes. She buzzed for the governor.

'Well,' he said, 'I hope it was of some help.'

'I cannot say, at present, whether it will help us or not,' she
responded. 'It contains no clue to the whereabouts of the little
boy Manoel, and, in itself, it does not throw any *direct* light
upon what has happened to young Mr Ferrars.'

'The bit about visiting the lighthouse, and finding Ferrars'
clothes there, is incredible,' said the governor. 'On the other
hand, this man Marsh has no record of violence, and there was
no blood, only slight staining by sea-water, on the clothes when
we took them off him.'

'*Slight* staining by sea-water,' said Dame Beatrice, thoughtfully.

*   *   *

'Seems to me the Spaldings have got some explaining to do,' observed Laura, when Dame Beatrice has given her an account of the convict's story.

'Why?' Dame Beatrice enquired. 'As the governor indicated, what evidence is there that the man ever went to that lighthouse at all? The Spaldings have only to deny his statement, and everybody will believe them.'

'Everybody except you,' said Laura shrewdly. 'Now, if only he'd had the sense to leave his prison uniform behind in the tower, instead of fatheadedly throwing it down one of the quarries, we should know where we were.'

'Oh, no, we should not, not by a very long way. For one thing, we should need the police and a search warrant in order to obtain access to the room in the tower, supposing that the Spaldings objected to our searching it – which they would have every right to do – and, for another, even if the convict's clothes had been found there, there is no evidence to show that that is where he obtained Mr Ferrars' garments, is there?'

'You mean, the weather being what it is at this time of year, he may have preferred to strip and change in the tower rather than in the open? A bit risky, wasn't it? I mean, either Howard or Fiona might have heard him.' She paused, then added, 'It's a pretty circumstantial story, isn't it, though? I mean, it's quite unlikely he would have invented all that about the lighthouse, isn't it?'

Dame Beatrice did not answer the questions. She said, 'I wonder whether the police have got any further in tracing Manoel?'

'Will you want me this afternoon?' asked Laura, in an equally disconnected manner. 'I ask because, like Yvonne Arnaud in *Tons of Money*, I have an idea!'

'If it leads to equal devastation, I wish you would forget it,' said her employer, 'but I suppose you were born to be a law unto yourself, and to get into trouble as the sparks fly upward.'

'Bless you for those few kind words,' said Laura. 'Do you think the convict killed Ferrars to get his clothes?'

'If so, he did not kill him in the lighthouse.'

'Mrs Spalding was in a blue funk when we called there. Something has to make sense somewhere or other, hasn't it?'

'Slightly stained with sea-water,' said Dame Beatrice.

'Sounds as though Ferrars went swimming, leaving his clothes on the rocks, and got himself drowned, and the Spaldings found the clothes and took them back to the lighthouse. Oh, *I* don't know!' said Laura.

CHAPTER TWELVE

In a Beautiful Pea-Green Boat

'We'll have favourable winds, a quick passage, and not
the least difficulty of finding the spot . . .

When three more days had gone by and no trace of Manoel's
movements had come to light, Mr Eastleigh telephoned the
Querigua Montes embassy in London to give them the information that the son of the president was missing. Their reply,
although reassuring in one sense, was the reverse in another.
Querigua Montes was, for the fifth time in nine years, the scene
of a revolution, and the president's troubles and anxieties were
such (and his future, the caller indicated, so uncertain) that
the headmaster was urged to leave matters in the hands of the
English police and to refrain from worrying either the embassy
or the president himself until the outcome of the revolution
was known.

'Well, at least we shan't have the embassy giving us the run-
around, or the president coming over here to badger us,' said
the headmaster to his wife, Dame Beatrice and Laura, 'Neither
does it seem likely, under the circumstances, that the child has
been kidnapped.'

'I have believed, from the beginning, that he ran off on his
own,' said Mrs Eastleigh. 'That being so, I should have thought
the police would have found him by now, though. Surely a boy
of his age, and with a markedly foreign accent, at that, cannot
have got very far?'

'There's a feeling abroad that he had a good deal more cash
on him than the ordinary school allowance of pocket-money,'
said Laura. 'It's only a rumour, but, where boys are concerned,
rumours are apt to be based on facts, however much distorted
in the telling.'

'True,' agreed Mr Eastleigh. He looked gloomy. 'I don't
much like the sound of that.'

'I suppose he didn't meet that escaped convict and get set upon and robbed?' suggested the headmaster's wife, her eyes widening. 'If so, he might be lying injured, or even dead, in one of the quarries.'

'The quarries are being methodically examined,' said her husband, 'but, of course, that sort of search takes time. Anyway, it is a task we must leave to the police.'

'There was no money on the convict when he was caught,' said Dame Beatrice. 'Laura, I think, has her own ideas on the subject of the child's disappearance, and they may be worth a passing thought.'

'I've talked it over with Dame Beatrice,' said Laura, in response to a keen, half-hopeful glance from the headmaster, 'and, if you agree to release me for a few days, she is willing to take over my classes while I'm away.'

'No, no, I could not think of her troubling herself to that extent,' protested Mr Eastleigh. 'The Extra English boys can remain with their own forms, as they have been doing for the past few days, and that leaves only twelve periods unaccounted for. I will continue to look after those myself. But what is your scheme, Mrs Gavin?'

'Not so much a scheme, actually, as a hunch. Could we have a word with Colin Spalding after breakfast?'

'Certainly. I will send for him. How do you think he can help us?'

'I don't know that he can, but it's worth trying.'

'Anything is worth trying,' said the headmaster. He sent for Colin before Assembly, beamed at him and handed him over to Laura. Mrs Eastleigh went out, but Mr Eastleigh and Dame Beatrice remained in the room. Colin seemed nervous.

'Cheer up,' said Laura. 'Nobody's feeling cannibalistic towards you.'

'Sit down, Spalding,' said the headmaster kindly, 'and give Mrs Gavin your fullest attention, for she thinks perhaps you can help us.'

'Well,' said Laura, 'I expect you're sick of doing it, but could you cast your mind back to that evening at tea when you told your tales? There should have been nine boys and yourself, you at the head, a prefect at the foot, and four boys on either side. Right?'

'Yes, that's right. Peters was the prefect, then I had Sanderson and Rogers on either side of me, Peters had Redwood and the younger Geoghan, and next to Sanderson was the missing boy, de Roseda. Opposite him (I think) was Sculley and the other two boys—' he frowned in concentrated thought – 'oh, yes, were Conelly and Philips. Why?'

'Just so that we know de Roseda was there,' Laura replied. 'Can you remember what you talked about?'

'Smugglers, mostly. That's what led to the game of hide-and-seek afterwards. We left out Peters, of course, because he's older, and has his own friends, but when tea was over I raked in the rest of my chaps and we began the game.'

'Can you remember mentioning any particular smugglers' coves and so forth? – any special localities, you know?'

'Only vaguely. I promised them – that's how it all began – that I'll read *Moonfleet* to them in the half-hour after prep. – just for the fun of it, you know, sir,' he added, turning to his headmaster. 'I thought I'd get them looking forward to the book, that's all, so I talked about smuggling and the excisemen in a general sort of way, and told them something about smugglers' caves and pack-horses, and then somebody suggested this game of hide-and-seek, so I got it organised. I'm sorry it's led to so much trouble. Of course, if I'd had any idea—'

'Nonsense, my dear chap! No fault of yours, and nobody blames you in the slightest,' said Mr Eastleigh. He looked expectantly at Laura. She turned again to Colin.

'*Moonfleet*, as I remember it, is set somewhere along the great bank of shingle which ends by carrying the causeway over to this island, isn't it?' she said.

'Yes, of course it is. I told the chaps that.'

'So it's a real place. Do you remember any other real places you may have mentioned?'

'Oh, I told them about the Cornish wreckers and I believe I mentioned various smugglers' holes between here and South Devon, and then I talked about the Channel Islands and the smugglers on Jersey and Guernsey, but I don't remember an awful lot of what I said. I was interrupted by questions and by boys getting up from table to pour themselves out more tea from the pot on the sideboard, and I was giving a general eye to things as well – you know, making sure everybody had his fair whack at the fishpaste sandwiches and didn't hog all the cake...'

'I know how it is,' said Laura. 'Right. Thanks a lot, Colin. Well, that's all from me.'

'Thank you, Spalding,' said Mr Eastleigh. Colin hesitated, looking puzzled, but, as nobody volunteered any other remark, he bowed awkwardly and went off.

'Well, that only took us about as far as I thought it would,' said Laura. 'Next on my list are Sanderson and Rogers, taking Sanderson first. He's got a retentive memory, judging by the answers I get from him in history lessons. He's also a natural criminal, so smuggling should be right up his street.'

Sanderson proved to be a small, composed, straw-haired child in glasses.

'If it's the white mice, sir, yes, sir,' he said, addressing the headmaster. 'But I've sold them, sir. They won't cause any more trouble, I assure you, sir.'

'Never mind the white mice, Sanderson,' said Mr Eastleigh, to whom this saga was new. 'We can deal with those later, if necessary. Kindly give your full attention to Mrs Gavin.'

'If it's the rude drawing on the history time-chart, Mrs Gavin, yes, Mrs Gavin,' said Sanderson. 'But I can clean it off with my new soft indiarubber, and I solemnly promise to do so.'

'Goodness me! How many crimes *are* you going to confess to?' demanded Laura. 'For goodness' sake keep the rest of your guilty secrets to yourself, or we shall be here until lunch-time. Now, then.'

'Yes, Mrs Gavin?'

'Do you remember a game of hide-and-seek – only it was called Smugglers and Excisemen – which you played with Mr Spalding a few days ago?'

'Oh, yes, Mrs Gavin. And, of course...'

'No!' said Laura firmly. 'You confine yourself to answering my questions. I've no doubt whatever that there was mayhem and general fratricide as an accompaniment to the revels, but I don't want to hear the details now. Listen – and *think*! When

Mr Spalding at tea-time was talking about smugglers' holes, which did he specifically mention?'

'He was telling us about the book *Moonfleet* – it's very good, but I read it when I was seven – and then he mentioned – let me see, now—' He took off his glasses. Laura waited. The tip of a red tongue appeared between Sanderson's thin and resolute lips, and his greenish eyes fixed themselves on the past.

'Well, boy?' said Mr Eastleigh, when he judged that the moment had come.

'Yes, sir. Yes, Mrs Gavin.' Sanderson closed the greenish eyes and recited at speed. 'He – Mr Spalding – mentioned Banks Cove, Sandy Bay, Greenland Hole, Hales Head, Dead Man's Dunes and some places in the Channel Islands on Jersey and Guernsey. I don't think they had actual names. They were caves in coves, he said. '

'Many thanks. That's fine,' said Laura. 'Did the boys seem to know any of these places?'

'Some of them had been to the Channel Islands, and I think Philips had been to Dead Man's Dunes.'

'Did the missing boy, de Roseda, speak about any of these places?'

'He said his tutor – he has a tutor to look after him in the holidays – had taken him to the Channel Islands, but he didn't say which ones.'

'Were all the boys interested in smugglers?'

'Oh, yes, Mrs Gavin, of course. Conelly said his mother once smuggled in some silk stuff from Italy by showing the Customs a ticket for admission to the Roman ruins at Pompeii, and when the Customs saw the price on the ticket they thought it was the price of the silk, and she didn't have to pay any duty. We thought it was a wizard idea. Conelly said his mother honestly thought she was showing them the proper bill for the silk stuff, but I should doubt that very much, Mrs Gavin, wouldn't *you?* Besides, it spoils the story.'

'Get along, if Mrs Gavin has finished with you,' said Mr Eastleigh. The literary critic put on his glasses and took his departure.

'A brilliant child,' said the headmaster indulgently. 'but a rather naughty one. His father is a professor of Greek and his mother models waxworks for Madame Tussaud's.'

'Well, that's my hunch, for what it's worth,' said Laura, when the door had closed behind Sanderson. 'Manoel is reminded of his visit to the Channel Islands, remembers (I'm prepared to bet) that there are two Roman Catholic churches in St Helier alone, and makes his getaway with the dual purpose of going to church and tracking down the smugglers' haunts.'

'But how would he get himself there – a boy of nine?' asked Mrs Eastleigh.

'By paying his fare, I suppose,' said Laura, bluntly. 'It seems he had plenty of money. I take it you wouldn't care for me to go after him and see whether I can chase him up and bring him back? This is what I meant when I asked you to release me for a few days,' she added, turning to the headmaster. Mr Eastleigh looked doubtful.

'It isn't that I won't release you,' he said, 'but I think you would be going on a wild-goose chase. The police are doing everything they can to trace the boy, I am sure.'

'They haven't got around to the Channel Islands,' said Laura. 'They still think he's about here or perhaps has managed to get as far as the mainland, you know. I suppose they asked how much money he was likely to have had on him, and based their deductions on that, not knowing that probably he had a lot more. How about it, then? Do I get leave of absence for a few days?'

'I suppose you're tired of routine and want a jaunt,' said the headmaster, with the smile he kept for her. He found her refreshing after the brash or apologetic young University men he usually had to recruit. 'If Dame Beatrice is agreeable, it's all right with me. I think you'll find the sea and air services a bit restricted at this time of year, but you would have to enquire about those.'

'I'll manage,' said Laura, thinking with glee of the diesel-engined cruiser she could charter. 'I have my methods, and they're pretty good, at that.'

'Ship you over to St Peter Port, with maybe a chase round the other islands?' said the owner of *Pronax*. 'Well, don't blame me if it's rough. Couldn't you take your holiday later on in the year?'

'It's no sort of holiday,' said Laura. 'I'm chasing a run-away.'

'Daughter or son?'

'Neither, as it happens. It's simply a kid who's vanished from the school where I work, a boy of nine.'

'Gone off on his own, has he?'

'We don't know. What time will you start in the morning?'

'Tide's right at about ten. How long do you reckon to be away?'

'I have no idea. Does it matter? You haven't any other commitments, have you?'

'Only a new-wedded wife. You being you, I think I'd better bring her along. We've only been married eight months, and I don't want her getting ideas.'

At ten on the following morning they left the harbour and soon were out in the bay. They stood well away from the island, which, from the sea, presented a stark, forbidding outline of cliffs and headlands, and by noon they had left it far behind and were bucking along through heavy seas which reminded Laura of large, well-intentioned but formidably powerful horses.

The wife was also large and well-intentioned, a plain, sensible, motherly girl, active and competent in the tiny galley and capable of taking her turn at the wheel. Laura, who was an excellent sailor, thoroughly enjoyed the trip and was sorry when, after a very rough passage, they made St Peter Port, with its jetties, piers, castle and lighthouse.

'I'll come with you when you go ashore,' said the wife. Her name was Lilian. 'Two people making enquiries always seem so much more convincing than one. What will you do, Thorvald?'

'Juice up the boat and then go ashore for a drink, I expect. See you later.'

The advantage of a private charter, apart from avoiding the tedious business of booking a flight or a passage on a boat, was that the big cruiser could be used as an hotel. Laura had foreseen this, and soon decided that she could not have made a wiser move than to have hired the *Pronax* for her trip, very expensive though it was.

Enquiries for a lost boy answering to Manoel's description, and made first at the official information bureau on the Victoria Pier and then at the police station in St James Street, proved abortive. It was most unlikely, said the island police, that a small boy would have been able to land unnoticed, either from an aeroplane or a boat, if he was unaccompanied. They were very properly guarded in their reception of Laura's admission that she did not know whether the child had been alone or had been accompanied. She gave a description of Ferrars, but it could have applied, the police pointed out, to hundreds of young Englishmen who visited St Peter Port every year.

Laura's next and last call was at the presbytery of the Roman Catholic church. Here she was far more sympathetically received, particularly when she gave her reasons for approaching the priest. He was unable to help. He would surely have noticed the boy, he said. He made a point of having a word at the church door with all newcomers, unless, as, for instance, during the peak holiday periods, this proved impossible owing to weight of numbers. In a slack time such as the present, visitors were so few and far between that little Manoel could not possibly have escaped notice.

'Of course,' said Lilian, 'if this church lark is going to pay off, you have to be pretty sure the kid came on his own and in order to attend Mass. If he's been kidnapped, either by this Ferrars or somebody else, the last place he'd be taken to is a church, where the priest (and probably others at this dead and alive time of year) would be sure to remember him.'

These reasonable words did nothing to help matters. They returned to the *Pronax*, had supper and the drinks brought aboard by her owner, and then turned in.

'Another snag,' said Thorvald, as they breakfasted on the following morning, 'is that there's a very poor chance of running him to earth if his companion (supposing he's been abducted) had his own boat. I don't suppose I'm the only yachtsman from the other side who knows these waters. I always was in sail until our marriage, and, believe me, you've got to know an awful lot about these coasts if you don't want to run into trouble. The tides can rise forty feet in some places, and there are rocks everywhere. All the same, it's possible, if you know your way around, to lie up in little anchorages that the island fishermen use. There are lots of caves, too. You'd never explore them all, even if you could get to them – and I'm not risking my boat, let me tell you. Personally, Laura, I think you're on a wild-goose chase. If I were you, I'd cut my losses and decide I'd only come for the ride.'

'I don't leave avenues unexplored,' said Laura. 'I'm going on with the search for a bit. There's somewhere called Smugglers' Lane over in the direction of Moulin Huet and Saints Bay.'

'I don't see what you're going to gain. I agree with Thorvald,' said Lilian. 'The kid would be dead by now if he's been trying to sleep rough at this time of year.'

There was no cave. Laura, who had purchased a guide book, did not expect one, but she thought that the name 'Smugglers' Lane' might have proved an attraction to the child. She rode on a bus part of the way, and then walked. She had a reward, although it was not the one she sought. At St Martin's Church one of the gate-posts to the churchyard was formed by a statue of the Earth Mother, possibly of Bronze Age origin, representing an old woman, hooded, it seemed, and distinguished, apart from her crudely carved, surprisingly life-like face, by two cannonball bosoms placed each to each to solve the problem of carving them separately in the harsh, unyielding stone. The rest of her was a menhir with a large crack going from the left hipbone diagonally across the stomach. She was impressive and Laura loved her. The islanders called her La Grandmère de Chimquière and at one time had offered flowers to her until, at the beginning of the nineteenth century, this pleasant pagan custom was written off as being idolatrous.

'At least, to make her acquaintance is something,' thought Laura. Apart from La Grandmère and some magnificent coast scenery, the quest was of no value. Laura found a road past La Fosse Chapel which continued as the winding, hedge-protected Smugglers' Lane, but it ended only in a gate, a turning on to the cliff-top and a view of the small inlet called Saints Bay.

'So much for Guernsey, for the time being,' she said, upon her return to *Pronax*. 'It was worth a trial, but I think I'm more likely to be successful in Jersey.' They slept on board again that night and set off, as soon as the tide was right, on the following day.

CHAPTER THIRTEEN

Les Ecrehous

'There was a great, smooth swell upon the sea. The wind
blowing steady and gentle from the south, there was no
contrariety between this and the current, and the billows
rose and fell unbroken.'

At St Helier Laura obtained the first clue – if clue it could be
called, for at first she was inclined to dismiss it for reasons which
appeared to her to be obvious.

At the police station she drew a blank. They were sym-
pathetic, but were certain that no unaccompanied child, let
alone one as young as nine years, had landed on Jersey, either
from the sea or the air, within the stated time. They knew of
a missing youngster, having been alerted by the Dorsetshire
police and given a description which tallied with Laura's, and
they were keeping, they said, a look-out. Beyond this they could
not help her.

'Well,' she said, when she returned to *Pronax*, 'I suppose
it's something that the police here have been notified that
Manoel is somewhere at large. I expect Mr Eastleigh or Dame
Beatrice got on to them as soon as I left. I'm going to comb
this island. It's much the most likely one for him to have come
to.'

'I shall charge you waiting-time, but go ahead,' said
Thorvald; so Laura toured the island in a self-driven hired car.
She drove from St Helier in the south of Bonne, explored the
Wolf Caves, then went round to Grève le Lecq, then across
the island to St Aubin's Bay, thence to St Brelade's Bay, along
the coast road from Corbière Point to L'Etac and out to
Grosnez Castle. After that she went to the hotel out by Plémont
Point, drove inland and out again to Grève le Lecq, inland
once again to St Mary's Church, and so on and so forth until
she had covered, in two days, sometimes driving, some-

times on foot, more than three-quarters of the island and its coastline.

She spent the third day in St Helier itself, enquiring at hotels and guest-houses, a dreary, exhausting, completely unrewarding task. No little boy answering to Laura's description, or anything even remotely like it, had been seen either alone or accompanied by a young man. Everywhere she was received with patient courtesy, her story given attention, herself offered sympathy, but 'no dice', said Laura dispiritedly to Thorvald and Lilian, when she gave up at last and went back to them.

'You know, you'll knock yourself up,' said the motherly girl. 'It's obvious that the kid can't be here. You've searched and you've asked. You can't do any more. Pack it in, and let's go home. You look just about finished, old love.'

'You go if you like,' said Laura. 'I suppose I can always fly back.'

'No,' said Thorvald, 'my time's my own until I start filming again in June. You carry on if you want to. Lilian and I can bear it.'

So, on the following morning, Laura 'did' St Clement's Bay as far as La Rocque Point, then went to Grouville Bay with its golf-course, and on to Gorey and Mont Orgueil Castle, and so rounded St Catherine's Bay to the breakwater at Verclut Point. She made enquiries wherever there was anybody to question, and then, leaving the car at the quarries, she walked as far as the way could take her round the rocky coast of Fliquet Bay. There was nothing to help her, so she returned to the car and drove inland to St Martin's Church and then north to Rozel Bay and as close to Bouley Bay as the road allowed. After that, she walked and explored again.

It was that same evening, when she had given up any hope of finding the boy, that the clue came and was, at first, rejected. She went back to the boat weary, disgruntled and famished, for she had eaten almost nothing since breakfast. When she had had a late supper, Thorvald suggested that they might as well go ashore for a drink.

The *Pronax* was moored almost opposite a small hotel. Its cocktail bar had an attractive interior, being very clean, and having red-patterned carpeting on the floor and a hooded fire-place hung with warming-pans and horse-brasses. A broad picture-rail, painted dark brown to match the seating, held patterned plates and one or two jugs, and there were spring flowers in bronze-coloured vases on the deep window-ledges. The cushions on the wooden chairs and a wall-long settle were patterned, too, and every table, in addition to its small circular mats for glasses, was provided with a soda siphon and a flask of clear water.

'I'll order,' said Laura. 'It will give me a chance to question the barman. I don't know what the rules are here about allowing kids in bars, but this is an hotel, not a pub, so, if Manoel *is* with Ferrars, maybe they came in here.'

'No, I'd better do the ordering,' said Thorvald. 'Oh, it's all right. A chap's coming over. What are we having? Whisky for you? Bloody Mary for Lilian. Beer for me.' He gave the order. When the waiter brought over the tray of drinks, Laura put down a pound note and said:

'Do you allow children to come in here?'

'Not in this room, madam, but there is a garden.'

'Bit chilly at this time of year, isn't it?'

'It is never really chilly in Jersey, madam. In any case, we have a summerhouse with a heater. Your child would be happy with you there.'

'It isn't my child. A friend of mine brought him. I was hoping to run into them. Boy of nine, dark-skinned, very thin, large brown eyes and speaks with a Spanish accent.'

'I will bring your change, madam.' He did this. Laura left a lavish amount of the change on the tray. 'Thank you very much, madam. A little boy, not English, not French? I took out watered wine and a sandwich to him. He was with a gentle-man of middle age who had brandy and soda.'

'Of middle age?'

'Yes, madam. The gentleman had grey hair and spoke in a thin voice.'

'When did you see them?'

'Two days ago, I think, but it might be three. I did not notice them particularly. We are always busy at the time of day when they came.'

'Did you hear the man call the boy by name?'

'Not that I remember, madam.'

'They didn't stay here at the hotel?'

'No, madam. I think I heard the gentleman mention that they were going to some of the other islands to photograph seabirds.'

'Les Ecrehous!' said Thorvald. 'Yes, that's it!'

'Les Ecrehous? Whereabouts is that?'

'They are a group of small islands, madam, about half-way over to France,' said the waiter, before Thorvald could answer. When he had left them, Lilian said:

'I thought the kid's escort was a *young* man.'

'Yes,' said Laura. 'I don't think it's much use going to these islands. The boy can't be Manoel. I thought at first we were on to something, but we're not.'

'I still think it's worth trying,' urged Thorvald. 'I mean, think of the description of the boy – not English, not French. I think you'd be greatly mistaken not to follow this up.'

'Well, what are they like, these islands?'

'They're dependencies of Jersey, so you see the connection. They're actually part of the parish of St Martin. Three of them are habitable. People go over for week-ends, so that means they're quite accessible. Besides, they're a paradise for a romantic sort of kid. There's a ruined priory on one of them, and there's good fishing and tremendous colonies of black-backed gulls and terns, and not much else. A youngster would love it there. Best of all, from a kid's point of view, the islands were great places for smugglers in the old days.'

'Smugglers?' said Laura. 'They were playing at smugglers when Manoel disappeared! He'd been to the Channel Islands before, and may have heard of Les Ecrehous. I'll take a chance. Can we go over there tomorrow?'

'Easiest thing in the world! We'll get round to Gorey first thing in the morning, provision up, and off we go.'

Laura never needed much sleep. She lay on her bunk and turned over in her mind the chances – they now seemed slight – of tracking down Manoel and his abductor. The picture of the latter had changed. Something began to add up. The new picture formed itself into a mental image of Howard Spalding.

In vain she told herself that this was nonsense, but the waiter's description of a middle-aged, grey-haired man with a 'thin' voice had taken shape in her mind and she could not dislodge it. She was up, and out on deck as soon as it began to get light, and began to prepare the breakfast. She woke the others and at just after sunrise the *Pronax* was edging first east and then north, to lie under the shadow of Mont Orgueil Castle, the formidable edifice of weathered stone which crowned a projecting headland at the northern end of the bay.

While the other two did the marketing for lunch, Laura climbed to the heights and looked out to sea. It was a clear morning and she had binoculars with her. Through them she could see Les Ecrehous, which were about fifteen miles from where she was standing. She thought that she could also pick out the coast of France. She got back to the boat before the others had finished their marketing, did some swabbing down and at the same time tried to rid her mind of the image of Manoel and Howard trudging about the islands in pursuit of the haunts of gulls, terns and smugglers.

When the others came back to the boat she said:

'Is there a post office? I want to telephone a telegram.' She addressed it to Dame Beatrice at the school. It read: *Find out where Howard Spalding is Laura*. At half-past ten the *Pronax* backed gently out from the quay and soon the houses and hotels began to lessen in size, and the castle to change perspective, as the twin B.M.C. Commander diesels buckled down to their work and Les Ecrehous gradually grew larger.

Two of them, in particular, it was decided, might repay a visit, the isle of Le Maître and then Marmoutier. There were holiday cottages on both, although, according to the guide book, many on Marmoutier were derelict. Some, however, were habitable, and, in the high season, these were used at week-ends by the owners. Others belonged to fishermen, for the fishing-grounds off Les Ecrehous supplied (although not as lavishly as in earlier times) lobsters and shrimps, and also bass, bream, ray, mullet, rockfish, whiting and conger eels.

Maître Ile yielded nothing to Laura, however, except a passing interest in the ruins of the priory built by monks from Val

Richer in Normandy in 1203 and suppressed as an alien monastery in 1413. To any enquiries she was able to make of people she encountered on the island (and these, at that early time of year, were few) there was no helpful answer.

On Marmoutier, however, she found fishermen who had seen Pierre Logard's boat carrying away from the island a little boy and a middle-aged man. Pierre Logard? Oh, yes, he lived on Jersey. He kept his boat at the breakwater on Bonne Nuit bay.

'Might be worse,' said Thorvald, as the *Pronax* put to sea again. 'I know the way in, and it's a nice little harbour when you get there.'

Laura's quest was by no means over. Pierre Logard was not at home, but he had told his wife about his passengers. No, she could not describe them. She had not seen them. That they were a little boy and a man – his grandfather, perhaps – was as much as she had learned from her husband. Where had they gone? Where else than to Alderney? No, it was not such an easy passage, – the passage of the Swinge was never good, and most people flew, but there was the money to be considered. Pierre had very few such commissions, and the money offered had been enough. Besides, the old one had said he was afraid to fly.

Laura learned that Pierre had landed the two passengers at Braye, and hoped that at last she was on the trail. The *Pronax* spent the night in Bonne Nuit bay at the sturdy stone breakwater built out from an arc of sand in the shelter of Frémont Point. It was a fine, bold bluff, green here and there, which ran out in naked rocks and sheltered a larger beach on the further side of it. As soon as it was light enough, Thorvald was prepared to put off for Alderney.

Laura had other ideas. She had not argued with him, but she was not prepared to have his valuable boat risk the passage of the Swinge, so she rose before dawn and, by the light of an electric torch, left him a note to say that she was going to fly to Alderney and would back as soon as she could. She left the money which he was charging for the trip – it had been agreed that she would pay so much a day, as nobody could tell how long her search would take – and, having also asked him to wait for her, for she would certainly come back, she left the vessel at sun-up and made for the airport at St Helier.

It was a goodish walk – at least seven miles, she judged from the map in her possession – and from the granite quarries through Haûtes Croix to Les Ornes it was hilly. Even after that the land did not drop below three hundred feet. She stepped out briskly and reached Fort Regent and the airport after having stopped for a late breakfast and to make enquiries about the next flight to Alderney.

The airport was outside St Anne. She took a taxi into the town, the only place of any size, and booked a room. Enquiry at the reception office produced no information which was of any use to her except that Braye Bay, where she desperately hoped her quarry had been landed by Pierre Logard, lay directly north of St Anne and that there was a good road to it. Laura ordered the hotel taxi for nine o'clock on the following morning, and learned from the driver that there was no hotel at Braye, so far as he knew, and that there was little chance that her friends had remained there.

Laura paid off the taxi at the Old Harbour and began her enquiries. She thought that, at that time of year, and the fact that comparatively few people visited Alderney in comparison with those who spent holidays on Jersey and Guernsey, a boat landing two passengers, one of them a little boy, would surely have excited interest. She was right. Manoel and his elderly companion had been seen. They had obtained a ride in Jean Longville's car.

Jean Longville was tracked down He was at the inn. Yes, he had driven an elderly gentleman and a little dark-skinned boy to Essex Castle, on the opposite side of the island. What would they do at the Castle? They would rent an apartment. The castle had been modernised and was now let out in the form of flats. Certainly Jean Longville's car was at the lady's service. Back to St Anne's for lunch, and to Essex Castle at half-past two? Why, certainly. Nothing easier.

It was the end of the trail. Manoel, tearful and apprehensive because Don Quixote, who had taken him there, had gone off on the previous day and had not returned, was in the care of the porter's wife. The rent for the flat had been paid in advance. The flat had been taken for a week. No, such bookings, for so short a time, were not usually accepted, but there had been a vacant flat and it was out of season, so a week's rent was better than nothing. Yes, the porter's wife was looking after these particular tenants, marketing, cooking and cleaning for them.

As it was clear that the child not only knew Laura, but begged her to take him back to the school with her, there was no problem about getting the boy to St Anne and subsequently to St Helier. From the airport they went by taxi to Bonne Nuit Bay and boarded the *Pronax*. Laura left a note in the flat to tell X – whom she now identified, without a doubt in her mind, as Howard Spalding – what she had done.

No very coherent story could be obtained from Manoel. He had left school because he was unhappy. (Not a word would he say about his Church or about the smugglers.) He had walked and walked – he could give little account of the direction he had taken because it was dark. Then he became tired and frightened. Then he had seen a light. He had made for it. It was a house. There was a woman there. She had given him supper and put him to bed. She said there was no car. He must walk back to school in the morning. He did not want to go back to school. He was sure Mr Eastleigh would be angry because he had run away. In the morning he had slipped away before the woman was up, and had run and walked, run and walked – he did not know how far or in what direction.

After this, the narrative had become more and more confused. He had walked along a cliff. That was where he had met Don Quixote. No, he had heard no other name. The man had said, 'I had better be Don Quixote. You can come with me if you want to see some smugglers' caves. I am going to the Channel Islands.'

Of one thing Manoel was positive. Don Quixote had not been Ferrars. Don Quixote was a much older gentleman than Mr Ferrars, and one whom Manoel was absolutely certain he had never seen in his life before. He knew Ferrars very well. He could not have mistaken Don Quixote for Mr Ferrars. When the questioning, first by the headmaster and then by the police overcame him, he took refuge in tears.

'Well, at any rate, he's safe and well. That's the only thing that matters,' said Mr Eastleigh. 'He's had a shock, of course, feeling that he'd been deserted by this man on Alderney, so I think we'll just let it go at that for the present.'

CHAPTER FOURTEEN

A Reappearance

'. . . I'm a poor old hulk on a lee shore.'

'So what about Howard Spalding?' asked Laura, when she and Dame Beatrice were alone.

'I went to see Mrs Spalding, and her story is in accordance with your suggestion. Her husband had announced his intention of visiting the Channel Islands in quest of the roseate tern.'

'But roseate terns don't nest there any longer. There used to be a colony of them on Marmoutier, but they've gone, so the guide book says. Anyway, they winter in Africa and the eggs aren't laid until June, so, if he thought he would see them in the Channel Islands before Easter, he must be an optimist. I don't believe that is why he went. He knows all about terns and their ways. And what price picking up young Manoel and calling himself Don Quixote? Do you know what I think?'

'You probably think the same as I do.'

'Some sort of smoke screen. Exactly. But why?'

'Well, Mr Ferrars is still missing,' said Dame Beatrice.

'I gaze at you in wild surmise,' said Laura. 'Do you really think there is any connection between Howard's going to the Channel Islands, and the boy being with him, and Ferrars being absent without leave?'

'I do not know.'

'Oh, well, Ferrars is no business of ours, thank goodness. Neither is Howard Spalding, come to that.'

'Neither was Manoel, yet you went to look for him, and appear to have spared no pains.'

'A small kid's different. And there's another thing. Reverting to Howard Spalding, and assuming that he may have told the truth, why the Channel Islands?' pursued Laura. 'He could have seen the roseate tern in lots of other places, if that's what he really hoped for.'

'But, except for the Scillies, nowhere to the south of us, you know. He may have hoped for early visitors.'

'Yes, I suppose so, if you put it like that. All the same, I still think it's extremely fishy. Has Colin said anything about his father's absence?'

'Not to me, and, realising that they are not always on the best of terms, I have not approached him on the subject. He may not even be aware of his father's absence, if he has not visited the lighthouse recently.'

'What did Fiona Spalding think about Howard's going off like that?'

'She said she was accustomed to it, and indicated that her husband is fanatical, impulsive and irrational where his bird-watching is concerned.'

'Fair enough, from what I know of him. Had she any idea of when she might expect to have him back?'

'I did not ask her. It was nothing to do with me. I showed her your telegram and she said that there was nothing to worry about – this in spite of the fact that she is in a state of anxiety. You did not mention Manoel, so, of course, I did not mention him either, although, knowing of your quest, I guessed that you thought you had found some connection between him and Howard Spalding.'

'Oh, well, I suppose Howard will turn up again in his own good time. I wish Ferrars would, too. There's only one thing I can't make out. I can't understand why Howard deserted the kid like that. It doesn't seem to fit in with his character as I read it.'

'Really? That is very interesting. You have a *flair* for distinguishing the sheep from the goats in a way which I cannot sufficiently admire.'

Laura gazed suspiciously into the bright black eyes of her employer.

'Hm!' she said. 'That sounds a double-edged compliment, coming from you. Are you staying on here now that Manoel has turned up? I wish you would. It only wants five more days to the end of term, and, as I don't like the way things are going,

I'd be much happier if you were here. I mean, why did Howard need the kid as a smoke-screen? It stinks a bit, that.'

'I will invoke Mr Eastleigh's hospitality and travel home with you in your car. That will enable me to send George before us in mine, so that he may alert the domestic staff. I must say Zena seems to have settled in well, and has already acquired a fair proficiency in the French tongue.'

'Stay until the end of term? Why, of course you must stay,' said Mr Eastleigh. 'I've had Mr and Mrs Ferrars to see me. They are naturally most concerned about the continued and inexplicable absence of their son. I feel extremely sorry for them. It is a very odd business altogether. I cannot account for the finding of Ferrars' clothes in possession of that convict. Mr and Mrs Ferrars knew about that, of course, and fear the worst. They think the convict may have killed their son in order to obtain the change of clothes, and that the body may be in the sea. I confess I share their anxiety, particularly as, by this time, there seems very little chance of finding the young man, alive or dead. The search has been a most exhaustive one, and I understand that it will be abandoned very soon, so far as the quarries are concerned, and the coast watched for a washed-up body.'

'Oh, well, in a few days' time, our part in all this will be over. I shan't be sorry to get back to normal, although I've rather enjoyed the school,' said Laura, later, to her employer. 'What are you going to do with yourself during the time that's left? I won't see much of you, I'm afraid. You know what the end of term is like.'

'I shall find ways and means of occupying my time,' said Dame Beatrice.

She spoke more truly than, at the time of utterance, she knew. The first report came from Colin, the second from the police. As it happened, Dame Beatrice had been prevailed upon by Skelton, Robson and Heathers to recount some of her cases to them. Skelton, by virtue of being in charge of the physical education and games, had no examination papers to mark; Heathers, whose youthful charges were not required to sit for end-of-term examinations, was in the same happy state; Robson, who taught mathematics to the older boys, had made very short work of the few dozen papers sent in, and so all three were free at a time when their less fortunate colleagues, including Laura and Colin, were kept extremely busy.

Laura had seen very little of Colin since her return from the Channel Islands. She had sought him out to give him such news of his father as she had gathered, but he seemed neither interested nor excited. His sole comment had been, 'Went off with the beastly kid and then abandoned him? I don't believe it.' As this was Laura's own reaction, except that, on the evidence, there was nothing more creditable to believe, she had merely retorted, 'All right. I've no proof. I don't even know that the man *was* your father. I just thought you might like to know what I'd been told.' After that, he had appeared to avoid her, and was seen heading for the Point whenever it was his free afternoon. Laura thought she knew why, and despised him for taking so obvious an advantage of his father's absence.

On the third evening after Laura's return, the headmaster came to the Staff Common Room. Laura, Pocock and Grange were marking papers, making out lists and jotting down notes for the boys' end-of-term reports. It was unusual for Mr Eastleigh to go to the Staffroom. It was on the house telephone, as were most of the rooms in the hotel, and it was his custom to use this convenient method of getting in touch with the masters if he needed to contact them when they were not actually teaching, so that his appearance, to the occupants of the Commom Room, was a dramatic one.

'Oh, Mr Spalding, can you spare me a minute?' he asked. As this amounted to a royal command, Colin put down his marking pencil and followed his headmaster out of the room. 'My sitting-room will be best, my dear fellow,' Mr Eastleigh went on. 'That's it. Sit down. My dear, a glass of sherry for Mr Spalding.'

'I'm so sorry about the news, Mr Spalding,' said Mrs Eastleigh, bringing the glass to Colin, 'but while there's life, there's hope.'

'Not . . . what's happened to her? She isn't . . . she hasn't . . .' babbled Colin.

'She? We are talking about your father, my dear fellow,' said Mr Eastleigh. 'He appears to have been a little too venturesome, and to have exposed himself to danger. In short, we have had a message from the police to say that he was picked up at sea by fishermen and is in a rather serious condition and in hospital on Jersey. It is thought that he must have fallen from cliffs and injured himself, and that the tide, which, as you probably know, can be extremely strong in those parts, must have swept him out to sea. It is a miracle he was not drowned.'

'Does my stepmother know?' asked Colin.

'No. The police here, having received this information from the Jersey police, passed it straight on to me.'

'Seems a funny thing to have done.'

'What does? Drink up your sherry, my boy.'

'Yes . . . thanks.' He sipped. 'I mean, I should have thought they would have sent to my stepmother direct. My father would have carried plenty of papers and things by which they could identify him, I should have thought.'

'Oh, well, it is a minor point,' said Mr Eastleigh. 'No doubt, if he had papers on him, they were so saturated with sea-water as to supply very little information. Possibly the only means the authorities had of identifying him was to trace him to an hotel, or wherever it was that he stayed, and obtain what information they could from the hotel register. This would give little more than his name and the fact that he had been in residence on this island.'

'That means he's unconscious, then. Otherwise, he'd have given them the address of the school or the lighthouse. And that's another thing . . . how did the police . . . I mean, what made them think of coming here to the school?'

'The disappearance of Manoel de Roseda y Lambre, I imagine, gave them the necessary data. The police took down the name of every adult in this house, and your father's name being the same as your own, it would be the obvious thing to bring me the information. That is how it happened, I should think.'

'Well, I suppose I'd better let my stepmother know what's happened. Thanks for telling me, sir. Do you mind if I go to her at once?'

'That is what I would suggest, and, if you think it best, perhaps you had better stay the night there, unless she has friends she can contact. I am afraid the news will be a shock to her.'

'Isn't my father likely to recover, then?' asked Colin, bluntly.

'Oh, my dear boy, we must never lose hope,' said the headmaster. Colin, outwardly unperturbed, got up.

'I'd better take my examination papers with me, sir. I expect I can get them marked some time tonight,' he said.

'He doesn't seem unduly upset,' Mr Eastleigh remarked to his wife, when Colin had left them.

'He has to break the news to his stepmother, so I suppose he feels he must try to keep calm for her sake,' said Mrs Eastleigh. 'I expect she will want to go out to the hospital immediately.'

Colin's first action, upon leaving the headmaster, was to interrupt Dame Beatrice's talk to his colleagues. Skelton answered the door to him.

'Sorry to barge in,' he said, 'but something's happened. Could you possibly come home with me, Dame Beatrice? I hate to bother you with my affairs, but, well, you see, I've – there's some news to give my stepmother, and I'd rather have another woman there, if you wouldn't mind. Laura – Mrs Gavin – is tied up with marking, or I would have asked her to come.'

'Not your old man?' asked Heathers, coming forward. 'You don't mean there's something wrong?'

'Yes. Oh, he's not dead – not yet.' He looked at Dame Beatrice, and then at the concerned expressions on his colleagues' faces. 'I can't understand it,' he went on. 'He's got a good head for heights, and he never does anything dangerous. I can't believe he went rock-climbing, or whatever it was, and fell into the sea and got swept away by the tide. It doesn't make sense. He's the most cautious man on earth. There's something very odd about all this.'

Fiona Spalding's first question was a little surprising.

'Is he delirious?' she asked. 'Is he talking any nonsense, do you know?'

'There is no reason to think so,' Dame Beatrice replied. 'He has injuries, it seems, and was picked up half-drowned. Unfortunately, that is all we know at present.'

'I can stay the night,' said Colin, 'if you want me to. Then

I suppose I'd better see about getting you out there to visit him. I can't come with you, of course. Too much to do at school.'

'I don't want to go,' said Fiona. She began to cry. 'I can't bear people to be ill. He'll be all right if he's in hospital. If you'll get the address, I'll write to him.'

'Oh, no, hang it all!' protested the young man, obviously shocked by this approach. 'Look here, I'll get leave from Mr Eastleigh and go with you. He won't refuse me, the circumstances being what they are. He'll know you can't be expected to go alone. How about that?' But she continued to weep. He took Dame Beatrice into the hall, and added, 'She's had a shock. Of course she'll go and see him. I'll talk to her when she's calmer. Well, I'd better drive you back to school. Thanks a lot for coming with me.'

'I don't think you had better leave your stepmother. I am perfectly capable of walking back to the school.'

'Oh, no, dash it! It's all of five miles.'

As it happened, Mr Eastleigh had foreseen the difficulty almost as soon as they had left. He went back to the Common Room, detached Laura from her marking and sent her in her own small car to bring Dame Beatrice home. They met no more than a couple of hundred yards from the lighthouse.

'How did she take the news?' asked Laura, when she had picked up her employer.

'It is difficult to say. She wept, but more in rebellion against going to see her husband in hospital than from shock, I fancy. She asked, point-blank, whether he was delirious.'

'Extremely odd, that. What was she after? Afraid he'd babble the secrets of the marriage bed?'

'Or other, guiltier secrets, I should imagine.'

'You curdle my blood! What, exactly, do you mean?'

'Nothing definite, at present, but it was, as you say, an odd question. Mr Colin Spalding will ask the headmaster for leave of absence for the remainder of the term, I think, and travel with his stepmother to Jersey. Well, at any rate, we can now account for two of our three absentees. I wish we could locate Mr Ferrars. What is the last we know of him for certain? Something which can be checked?'

'Oh, simply that he was supposed to meet this girl and didn't show up. It's all extremely unsatisfactory. It's known that he left the school immediately after lunch, and, according to what she told Heathers on the telephone, he wasn't to meet the girl until six.'

'Do we know *that* for a fact?'

'Well, I suppose not, really, but they were meeting at the pub for a drink, and you can't do that before six. I mean, they'd have been too late to get one before afternoon closing time. Anyway, I expect the girl would be at work in the afternoon. No, I'm positive he went out to the lighthouse and then something stopped him keeping his real appointment.'

'Is there any way of getting in touch with the girl, I wonder?'

'The police are sure to have winkled her out. You could ask the Inspector for her address. With your Home Office job, he'd be bound to respect your wishes. Flourish your *bona fides* at him, and he can't refuse you.'

'With your usual acumen, you have nicked the matter. I will take your advice.'

The Inspector was not only pleased but flattered to be visited by so distinguished a personage as the consultant psychiatrist to the Home Office. It was not that he admired psychiatrists – like most policemen, he distrusted them, and called them, in private, the mumbo-jumbo merchants – but Dame Beatrice, he was aware, had solved some pretty problems in murder in her time, and had never expected to be given credit for this to the disadvantage of the Force.

He gave the girl's name as Miss Juniper Keggs and her address in the mainland seaside resort as 'Bunkies', Tideway. He offered to send Dame Beatrice there in a police car, but this she refused. Laura had finished her marking and was free until the school reports had to be made out, so, on the following afternoon, she drove Dame Beatrice down the steep incline and over the causeway and so to Miss Keggs' home in an unpretentious, respectable little street which ran alongside part of the harbour.

Miss Keggs was not at home, and her mother regarded the visitors with suspicion.

'I don't know you, do I?' she asked, when, at the front door, with its polished brass and white-washed step, she came face to face with them. Dame Beatrice produced a visiting card.

'I am attempting, with the goodwill of the police, to trace a certain Mr Ronald Ferrars,' she said, 'and I think your daughter may be able to help me.'

'She isn't in. She's at work. The police have been here, and she's told them all she knows.'

'I am not convinced that she has told them *all* she knows. Maybe they did not ask her as many questions as they might have done, but we know a little more now than they did then,' said Dame Beatrice. The woman flushed and said:

'My Junie's a good girl, and this Ronnie was – well, seemed – a most respectable young man. Oh, well, you'd better come in.' She gave them armchairs in a room which contained, among other things, a television set and a radiogram. 'Now,' she went on, 'what did you want to know?'

'How long has your daughter known Mr Ferrars?'

'Only since the school moved on to the island.'

'How did they become acquainted?'

'My daughter was at school with Nina Beverley, who used to teach at the school. Nina knew our address, of course, and brought young Ronald to see us. Then Nina and Ronald fell out because of Junie, and Nina kept trying to get him back, and, when she couldn't, she just threw up her job and went and stayed with somebody who lets rooms to summer visitors. Quite near the school – you know – the hotel – it was, but she didn't stay all that long. She wrote to Junie, rather a nasty letter, saying Ronnie was cutting a dash with a married woman.'

'Mr Ferrars was to have met your daughter, I understand, on the evening when he disappeared.'

'Yes, that's right. Junie was very put out about it. But the police have had all this out of her already.'

'Did she have any idea, at the time, of his reason for not keeping the engagement?'

'Well, I didn't mention it to the police, of course, it being none of their business, but Junie did say to me – being very annoyed, you understand, when Ronald, as she thought at the time, had broken their date – she did say to me, 'I bet he's with Nina, unless he's gone after the trolloping married woman again.' Of course, I checked her for language, but I did agree with her really. After all, I mean, a married woman and old enough to be, well, anyway, his aunt! It wasn't decent.'

'Mrs Spalding,' said Laura. Mrs Keggs gazed at her. 'They met on a cruise,' Laura went on. 'Mrs Spalding's stepson and Ferrars were at school together. If Ferrars was friendly with a married woman down here, ten to one it was with Fiona Spalding.'

'I wouldn't know the name,' said Mrs Keggs.

'And the police knew nothing of this friendship?' asked Dame Beatrice.

'It wasn't for Junie and me to sling mud,' said Mrs Keggs, virtuously. 'When Ronnie didn't turn up that last time, Junie acted dignified, and put him out of her life.'

'Your daughter did not suggest that the police should question Mrs Spalding when it was known that Mr Ferrars had disappeared?'

'How could she? – apart from not wishing to cast nasturtiums, I mean. I don't suppose for a minute she knows the woman's name, any more than I did 'til you mentioned it. If she does, she hasn't mentioned it to me. And, anyway, until the police came poking their noses, we didn't know he *had* disappeared.'

'How did Miss Beverley find out that Mr Ferrars was in the habit of meeting a married woman?'

'Followed him about, I wouldn't wonder. Just to be nasty, you know. She said (so Junie told me), "You needn't think you've taken him away from me. Neither you nor this married Martha he's taken a fancy to." Of course, Junie asked her straight out what she meant, and then it all came out, everything except the woman's name. I wonder,' she concluded, looking thoughtful, 'whether Junie *does* know who the woman was, and didn't like to say? After all, Junie was very fond of him. She wouldn't like to give him away, even if he done something wrong and had to clear out in a hurry.'

'Be that as it may,' said Dame Beatrice, 'I have a feeling that Miss Beverley, as she had found out so much, would have known the woman's name, whether or not it was Mrs Spalding,'

'But you mean she might not have told Junie? Of course, Nina was a deep one. Spoilt, you know, and used to getting her own way. Maybe she thought she could even up things better for Junie not knowing the whole story. If it was in a book, you might think blackmail was at the bottom of it.'

'Blackmail? Do you really think Miss Beverley would stoop to that?' asked Dame Beatrice, as though she found the idea incredible.

'Well, perhaps she wouldn't think of it like that,' said Mrs Keggs, 'but she wouldn't be the first girl to put a bit of pressure on a young man, if there was something she really wanted. What was to stop her saying something to the effect of if he didn't stop playing around she would report him to his head-master for making passes at a married woman? That wouldn't have done him much good in his job, would it?'

'I see what you mean,' said Dame Beatrice.

'What's more,' pursued Mrs Keggs, 'if he's disappeared, ten to one that's what she *did* say – or to that effect – and so he thought he'd get away while he could, not to have to face being disgraced and sent away from the school.'

'I don't think Mr Eastleigh would be as harsh as that,' protested Laura. 'He would probably have given him a stiff ticking-off, and warned him, and left it there. I can't imagine him sacking anybody for a thing like – well, for the sort of thing young men do before they've settled down.'

'I don't know so much,' said Mrs Keggs. 'If you ask me, these private schools have got to be like Potiphar's wife.'

'I thought that was Mrs Spalding's rôle,' said Laura. 'You mean Caesar's wife, I fancy, but no matter.' Mrs Keggs glared at her, and Dame Beatrice, murmuring thanks and civilities, took Laura back to the school.

CHAPTER FIFTEEN

A Mother – Naked Man

'I could scarce persuade myself that murder had actually
been done.'

'Well, it looks as though we can give up worrying about
Ferrars. He's just simply hopped it. I never quite swallowed
that tale that he and the Beverley parted because he'd smacked
one of her little boys,' said Laura, after they had left Mrs Keggs'
house. 'She wouldn't have given a hoot about anything of that
sort. I think at last we've heard the truth. He'd done a Mac-
heath with three women and made the neighbourhood a bit too
hot for himself.'

'I think, all the same, that I must have a word with Mrs
Spalding before she goes to Jersey,' said Dame Beatrice.

'I thought she told you and Colin that she wouldn't go to see
her husband. Wasn't she sending a letter?'

'I am sure she will change her mind. Mr Ferrars has made a
significantly successful disappearance, don't you think? I do
not like it very much. Let us drive at once to the lighthouse.'

'To do what? To tell her " 'tis pity she's a whore"?'

'To ask Mrs Spalding to tell us what she knows about the
disappearance of Mr Ferrars.'

'What have you got on Mrs Spalding? There's something up
your sleeve.'

'I hope that I fail to understand you.'

Laura grinned.

'A hope doomed to crash at the first fence,' she said. Her
expression altered. 'You don't think she really knows anything,
do you?' she asked. 'About where he is, I mean.'

'Time will show.'

Time, with its accustomed liberality, showed more than even
Dame Beatrice had envisaged. She and Laura arrived at the
rented lighthouse less than half-an-hour before the police turned

up. Fiona was not expecting visitors. She had just finished washing her hair, she explained, when, turban-towel on head, she
opened the door to Laura and Dame Beatrice. She was alone.
Colin, she explained, had gone to the mainland to book two
passages on the Channel Islands boat for St Helier.

'I *couldn't* fly,' she added, with tremendous emphasis, 'and
the boat gets there in less than a day. Of course, we shan't go
until after the school breaks up. My husband is not on the
danger list.'

'We are glad you will find your husband sufficiently recovered,' said Dame Beatrice, 'but we came for more reasons
than to tender our good wishes.'

'Oh, yes? Would you like a cup of tea? No? What is it, then?
You haven't any more news of Howard, have you?'

'I regret to say that we have not. Our errand is in connection
with the prolonged disappearance of Mr Ronald Ferrars.'

'Yes – yes, well, I suppose it *is* prolonged. But what has that
to do with me?'

'I am hoping that you will be good enough to answer that
question yourself.'

Fiona's expression was one of extreme alarm.

'I don't know what you mean,' she said. 'I know nothing
whatever about his disappearance.'

'Very likely not,' said Dame Beatrice briskly, 'but he was a
fairly frequent visitor here, I believe.'

'Oh, Colin brought him over once or twice. They were at
school together, you know, and then we met him again on a
cruise some years ago. But I'm sure I've told you all this.'

'Oh, yes, of course you have. There is more. He was not
always accompanied by your stepson when he came here, was
he?'

'He may have looked in a couple of times on his own,'
admitted Fiona, glancing from one of them to the other. 'There
isn't much for them to do on their free afternoons, and he and
Colin didn't often have those together. I really couldn't say.
Why does it matter? I don't know anything about his disappearance, I tell you. How should I? He was only an
acquaintance. I don't see what you think I can tell you. What's
it to do with you, anyway? You're not related to him,

are you? Did his parents send you? Oh, but he wouldn't have told them anything. It was – I mean, there wasn't anything to tell!'

'Do you remember the dates on which he came?'

'No, I don't.'

'I wonder whether your husband would remember? – Not that I should think of worrying him in his present state, of course.'

'Howard?' Her first appearance of panic was giving way to wariness, Laura thought. 'It wouldn't matter whether you worried him or not. He's even more vague about dates and things than I am. Besides, he spends so much time up on the lighthouse gallery that he may not even have been down here when Ronald called. But what's this all about?'

Before Dame Beatrice was able to answer this question, there came the sound of a car. It pulled up and the ensuing silence was broken by a knocking on the door. Fiona answered it. Her voice came clearly to the visitors.

'The police? Have you brought me news of my husband? Is he – is he – is it bad news?'

'We have no further information about your husband, madam. We should be glad of permission to search these premises. I'm sure you won't make any difficulty.'

'Search the premises? But why?' There was no doubt about the panic in her high-pitched, unnatural voice.

'If we may come in, madam, I shall be glad to explain.'

He was shown in by Fiona, and Dame Beatrice, who had recognised his accents, found herself greeting the Inspector. He was followed by his sergeant and by two constables.

'Well?' said Fiona. 'I can't tell you any more than you already know. What do you want this time? I don't know where Ronald Ferrars is! Why are you pestering me again?'

'No, I don't imagine you can help us more than you have done, madam,' said the Inspector, a large, calm man with blue eyes and a Dorsetshire burr. 'Not about Mr Ferrars, I mean. Until his body gets washed up somewhere – and where that'll be, and when, is known only to the Race and the Almighty – we're rubbing the poor young gentleman off our slate, as you might say.'

'Then what *do* you want? I'm trying to get myself ready to go over to Jersey to visit my husband. This is a most inconvenient time to have people call.'

'You have come to the conclusion that Mr Ferrars is drowned, then,' said Dame Beatrice.

'Doesn't seem much else to think, Dame Beatrice. We soon tore up that convict's tale as how he found those clothes in the lighthouse tower. He's come clean about that. Now says he found 'em in a little, half-dug quarry t'other side of the island, out beyond those cottages at Casley. We argued it this way: if the cove had croaked Mr Ferrars he would never have stopped to strip him to the buff. He'd have taken his jacket and trousers, and his shirt and pullover, and likewise his shoes and socks, but not the rest of the clobber. He's been put through it properly by us and by the prison governor, and we reckon he's telling the truth. The poor young gentleman must have fancied a swim. It looks easy enough to get into the water if you scramble down the rocks. Those long, flat blocks that are only about a couple of inches or so above water-level at high tide might look ideal to bathe off to anybody who didn't know this coast and thought he could keep his head above water a-swimming in the Race. We've had it happen before. You can't stop people being foolhardy. Although why anybody should fancy a swim *this* time of year ...!'

'Oh, I don't know. I had a swim myself the other day,' said Laura. The Inspector gave her a look of fatherly disapproval, and turned again to Fiona.

'But if it isn't about Mr Ferrars, what *is* it about?' she asked. 'As for searching the place, well, it isn't for me to say. You'll have to get my husband's permission. He's the tenant here.'

'In that case, madam, a search-warrant may be the answer.'

'A search-warrant? Oh, but, really!'

'Perhaps I should explain. We have reliable information that this place was used, before you came here, of course, as a repository for smuggled goods. Naturally, we are anxious to confirm this, as it seems doubtful whether all these goods have been removed.'

'But that has nothing to do with us!'

'Of course not, madam.' In the face of her obvious terror,

the Inspector's voice had become suspiciously soothing. 'We wouldn't think of suggesting that you and your husband are implicated. But we've had this tip-off, as I say, and we can't afford to ignore it. Well, I will proceed to obtain the warrant, madam. You will have no objection to my leaving the sergeant here, of course?'

'Oh, well, I suppose – well, you'd better carry on,' said Fiona. She looked so pale that Dame Beatrice took her by the arm and led her to a chair. As she sank into it, and the strong yellow claw released its hold on her arm, she clutched at it. 'Please don't go! Please don't leave me!' she said. The constables made an unostentatious move towards the door and went out to the base of the tower. The Inspector nodded to his subordinate and the sergeant made short work of turning out the living-quarters. When he returned empty-handed the Inspector said:

'Before we check the tower, madam, perhaps you would kindly assure yourself that everything in the rooms here has been left as the sergeant found it.'

'Check the tower?' cried Fiona. 'Why – why would you want to do that? Nobody but my husband uses the tower. You won't find anything there but a lot of old junk.'

'Very likely, madam. But, you see, if there *is* any contraband on the premises, the tower is the most likely place for it. We've gone over your quarters more as a matter of form than anything else, not expecting to find what we're looking for. So now for what we think is the real hiding-place, if any. You are welcome to come with us, if you wish.'

'Good Lord!' exclaimed Laura. 'The lugger in Kitt's Hole!'

'I beg your pardon, madam?' said the Inspector, swinging round on her. Laura waved a shapely palm.

'A sort of quotation,' she explained. 'I was wondering whether there might be any connection.'

'With the smuggling, madam?'

'Well, yes.' She told him about the large, sea-going vessel she had seen early one morning standing off the little cove where, later on, she had swum.

'There could be a connection,' said the Inspector. 'Your

description ties in very well with some other information we received about this boat. We think she brought over tobacco, in the form of cigars, from Holland, and brandy from France. We also believe that the stuff was taken off her in rowing boats and winched to the cliff-top by means of the derricks the fishermen use in these parts where there aren't any beaches.'

'A neat idea,' commented Laura approvingly. 'None of that nonsense about concealing the booty in caves and then having all the sweat of manhandling it up the cliff-face. I call it an intelligent use of the local amenities, don't you?'

'Yes, madam, but not intelligent enough to allay the suspicions of anybody who happened to see them at work. Of course, they're amateurs,' he added, in an indulgent tone. 'The pros would be running drugs or diamonds.'

'Oh, you've got witnesses, have you? People who've spotted them at work?'

'Not eye-witnesses, madam, unfortunately, but have you ever ridden your bicycle, or used your typewriter, or handled your fountain pen after somebody else has had a go with them, madam?'

'Oh, the kineaesthetic sense in reverse, so to speak? The genuine island boatmen got the feeling that alien hands had been operating their pulleys?'

The Inspector did not answer, but permitted himself a sly Dorsetshire smile. Then he turned back to Fiona, who was still clutching Dame Beatrice's hooked, yellow fingers.

'With your permission, then, madam,' he said, and led the way out, followed by the sergeant. A constable came into the room and fixed a stolid, non-committal gaze on the fireplace.

'Please go with them,' said Fiona, releasing Dame Beatrice's hand. 'I'd like somebody to – to see what they're up to. I don't know what Howard will say when he finds out they've gate-crashed his precious lighthouse.' She attempted a laugh, but it was unconvincing. It was clear that she was in a state of terror.

'Laura will go,' said Dame Beatrice. 'I think I will remain here with you.' Eager to be in the picture, Laura followed the policemen out of the room. The Inspector seemed to have his plan of campaign cut and dried.

'We'll start at the top and work down,' he said to the sergeant. 'You two chaps—' to the constables – 'stay down below. If we need anything we'll call you. Hullo, Mrs Gavin, are you coming along?'

'Just to keep an eye on Mrs Spalding's interests,' said Laura, grinning. She followed the two men up the iron staircase, thinking of Howard and his discourse upon the seabirds. From the gallery, where the Inspector took a survey and some notes, they went into the lamp room and then, as they descended, flight by flight, they inspected the bunk-room, the living-room and the galley. These, it was obvious, had indeed been used as junk-rooms by previous owners of the property. The two officers methodically turned over the contents of cardboard boxes, packing-casses, battered and handle-less suitcases, store-cup-boards, the oven, and some shelves piled with old books and disused crockery. It took a considerable time before they were satisfied, but at last they descended almost to the foot of the tower.

'Looks as though, if there ever *was* anything, they managed to get it away before the tenants moved in, sir,' said the sergeant.

'I don't believe there ever was anything here,' observed the Inspector. 'All that junk we've been looking at wouldn't leave any room for anything else, and it wasn't put there yesterday, either. Oh, well! Last lap!' He turned the handle of the lowest door. 'Hullo! This is locked. Perhaps we've struck oil after all. Sergeant! Trot back to Mrs Spalding and ask her for the key of the store-room.'

'Right, sir.' The sergeant removed himself with stately, official tread, to reappear almost immediately. 'The lady says it's always been locked, so far as she knows. She says her husband may have a key, but she hasn't one.'

'Oh, well,' said the Inspector, withdrawing from a pocket a set of keys of various sizes, 'let's see what we can do without their help.'

At his third attempt the heavy door opened. Laura, peering over his shoulder, saw a room larger than those they had already inspected, for the lighthouse tapered towards the top. The room was empty except for one thing. In the middle of the floor, face downward and with outspread arms, lay the purplish and greenish body of a naked and extremely dead man. The Inspector turned and ordered her out of the way.

'No place for you, madam,' he pronounced austerely.

'Well, it wasn't, actually,' said Laura to Dame Beatrice, when they were on their way back to the school. 'I only got a glimpse of the *corpus,* but it looked absolutely beastly and the smell was horrible. I went out and catted. What did you make of it when they called you in to look at it through forensic spectacles?'

'That fatal injuries had been sustained as the result of a heavy fall, and that there may have been a fight, but none of us cared to linger in the room for very long. My examination was cursory.'

'I suppose it's Ferrars?'

'I have no idea. It is logical to suppose so, but a formal identification will be necessary.'

'I should think it's a foregone conclusion that's who it is. I mean, he's been missing and the convict had all his clothes. Looks pretty bad for him, doesn't it?'

'The convict? I should say that it looks infinitely worse for the Spaldings. For one thing, it would seem to explain Mrs Spalding's acute fears when she knew that the police intended to search the premises. Her obvious panic is bound to have coloured the Inspector's views.'

'You mean she *knew* the corpse was there? I say, it might explain why Howard made his getaway to the Channel Islands, mightn't it? – and why he picked up Manoel as a sort of smoke-screen on his way out. What do you suppose will happen now?'

'Mrs Spalding will be closely questioned, of course, and so will her husband, as soon as he is well enough. I cannot imagine what explanation they will be able to offer.'

'Bland, blank ignorance of the goings-on, coupled with stout denial of having had any part in the disposal of the body, I should think. Faced by similar circumstances, that would be *my* line of country. And, of course, it might be true.'

'Yes,' said Dame Beatrice, doubtfully. 'It *might* be true, of course, except for the fact that the room was locked. I cannot see,' she added, 'what anybody had to gain by hiding the body in the lighthouse. It can lead to only one conclusion.'

'That Howard Spalding killed Ferrars when he found him making passes at his wife? I can't see Howard doing any such thing. But who else would want to murder a silly young bloke like Ferrars?' demanded Laura. 'Oh! – Oh, Lord!' Her voice broke in dismay.

'You are thinking of Mr Colin Spalding,' said Dame Beatrice. 'If only,' she added, disapprovingly, 'people would learn to leave things alone! More than half the trouble in this world is caused by their apparent inability to do so.'

'What do you think actually happened, then?'

'The likeliest thing, from what I saw of the body, is that Mr Ferrars was attacked and pushed off a cliff on to the rocks below.'

'That does away with the theory that Howard caught Ferrars sporting with Fiona, then, doesn't it? I mean, they would hardly have been love-making out of doors at this time of year. Lady Chatterley might have done it, but not Fiona Spalding.'

'If only Mr Howard had not picked up that small boy and run away with him!' Dame Beatrice shook her head sadly.

'Yes, as damn-fool an action as Crippen running off with Ethel le Neve,' agreed Laura. 'Bound to cause the dicks to scratch their heads.'

CHAPTER SIXTEEN

Findings

'This is the black-hearted hound's account book.'

'Well, I suppose they've got a day or two before the balloon goes up for the Spaldings,' proceeded Laura. 'The police will have to get the body identified, there will be a post-mortem and an inquest, and so on, before there's a formal charge, I imagine. Are you taking any further interest in the proceedings? I mean, granted that it *is* Ferrars, it seems to me that the job Mr Eastleigh asked you to do is done, especially as Manoel has appeared among us safe and sound.'

'Is it possible to establish what Mr Colin was doing when Mr Ferrars disappeared?'

'Well, that's the rub, isn't it? We don't know when Ferrars *did* disappear. We can account for him up to the end of school lunch, but, once he'd gone off, that was the end of him, so far as we know at present. I mean, the fact that he failed to turn up for the *rendezvous* with Miss Keggs doesn't necessarily mean that he was dead, does it? He may just have decided to stand her up, or found himself too late to keep the appointment.'

'What you say is very just. All the same, I shall be interested to find out, if I can, what Mr Colin Spalding was doing that afternoon and evening.'

'If he *did* kill Ferrars, he'll probably tell you a lot of lies, but you'll be able to sort those out. Personally, I don't believe he's got it in him to kill anybody.'

'Everyone has it in him to kill somebody, child. Fortunately, in the case of most of us, the temptation to commit murder is not strong enough to cause us to give way to it, but that is all it is safe to say.'

'There, but for the grace of God, go I, you mean? Something in it, I suppose. But I think I see what you're after. If we can give Colin a clean bill for that afternoon, and show the Spaldings that he's completely in the clear, they'll tell us what really happened, so far as they themselves are concerned. Of course, they *may* not have been the people who put the body in the tower, you know.'

'Oh, come, child! Mrs Spalding's terror of the police! Mr Spalding's flight, taking Manoel with him!'

'All right, you win. So they put Ferrars in the tower and locked the door on him and chucked away the key because they thought Colin had done him in.'

'Colin was known to have been in love with his stepmother, was he not? I understood from you that Mr Howard realised that such was the case.'

'And Ferrars had been over there more times than Fiona is willing to admit. We don't know how much Colin knew about that, though, do we? Neither do we know how much of it Howard either knew or guessed.'

'A jealous lover is a suspicious man, do not forget, and Mrs Spalding, if I read her aright, is not the most discreet and careful of women.'

'A bit idiotic, you mean, to entertain young men in the bedroom while her husband was on the premises, albeit on top of his ivory tower? Yes, I must say I agree. So we sift Colin. The trouble about doing *that* is that I don't suppose for a second he'll remember anything about it, if he's innocent. I speak from my own experience. I couldn't possibly tell you what I was doing on any particular day at any particular time.'

'If he is guilty, I have methods to ensure that he gives himself away. But I am proceeding first on the assumption that he is innocent.'

'But I suppose that means he doesn't remember the afternoon in question, and what he did on it?'

'We have one strong card to play, you know. Whatever he does *not* remember, he is certain to remember the game of Smugglers and Excisemen, after which Manoel was not to be found. We shall work back from there. I have no doubt that we shall be able to pick up the threads.'

'And then, I suppose, you'll check them against what the

rest of the Staff can tell you. Fair enough. How will you break
it to Colin that the body has been found at the lighthouse?'

Soothed by Dame Beatrice's presentation of the news, Colin
took the information better than Laura would have expected.

'Of course, they won't agree they *did* hide the body,' he concluded, 'but nobody will believe them except me.'

'You will believe them, then? Why?' demanded Dame
Beatrice. Colin stared at her.

'They're – they're not those sort of people,' he said. 'The
police must be mad! It's plain enough what happened. That
convict fellow pushed Ferrars over the cliff, robbed the body
of the clothes and things, and dumped it in the lowest room
of the tower.'

'To which he had the key?'

'Those junk-rooms were never kept locked.'

'Yet the room in which the body was found *was* locked,'
Dame Beatrice pointed out.

Colin gave something between a snort and a groan.

'It doesn't make sense. None of it makes sense,' he said. 'I
mean, suppose my father and Fiona *did* find Ferrars' body.
Suppose it was accidental death, as the coroner's jury are bound
to find. *Why* should they hide it up? The whole thing's crazy,
and my father isn't crazy except about his beastly birds. What
should he have made him act against his whole nature? We've
had our differences, and plenty of them, but I know him and I
know the sort of things he would and he wouldn't do. His first
thought, if he came across the dead body, would be to go
straight to the police. Why on earth should he do anything else?
He's about the most meek and mild citizen I know. It's one of
the things that's always riled me about him. He conforms to
everything, and in every possible respect.'

'There are three very good reasons why he would not have
gone to the police,' said Dame Beatrice mildly.

Colin stared at her, horrified and incredulous.

'*Three?* Do you mean – but you don't think one of the three
of *us* killed Ferrars, do you?'

'Suppose your father thought that *you* had killed Mr
Ferrars? Do you believe that, in such a case, he would *still* have
gone to the police?'

Colin could do nothing but gape at her. She waited while he assimilated her words.

'But I didn't kill him!' he said at last. 'It's obvious that his death was an accident. They *must* think he fell down the cliff. There isn't any other explanation.'

'Was he the sort of young man who would be likely to fall down the cliff?'

'How on earth should *I* know?'

'Well,' said Dame Beatrice briskly, 'I am proceeding, for the present, on the assumption that neither you nor your father is guilty, and that the death was accidental, as you say. I am arguing, therefore, that your father hid the body, believing that Mr Ferrars' death was *not* an accidental one, but that you yourself occasioned it. If you will search your memory and, perhaps, your conscience, you may realise why he may have come to such a conclusion.'

Colin flushed, and was silent.

'So what we've got to establish, old lad,' said Laura, 'is where you were, and what you were up to, on the afternoon when it seems that Ferrars must have died. If we can put you in the clear, you see, with an unshakeable, unbreakable alibi, your parents will no doubt give us the low-down on their part in the affair, if any – and it really does seem as though they had a part, so toil your unbreathed memory, and, if you never laboured in your mind 'til now, go to it, and that with a will.'

Colin groaned again and looked at her with troubled eyes.

'How on earth can I remember all that time back?' he asked. 'You know the school routine as well as I do. I suppose I just simply followed it, that's all. As for proving that I did – well, other people would have to do that, and I don't suppose they'll remember details any more than I do.'

'I propose to begin at the end of that particular day and work back,' said Dame Beatrice. 'Let us repair to the room in which you instituted the game of Smugglers and Excisemen.'

'Oh, that was in my own form-room.' He led the way to it. It was a first-floor apartment converted from a large and handsome bedroom to its present use. Traces of its original purpose were still present in the form of a washbowl and an electric point for a razor in the south-east corner of the room, together with a fixed wall-mirror above the bowl and a towel-rail to the side of it. 'Here we are. I take the Nines, you know, but I chuck them out as per time-table so that the chaps taking Russian can come along here to get their lessons from me, and my own mob go along to the form-room of whoever's taking them on. Sit down, won't you?' He dragged two chairs out from behind school lockers and placed them for the visitors, and then seated himself on his table. Dame Beatrice took out a small notebook and poised the ball-point to which Laura, with some difficulty, had converted her.

'Now,' she said, 'at what time did you call your boys in here to arrange this game?'

'Oh, pretty well as soon as tea was over. We played it between tea and prep.'

'What does "pretty well" mean?'

'The chaps are supposed to rest for a quarter of an hour after tea. Not that they do, of course, but the Man has theories about violent activity immediately after meals.'

'You were present at tea, I believe?'

'Oh, yes. It was at table, if you know what I mean, that the game really started. I was yarning to them about smugglers and so forth, in preparation for a book I was going to read them.'

As Dame Beatrice had already learned this from Laura, she passed on to her next point.

'Tea begins at . . . ?'

'Five o'clock, as soon as they've cleaned up after games, you know.'

'Do you assist with the games?'

'Well, actually, no. When Mr Eastleigh heard I'd been ill, he excused me from them. All I have to do is to stick my boys under the showers before they have their tea.'

'So now we have to account for your movements between lunch, and showers and tea.'

'That means most of the afternoon. Oh, yes, of course! I know! I wrote a letter.'

'Yes? Where would you have been when you did that?'

'Up in my room.'

'Have you any idea of the time?'

'When I went up there, you mean? No, not really. All I remember is that I chucked the last draft of the letter away when I heard the chaps coming in from games.'

'The last draft?'

'Well, yes. You see, I decided not to send the letter, after all. I couldn't seem to word it properly. I couldn't seem to say what I wanted to say.'

'Would it be seemly to ask . . .?'

'Oh, it doesn't matter telling you that, now she's in such an awful mess. The letter was to Fiona to tell her . . . well, to tell her I shouldn't be pestering her any more.'

'Thank you for telling me that. If I may presume further, could you recount to me your reason for writing such a letter?'

'Yes, I suppose so. I found out she was seeing rather a lot of Ferrars.'

'I wonder whether you put that in the letter?'

'No, of course I didn't. That's what made the letter so hard to write. I could hardly call her a whore on paper, could I?'

'Is that how you thought of her?'

'At times, yes,' said Colin, sullenly. 'All the same, I don't want her had up for murder.'

'She was fond of Mr Ferrars, you think?'

'I begin to wonder whether she was fond of anyone,' said Colin, bitterly. 'Anyway, I found I couldn't write the letter, after all. She'd . . . well . . . I mean . . .'

'You've been a fool where she's concerned,' said Laura sternly. ('It's all right. I had a Presbyterian upbringing,' she added, for the information of her startled employer.) 'I'm glad you've stopped being a baby, Colin, always wanting the moon,' she went on, swinging round again on him. 'You wouldn't be at all a bad kid if you'd only show a bit of independence. Fancy letting your father choose your woman for you!'

Colin was seldom dumbfounded. He gurgled. His eyes bulged. Then he capitulated.

'Just as you say,' he gloomily agreed. His immature but pleasing countenance brightened. 'Actually,' he added, 'I must say you look rather beautiful when you're angry, Laura. You don't mind if I call you Laura, do you? After all, you did compromise me down on the beach.'

F

'Well, really!' said Laura, beginning to laugh. 'Perhaps there's hope for you yet!'

'That being settled,' said Dame Beatrice, 'perhaps we may be permitted to return to the matter in hand. At what time do you think you settled down to write this letter?'

'After I'd had the row with Ferrars.'

'Oh, you quarrelled with Mr Ferrars, did you?'

'We exchanged a few rough words.'

'May one enquire . . .?'

'He was a sock and tie sneaker.'

'Oh, I see. You quarrelled with him, but not on the subject of his paying his attentions to Mrs Spalding?'

'No, not exactly, but I didn't see why he should fascinate her wearing my woven cravat and domino-patterned *chaussettes,* so I waylaid him and ordered him to divest himself of the trappings.'

'Good for you,' said Laura. 'How did he respond?'

'Oh, quite decently. He said, "Sorry, old man. No idea that you'd object." '

'To which you replied?'

'I said, "Well, I wouldn't object so much if you'd had the decency to ask for them." So he said, "Well, I do ask for them, and I'm in the deuce of a hurry, so do you mind not pressing to have them back at this particular moment?" I said, "You're a louse and a rotter." He said, "Righty-o, old boy. I'll paste it in my hat and play it on my tambourine. By seeing you." And, with that, he buzzed off and, of course, I've never seen him again.'

'How long after lunch did this exchange take place?' Dame Beatrice enquired.

'Almost directly. As soon as he'd gone I went to my room and started trying to word this letter. I pretty well guessed he was going straight over to the lighthouse, you see.'

'What reason had you for guessing anything of the sort?'

Colin turned to Laura.

'I wonder whether you remember my inventing an outing to Bournemouth while you were over at the lighthouse that time? Well, of course, there wasn't anything planned. It seemed an opportunity to get Fiona to myself and put things to her without wondering all the time whether my father would burst in and catch us. We'd had a row that day you came, you see – about you, actually. Well, I picked her up in the car, but in Bournemouth we ran straight into Ferrars and Miss Beverley, who'd just left the school, and, before I knew what was happening, we'd switched partners and I found myself landed with the Beverley for the rest of the afternoon and evening. The other two slipped us in the Arcade and we met again in the car-park, so that I could run Fiona back to the lighthouse. I didn't speak to Fiona all the way home, and on Ferrars' next free afternoon I followed him. He was on foot and so was I. I watched him go into the lighthouse. I spotted my father up on the light-house gallery, and I crept to the window of the bungalow. I didn't have to wait long to see what I expected to see.'

'How did Miss Beverley view the exchange of partners at Bournemouth?' Dame Beatrice enquired, offering no comment on Colin's confession of spying.

'She made a few brief remarks about Ferrars, and told me next time they met she'd make a row. She said she'd finished with him, anyway, and was glad to be quit of his company. I couldn't very well tell her that I'd be glad to be quit of hers, so I gave her tea, and we went to a film and then had dinner and a spot of dancing. She wasn't bad fun, and I enjoyed my-self after a fashion. She asked me a lot about Fiona and said Ferrars always had preferred mutton to lamb, which was pretty offensive, but I felt so mad with Fiona that I let it go, and ... well ... that was that.'

'Yes,' said Dame Beatrice, 'I suppose it was, except that you saw Mr Ferrars set off for the lighthouse on subsequent occa-sions, you say.'

'It doesn't mean I murdered him,' said Colin.

'So, on the afternoon of his disappearance,' said Dame Beatrice, taking no notice of this, 'we have the following cata-logue of your movements: at approximately two o'clock you quarrelled with Mr Ferrars on an unimportant matter. Very shortly afterwards you went to your room to write a letter to Mrs Spalding, and remained there, making various drafts of this, until, at about half-past four, you supervised your form while they bathed after games. You were at tea with some of your boys and played at hide-and-seek with them from five o'clock until preparation. Did you sit with them during preparation?'

'No, Pocock took his lot and mine for prep. that evening, but then, when they'd had prayers and their bedtime snack, I put my boys to bed. Prep. only lasts an hour, anyway. I couldn't have gone and murdered Ferrars while it was on.'

'Thank you, Mr Spalding. You have been most frank and helpful,' said Dame Beatrice. 'I will be equally frank. I shall check this story of yours, so far as I can, of course. You would expect that. If, as I think likely, it is supported by your colleagues, I shall remit it to your father and stepmother and obtain from them an account of how Mr Ferrars' body came to be found unclothed in a locked room at the foot of the lighthouse tower. I think there can be no doubt that your father put it there, and I think he did so because he believed, and your stepmother believed, that you had caused Mr Ferrars' death. When they are persuaded that you did not, I think they will reconsider their present attitude.'

'You won't be able to check that I˙was in my room from about two until half-past four though, will you?' said Colin miserably. 'And that's the time that counts.'

CHAPTER SEVENTEEN

The Wheat from the Chaff

. . . we saw ourselves at once in a difficult and dangerous position.'

'What do you think of all that?' Dame Beatrice asked, as they went to Mr Eastleigh's room to obtain permission to speak to Mr Heathers.

'It took him a darned long time to write that letter,' said Laura. 'All the rest of it was all right, but I find it difficult to believe he was stuck up there in his bedroom from just after two until half-past four. What's your idea about that?'

'I may be able to tell you when we have heard what Mr Heathers, and possibly others, have to say.'

'Heathers' evidence won't be any help. He was pretty busy that afternoon from two until half-past four, I expect, and that's just the time we want covered. He'd have been taking the Sevens and Eights for games, for one thing.'

'Where are the games played?'

'Mr Eastleigh rents a meadow about half-a-mile north of the school, in the opposite direction to the lighthouse, but the Sevens and Eights don't use it. They kick around in the entrance courtyard to the hotel. If you've noticed, there's quite a decent-sized patch of grass there. You don't need to play on the gravel, although small boys, with their usual cussedness, seem to prefer it. That's when they're on their own, of course. I was always mopping up gravel rashes during my short time as matron.'

'Then, surely, if Mr Heathers and these tiny boys were play-ing outside the front door of the hotel, Mr Colin must have been seen if he left the school during the time he claimed to have been trying to compose his letter to Mrs Spalding?'

'It isn't as easy as that. The Man would never think of allow-ing boys to play games immediately on top of a stodgy lunch. They have to put in two lesson periods of half an hour each before they're able to go to the field. This operates on every afternoon except Wednesday, when clubs and hobbies take up the whole of the time between lunch and high tea at six.'

'Then would not Mr Colin have been teaching from two o'clock until three? He did not mention that he was, although it would have helped him to establish his alibi.'

'Let's look at the big time-table. I can't answer that one off-hand. I know *I* was teaching. I had two history lessons, one with the Eights and one with the Tens. As the Tens come to me straight from French they have to be calmed down a bit before I can start.'

'I thought that to tease the French master was now a thing of the past.'

'Oh, the Tens don't *rag*! You wouldn't dare rag Mr Pocock, anyway. No, they come and tell me all about the lesson, and try out their French accent on me, and rehearse all their latest vocabulary, and so forth. Endearing of them, but rather trying when I'm wishing them to concentrate on the local history. It's all right, once I've quenched the *joie-de-vivre*, of course.'

Mr Eastleigh, who was busy, received them with his usual charm, and waved Laura towards the big time-table.

'There will be people marking and making out reports in the Common Room,' he said, 'so you will be better off in the housekeeper's room, where you can be perfectly private. My wife won't mind a bit. She'll probably park herself in here.'

'The big time-table has established one thing,' said Laura to Dame Beatrice, as they went along the passage to the room which had once been Laura's sanctum. 'Colin wasn't teaching that afternoon. You see what it means, though, don't you? Everybody else was on, including Heathers, so Colin could have slipped away at the beginning of afternoon school and, so long as he got back directly games were over and the front of the hotel was clear of Heathers and his Sevens and Eights, there's no reason why anybody should be the wiser. The games played on the field are packed up at a quarter past four, you see, but the older boys never hurry back, so it's always twenty to five before they come straggling in to get their showers before tea. Mind you, they may have been earlier that day, because of a heavy sea-mist which came rolling in.'

'You say that everyone except Mr Colin was teaching that afternoon, but it seems as though Mr Ferrars was also free.'

'I looked him up. He's down to take biology first period in the afternoon, so I expect he leaves them writing up their notes and takes the time off. Second period he's free, anyway.'

'But was Mr Eastleigh satisfied with this arrangement that Mr Ferrars should help himself, as it were, to a free period?'

'Oh, yes, I expect so. Any kind of science is a hell of a subject here, because, of course, we haven't got a lab., so Ferrars was pretty considerably handicapped and naturally got more than a bit cheesed off. He was always beefing about it in the Staffroom and hinting that he should resign, so, if his boys were reasonably quiet and were kept reasonably busy, Mr Eastleigh would wink at Ferrars taking a breather.'

'He seems a remarkably easy-going headmaster.'

'It pays off, you know. He's able to keep a first-class Staff. Skelton, who's in charge of games, has also had sculpture in the Academy, and the music man, Robson, who also takes some of the maths., is a Mus. Doc. and is guest conductor at the big music festivals. Mariana – Mr Grange – turned down a producer's job on B.B.C.2 in favour of teaching, and Heathers, for all that he seems such a nit, has already published a book on the geology of Norway and seems all set – so my spies inform me – for an F.R.S. later on.'

'I see. '

'And here,' Laura added, as they reached the housekeeper's room, 'is Mrs Eastleigh. I say, I do hope we shan't need to turn you out of your sanctum for very long,' she added, to the headmaster's wife.

'Now, Mr Heathers,' said Dame Beatrice, when Mrs Eastleigh had left them, and Heathers had answered a summons to the housekeeper's room, 'the truth, the whole truth and nothing but the truth. Consider yourself on oath, dear child, if you please.'

'Oh, yes – yes, certainly,' agreed Heathers, nervously taking off his spectacles, looking surprisedly at them and putting them on again. 'Just so. Of course. About what?' he asked, a note of apology in his voice. Dame Beatrice took out her notebook.

'Can you cast your mind back to the day on which Mr Ferrars was first reported missing?' she asked.

'Yes, I can,' said Heathers, eagerly. 'Yes, indeed, I remember it very well. I'm sorry to say that I was rather angry with poor Ferrars at the time. The arrangement was, you see, that if I took the games he would take prep. and then put the Sevens and Eights to bed, so, when he didn't show up, I had to do everything he ought to have done. I felt he'd let me down. It was a great shock to me when I realised that he wasn't to blame. Then, of course, there was the telephone call from some wretched girl to say he'd promised to meet her and had stood her up. That made me angry, too, because it meant that he'd never intended to come back in time to take prep. and see the chaps into bed.'

'Were you present when he left the school that afternoon?'

'Not when he actually left. I expect I'd gone to class before then. I did hear him having a bit of a fuss with Spalding. It was about some socks, I think, and a tie. Nothing, really. Just the usual give and take. Not serious. That would have been at about five minutes to two. I didn't hear the end of it because I knew my Sevens would be creating hell – making a good deal of noise – because they were looking forward to a double drama lesson on that afternoon, and the prospect of drama always seems to go to their heads.'

'I understand that Mr Grange took the school for play-acting,' said Dame Beatrice.

'Oh, yes, so he does – drama proper, as one might put it. I call what I do "graphic geography", actually, but the boys call it drama, to make it more exciting. We all act as mountains and rivers and railways and so forth, you know. The mountains make pyramids of three boys to each mountain, and the rivers meander round them, and the railways play at trains and try to make tunnels through the mountains – rather good fun for them, actually. There is always great competition to be a railway.'

Dame Beatrice said that she could well believe it.

'Do you know where Mr Spalding went when he and Mr Ferrars parted?' she asked.

'No. I didn't see Spalding again until we sat at tea. It's his afternoon off, you know. I do know he didn't leave the school while I was taking games on the front lawn and gravel.'

'Is there anyone on the Staff who might have seen him between two o'clock and half-past-four?'

'I could not undertake to say. Rather unlikely, I think.'

'So Heathers is a dead loss,' said Laura, when Heathers had returned to his form-room.

'I should be sorry to have missed the description of a graphic geography lesson,' said Dame Beatrice.

'I know. I wonder half his kids haven't broken their necks before now. Any good sending for anybody else?'

'These windows look out on to the drive. I wonder whether Mrs Eastleigh was in this room for the major part of that afternoon. If so, perhaps she can help us.'

Mrs Eastleigh returned to her domain.

'I met William Heathers in the passage,' she said, 'so I knew you had finished with him. Was he of any help in your enquiries?'

'No, but I wonder whether you may be,' said Dame Beatrice. 'Do you mind answering a few questions?'

'Of course not. What do you want to know?'

'To what extent, if at all, you can substantiate Mr Colin Spalding's account of how he spent the afternoon of the day on which Mr Ferrars disappeared.'

'Oh? Is it important that I should?'

'I know that you will not repeat this, except, perhaps, to your husband, but Colin's parents may have hidden Mr Ferrars' body. They could have had only one of two reasons for doing such a lawless thing. Either they themselves have guilty knowledge of how Mr Ferrars died, or they believe that Mr Colin killed him.'

'Good gracious me!'

'You have heard no rumours to this effect?'

'Certainly I have not. What a dreadful thought that Colin Spalding – But, no! He is quite incapable of such a thing. I'd as soon believe it of myself!'

'He claims to have remained in his bedroom from just after two o'clock until half-past four. Is there any way in which I can prove that statement to be true?'

'Two and a half hours? It sounds a long stretch, but perhaps he was putting in the time on his Russian. He is teaching Russian, you know. The boys are mad on it. My husband wants him to stay with us when we go back to Kent next term. I don't know whether he will. I think he might have done, but for all this upset about Ferrars.'

'You cannot help us, then?'

'I'm sorry. I'd like to have helped *him*, but I don't see how I can. I was in and out of here, and I made some telephone calls from the box in the entrance hall, and went to the kitchen, I remember, and on a tour of the dormitories to inspect pillow-cases and pyjamas and things. I do that regularly on a Friday. The laundry is collected on Mondays, so that gives the sewing-woman time to do any repairs. Boys are very hard on pillow-cases and pyjamas.'

'Yes. Well, thank you, Mrs Eastleigh. You cannot think of anybody else who would know whether Mr Colin stayed in that afternoon? He does not claim to have been studying Russian, but to have been composing a difficult letter of which, I gather, he made several drafts. In the end, it seems, he gave up the attempt, as he found he could not express himself as he wished.'

'Several drafts? That would mean a fair amount of waste paper. Just a moment! I'll send for the maid who looks after that set of rooms.'

The maid was able to establish one thing. Colin had been doing a considerable amount of writing, either on the afternoon in question or that same evening.

'Are you sure it was the day we are referring to?' Dame Beatrice asked. The maid, a dependable forty-year-old who had come with the school from Kent, was certain.

'I couldn't be mistaken, madam, not with all the fuss about the little boy that never came back to his dormitory that night. We heard about it next day, and it was the following morning as I done out Mr Spalding's room with all that mess of blacked and burnt-out papers on the hearth, the fire-grate being done away with in favour of the electric fire, as you know, madam. I wonder he hadn't burnt the place down! Took me the best part of twenty minutes to make a job of it, with all them dead matches and all.'

'It doesn't help very much,' said Dame Beatrice, when the maid had been dismissed. 'It does not prove that it was during the afternoon that Mr Colin did this writing and burnt the results. It could equally well have been after supper that same evening. It does not prove, either, how much time the writing and the destruction of the writing might have taken. My next step will be to get in touch with Mr Howard Spalding, supposing that he is well enough to be questioned. No doubt the police have been to the hospital to find that out already.'

Howard, in the private ward to which he had been transferred, was despairing but dignified.

'It is good of you to put yourself to trouble on our behalf,' he said. 'Kempson, too, my solicitor, has been more than kind. He tells me that if a case is brought against us, Fiona will be dropped from it. I can claim that everything which happened was my doing, and that she was entirely guided by me.'

'Suppose,' said Dame Beatrice, 'you tell me exactly what *did* happen? I have no official standing, so far as this matter is concerned, and I shall, of course, respect your confidence. I make no promises, but if I could hear the whole story from you, without reservations, something might suggest itself. What do you say about that?'

'I've told Kempson most of it.'

'Then why not tell me the rest? If it is of any comfort to you, I am convinced that your son is blameless of any attack on the unfortunate Mr Ferrars.'

'Thank you for saying so. I was utterly wrong to suspect the boy in the first place. I am now convinced that he had nothing whatever to do with Ronald's death.'

'Oh, you called him Ronald, did you?'

'Well, a school-friend of my son . . .'

'He wasn't really that, though, was he? I do beg of you, Mr Spalding, to be quite frank with me.'

'Very well. I suppose I have nothing to lose by telling the truth. Where do you think I should begin?'

'When did you first suspect that your son was in love with your wife?'

This bald query caused the sick man to make a gesture as

though he was warding off an enemy. Then he dropped his arm and, settling himself more comfortably in the narrow, high, hospital bed, he said:

'Very soon after we got to the lighthouse, I'm afraid. Colin had been ill, you know, and I suppose my wife had coddled him a bit, and this may have caused him to think she meant a great deal more than was seemly. He is an impressionable, sensitive boy, and, of course, my wife is fifteen years younger than myself, and, although perhaps I am prejudiced, she has always seemed to me a very attractive woman.

'Matters reached their first climax on the afternoon when Mrs Gavin visited us. I was extremely sorry afterwards that I had made a scene in her presence, but I was very angry with Colin. He had taken advantage of our being up on the lighthouse gallery to remain with my wife instead of going for the walk he had proposed to take, and had behaved, I considered, in a thoroughly deceitful fashion.'

'Oh, yes, I have heard about all this.'

'From Mrs Gavin, no doubt. I am afraid that, on that occasion, neither Colin nor I could have appeared in at all a favourable light.'

'You know, Mr Spalding,' said Laura, 'I had an impression –I don't altogether know why–that Colin wasn't feeling friendly (let's call it) towards Mrs Spalding that afternoon. *I* thought they'd had the father and mother of a row, but it was after that that Ferrars began coming here, I think, so the row couldn't have been about him.' She knew, from Colin, that it had not been. It was Fiona who had made the fuss.

'Whether or not,' said Howard. 'I've agreed to be frank with you, Dame Beatrice, so here is the truth. To my certain knowledge, Ronald had called here twice before Fiona and Colin went off to Bournemouth that day. Both times, as it happened, I was downstairs and helped to entertain him by taking him up to the lantern gallery and discoursing to him on the subject of birds, which, as you probably know, is my chief interest.'

Laura exchanged a brief glance with Dame Beatrice, a glance which, in a tenth of a second, spoke volumes.

'Yes, indeed,' said Dame Beatrice. 'I have been told about your all-embracing hobby, and now we come to the day on which Mr Ferrars died. Will you tell me exactly what you did on that day?' She spoke gently. Howard was, and looked, a sick man. He lay back on his pillows and closed his eyes. 'Take your time,' she went on, 'and remember that, until we obtain the whole truth, of which your narrative can give us, perhaps, the major part, we shall not be able to clear this matter up and remove suspicion from yourself and your son.'

'You mean you can clear us?' He opened his eyes and struggled to sit up as he asked the question.

'Take it easy,' advised Laura, 'but spill all the beans you can.'

'Very well. I am in your hands, and in yours, Dame Beatrice. Where do you want me to begin?'

'Well, can you remember what you did immediately after lunch that day? You see, we can account for Mr Colin's movements up to two o'clock that afternoon, and from half-past four that evening.'

'But you don't know where he was between those times?'

'No, although it scarcely matters at the moment. In fact, it may not matter at all. I am prepared to accept this story that he was up in his bedroom writing letters, although I cannot really confirm it.'

'Then why are you prepared to accept it? What is more, are the police prepared to accept it?'

'The police do not suspect your son. You see, you and I have a piece of evidence which is not yet in their possession. I refer to the fact that your son had shown a sort of calf-love for your wife.'

'Calf-love? Is that all you think it was?'

'Certainly I do. At his first meeting with Laura here, he immediately transferred his admiration to her. That, to me, has been obvious.'

'The fortunate woman bridled and preened herself,' said Laura. Howard looked from one to the other of them, bewildered by what he heard. 'Oh, yes,' Laura went on. 'One could spot the symptoms a mile off, so I set about effecting the kindly but definite choke-off. It probably caused him to go back to your wife for a bit, but then, of course, Ferrars stepped in, and Colin's masculine self-confidence received another nasty jolt. He's not the stuff of which either Don Juan or a murderer is made. At least, that's my opinion.'

'I seem to have been very foolish,' admitted Howard; but some colour had come back to his face, and his eyes had brightened. 'Very well, then: here is what I know. But, first, will you tell me – it will help me to get matters clear – why you are prepared to accept my son's story that he did not leave the school that afternoon?'

'I have been studying the time-factor. We know he was in school at two o'clock. That is amply confirmed. We know he was there, as I told you, at half-past four, and from then onwards it is certain that he did not leave the building. Now, how far would you say it is from the school to your lighthouse?'

'Oh, every bit of five miles.'

'So, if I can show that he did not use your car that afternoon, you will agree, I think, that Mr Colin is hardly likely to have walked five miles out, fought with Mr Ferrars, pushed him over a cliff near the lighthouse, and walked five miles back, all of this inside two and a half hours.'

'And *can* you show that he did not use the car? He is no sort of walker, I know that. He hates it.'

The nurse came in with a tray of tea and biscuits and put it on the table beside the bed.

'Ah, thank you, Nurse,' said Dame Beatrice. 'I will see to it that your patient does not over-tire himself.'

'He looks all the better for seeing you, Doctor,' said the nurse. Dame Beatrice cackled, and began to pour out the tea.

CHAPTER EIGHTEEN

The Chaff from the Wheat

'...about three o'clock of a bitter, foggy, frosty
afternoon ...'

'We always lunch,' said Howard, when the tray had been
removed, 'at one o'clock precisely. I have a great belief in the
value of regular meal-times. I can say, therefore, that on
the day in question I would have risen from the table at
a quarter to two, finished helping my wife with the washing-up
by two o'clock, and then, as is my invariable custom, so long
as the afternoon is fine, I would have ascended to the gallery
of the lighthouse.

'You may take it that this is what I did, although I have
no clear recollection of it. The rest of the day and night, however, I recall with singular vividness. After I had been on the
gallery for about an hour, seated on the tall stool I keep up
there and wrapped in my sheepskin jacket for warmth, I became aware that a thickish mist was sweeping in from the sea.
Besides obscuring the view, it was extremely damp and unpleasant, so I retreated with my stool and notebooks to the
lamp room and began to write up some notes I needed for my
forthcoming volume on the sea-birds of the Wessex coast.

'At the end of another hour I had finished my task. I looked
at my watch, realised that it was half-past four and decided
that I would like a cup of tea. I saw that the mist had rolled
away – when, in my absorption, I had not noticed – and that
a weak sun had broken through. What made me go out on to
the gallery again I cannot say, unless it was the attraction of
the sunshine, for the week had been one of dull, although rain-
less, weather. However, I did go out, and that is when I saw
a man lying on the cliff-top about thirty yards or so from the
lighthouse.

175

'He was so still, and his pose seemed so unnatural that I concluded he had been taken ill. I hastened down the stairs to call my wife to have blankets ready, and found that she had left a note on the living-room table to the effect that she had gone over to the other lighthouse for tea, and would be back in time to get the supper. (We have it at six-thirty, so I had no fear of her being out after dark.)

'Having read the note, I left the bungalow and ran to where the man was lying. To my extreme horror I discovered that it was Ronald Ferrars and that he was dead, and that the body had sustained various serious injuries. The most dreadful thoughts raced through my mind. I felt sick and faint, but, my thoughts being what they were, I realised that some action must be taken before others discovered the body.'

The thin, precise voice broke off its clichés. The eyes, which had lost their passing look of animation, gazed back at the horrific past.

'You say the body was lying *on top of* the cliff?' said Dame Beatrice.

'Yes, indeed. Had it been on the flat rocks below – I went to the edge and peered over – I should never have jumped to the dreadful conclusion which I did. I should simply have thought that poor Ronald had been baffled by the sea-mist and had missed his way to us and had sustained a fatal fall. As it was—' he paused again – 'as it was, there seemed only one possibility – that my unhappy lad had followed him, knowing that he was proposing to visit my wife, and had fallen upon him with some weapon or a lump of quarried stone, and, in a fit of jealous rage, had killed him.'

'Yes, I understand your feelings. What were your reactions?' asked Dame Beatrice.

'Finding a strength I did not know myself to possess,' continued Howard, 'I raised the body and staggered with it to the lighthouse tower. My first concern was to conceal it. I confess that my thoughts were chaotic. By far the best thing I could have done – as I realised many days later – was to have tumbled the body over the edge of the cliff and left it to be found by others, but I was quite distraught when I believed that my son was a murderer.

'I have a full set of keys to the lighthouse, so I dragged the body into the lowest room of the tower and locked the door on it. Then I went back into the living-room and poured myself out a modicum of brandy. Then I went back to the tower, in a sort of dreadful fascination – and, I think, in the vain hope that perhaps Ronald was not dead – and took another look at him. There is no window in that lowest room, so I took my electric torch with me. This time I saw something which seemed to bring my heart into my mouth. Ronald was wearing Colin's tie!

'All the stories, both real-life and fiction, which I had read in my younger days, came flooding back into my mind. I remembered how the discovery of a hotel duster – or some such thing – had helped to hang a man. At all costs, I decided, there must be nothing to connect my son with the body for whose death I believed him to be responsible. Dame Beatrice, I cannot describe to you how I felt as I essayed the terrible task of undressing the body. The socks, which matched the tie, were also Colin's. I bundled the clothes together and had just finished doing so when I heard my wife come back. She called out, "Are you ready for your tea, dear? I've come back early to give you a surprise!" She thought that I was still up on the gallery, of course, so I locked the door on the naked body, pocketed the keys, went up a few stairs to the next landing and then called out, "Just coming, dear!" Then I went into the living-room.'

'Yes?' said Dame Beatrice, when she thought the pause sufficiently prolonged for dramatic effect. 'That must have been a difficult moment.'

'So difficult,' said Howard, collecting himself, 'that, of course, I muffed it. Instead of trying to break matters gently to the poor girl, I blurted out, "Fiona, Ronald is dead, and I think Colin killed him." She was so stunned that she did not say a word. She sank into an armchair and lay back and closed her eyes. I said, "It's no good taking it like that. We've got to *do* something." She looked at me then, and said – people always do say rather silly things at moments of crisis, I've noticed – "Are you sure he's dead?" I almost retorted – for my nerves, you understand, were quite on edge: "If you don't believe me, come and look at him!'" Then I remembered that he was naked and that his clothes were bundled up where I'd dropped them on the floor in that room at the foot of the tower.'

'So you went back for them and went out and chucked them into a disused quarry,' said Laura.

'Not straightaway, no. I realised I must wait until dark for that. I made us a cup of tea and put some brandy in each cup, and made Fiona drink up. Neither of us said any more. I went out to the scullery with the tray and washed up the tea-things, and then she said, "What makes you think Colin did it?" I said, "He was wearing Colin's tie and socks." She argued that didn't prove anything, so I agreed that, in itself it didn't, but nobody but Colin had any reason to wish Ronald dead, and that she must know that as well as I did. Then she began to cry, and I couldn't bear that, so I went up to the gallery again and waited for it to get dark enough for me to go out and hide Ronald's clothes. Just as I was about to go down to do this, Fiona called out to me that she was afraid to be left alone.'

'That ties in with what the convict told the police,' said Laura to Dame Beatrice.

'The convict?' asked Howard.

'Yes, when you left the lighthouse and picked up little Manoel de Roseda, you were taking the chance of running into an escaped convict,' Laura explained.

'I see. That's what the gun meant, I suppose. I thought at one point, earlier in the day, I heard firing. But there is more to tell before I met the little boy. You will want to know all the details, I suppose. I went down when I heard Fiona call out. I could tell how frightened she was. I told her what I was going to do with the clothes, all but the tie and the socks. Those I decided to put among Colin's things in his dressing-chest. They could prove nothing to anybody who found them there. I was beginning to get a grip on myself, you see, and to make plans. These I broke to her, telling her that for my sake and Colin's she had to be very brave and agree to do as I told her.'

'That was when you'd decided to make tracks for the Channel Islands,' said Laura.

'Yes, that's right. I thought, you see, that if they accepted her story – suppose it came to the point and she were asked for one – the idea that I'd gone on a bird-watching expedition would seem reasonable enough to pass muster. If her story was *not* accepted, the pursuit of the murderer would pass from Colin to me. You see, I realised clearly that it would only be a matter of hours before Ronald was missed and a search made for him.'

'The convict gave you a few hours' grace there,' said Laura. 'We were forbidden to search for Ferrars while the convict was still on the run.'

'I see. Well, I packed up a rucksack ready for the morning, collected all the money we had – I knew that Fiona could get what she wanted from the bank in the town, and that one of the women from the other lighthouse would give her a lift in a car to go and get it – and, taking the clothes with me, I set out, making for the small village on the west side of the island, beyond which, I knew (from various walks abroad) that there was an abandoned but fairly deep quarry. Into it I threw Ronald's clothes. It was an easy enough descent, as stunted bushes had grown up round the sides, so I climbed down and, with the aid of my torch, made certain that the garments were more or less at the bottom.'

'This, of course, was before you met Manoel,' said Laura.

'Oh, yes. I did not meet him until the following morning. I soon realised that my wife would become hysterical if I left her that night, so I decided, having got rid of the clothes, to return to the lighthouse. I left at daybreak next morning, and on the road to the mainland I encountered the little boy. I could see, from his dress, that he was one of the preparatory-school children. He asked me the way to the ships which crossed to the Channel Islands. I said, "Shouldn't you be at school?" He replied, "I am going to church, but there is not my church here. I have money to travel. Please tell me which way to go." It was then, of course, that I was tempted to take him with me.'

'As cover, I suppose?' said Laura.

'Well, it occurred to me that if I were sought in connection with Ronald's disappearance – for, of course, there might be

those who would put two and two together' – Howard's
smile was a bitter one – 'the description given of me would
not include the fact that I was accompanied by a small
boy.'

'We thought he'd been kidnapped, and that Ferrars had gone
off with him,' said Laura. 'That gave you another good break,
because, of course, the description of the kidnapper was of
Ferrars, not of you.'

'Oh, dear! What a very tangled web! However, my son has
written to tell me that the little boy is safe and well. I am so
glad to know that. I had a dreadful time, when I recovered
consciousness after my accident, wondering what had become
of him in the flat where I had left him, and imagining what he
must have suffered when he thought that I had deserted
him.'

'And now,' said Dame Beatrice, 'we have persuaded you to
talk for long enough. Sleep well tonight, and we will come back
tomorrow to hear the rest of this enthralling story.'

The rest of the story did not take long to tell, because Laura
saved Howard from recounting a good deal of it, as she knew
it already from her own visit on the *Pronax* to the Channel
Islands.

'How did you come to meet with your accident?' she asked.
'We did rather wonder whether it *was* an accident,' she added.
Howard answered the unspoken question.

'Oh, up to that point, the thought of suicide was the last in
my mind,' he said. 'My hobby is such that when I fell into talk
with the fisherman who took us over to Les Ecrehous, where
I thought I might see the roseate tern, and he described to me
a bird he had seen on Alderney which, from what he told me,
I thought might be *Anthus spinoletta spinoletta*, the water
pipit, nothing, of course, would satisfy me but to stalk and
photograph this bird, which, although it is a frequent visitor
to England, I had never seen. Arriving on Alderney, I made
enquiries as to accommodation, and was recommended temporarily to take a flat which happened to be vacant in Essex
Castle. This place . . .'

'Yes, I went to it,' put in Laura.

'. . . was originally, it is thought, of Norman origin, enlarged in the sixteenth century and, apparently, rebuilt then, and now converted into flats. The child, of course, was delighted with the place, particularly when he learned from the porter that a tunnel once led from the castle to the fortress of the Nunnery, so named, I gather, from the original Longy Nunnery, now ruined and tide-washed. Like all little boys, he has a romantic and bloodthirsty mind. For my own part, I had no wish to listen to the tale. It involved a description of skeletons washed out of the burial-place of the fort by the high tides of the year 1923, and some other bodies which the builders unearthed when the nearby coastguard station was constructed.'

'Talking of coastguards,' said Dame Beatrice, 'the body of Mr Ferrars was discovered by the police when they were searching for contraband in your lighthouse.'

'Indeed?' said Howard, almost listlessly. 'Well, perhaps it's as well. The strain on my wife, knowing that the body was in the tower, must have been almost insupportable. Mind you,' he added, with some show of animation, 'sometimes, in my more sadistic moments, I have felt that to live in close proximity with the corpse of her lover was only her just deserts. I am very fond of her, but I don't really think she has treated me very well.'

'What about your accident?' asked Laura, dreading a pause after this statement of the obvious.

'Oh, yes, my accident. Well, when the woman who was to look after the child and myself – shop and cook and clean, you know – heard that I was to search the coast and perhaps climb the rocks and so forth, she told me that, for the little boy's sake as well as my own, I ought to wear a life-jacket, especially as I had to confess that I have never learned to swim. The porter's story of the tides and the skeletons caused me to take this suggestion seriously, and there is no doubt in my mind that it saved my life.

'I left the boy in this woman's charge, and, having possessed myself of the life-jacket by purchasing it at a marine store on the quay at Braye Harbour, I returned to Longy Bay and armed with camera and binoculars – two items without which I never travel – I began to tour the coast. I spotted gannets, puffins and storm-petrels, and took some photographs, but of my real quarry there was no sign.

'I do not know how far I went. I believe the full coast walk is one of about eleven or twelve miles, so I certainly did not walk as far as that. At one point, however, a path seemed to lead from the cliff-top to the beach. This I took, but it proved to be precipitous and slippery. Moreover, as I descended, I disturbed more stones, one of which struck me on the head. I remember nothing more until I recovered consciousness and found myself in a ward in this hospital. They tell me that I must have fallen into the sea just at the turn of the tide, and was fortunate to have been swept clear of the rocks. Later, of course, the orders were that I should be moved into this single room where the police, no doubt, will interview me as soon as the hospital authorities give permission for them to do so.'

'Well, one thing,' said Laura, cheerfully, 'the fact that you were wearing a life-jacket rules out the suggestion that you were attempting suicide, and that's a big point in your favour. Another thing is that we're as certain as can be that Colin is no more guilty than you are of causing Ferrars' death.'

'Thank you,' said Howard. 'Your visit, and what you tell me, have done me more good than all the medicine I've been given. Thank you from the bottom of my heart.'

'He does get his language off the peg, doesn't he?' said Laura to Dame Beatrice, when they were on their way back to the airport. 'Rather a hero, though, on the whole, don't you think?'

'Neither he nor his son will be out of the wood, though,' said Dame Beatrice, employing the worn-out metaphor with an evil leer, 'until it is discovered who *did* kill Mr Ferrars. The interesting point, of course, is that the body, which, in addition to some injuries – possibly minor ones – which I thought might have been inflicted before death, had been killed by a heavy fall, yet the body was found lying on grass on the top of the cliff.'

'Somebody winched the body up from those flat rocks which run out from the base of the cliffs thereabouts and left it on the cliff-top,' said Laura.

'Yes, but who? – and why?' said Dame Beatrice. 'The murderer had only to leave the body on the flat rocks for the tide to take it away and for the Race to do the rest. I think I must speak to the fishermen who use those winches, or cranes, or whatever they choose to call them.'

CHAPTER NINETEEN

The Beginnings of a Synthesis

'... we heard voices already drawing near us ... along the shore.'

On Laura's return to the school she was met by Colin, who informed her that Fiona had left the lighthouse.

'The police have taken our home address. That's where she'll stay until we go to Jersey,' he said. 'I expect they'll tail her, of course, but they don't really suspect her of anything. It's the old man who's in for it, I'm afraid, and he's the last person on earth to have done such a thing. I'm perfectly certain it's that convict. I mean, it stands to reason.'

'Dame Beatrice is going to do a lot more sorting out there, and she has more cards up her sleeve, so she tells me. Be of good cheer,' advised Laura. 'What's going to happen to you next term?'

'I've no idea. I'd like to go to Kent with the school. The building will be near enough ready by the end of April, it seems. Mr Eastleigh has asked me to stay on, but, of course, if my old man's in the jug, I can't, and I shouldn't think the school would want me, anyway. What would *you* do in my case?'

'Keep my chin up and act as though everything was going to be all right.'

'Excellent advice,' said Dame Beatrice, when she heard of it. 'Mr Howard has given up his tenancy of the lighthouse and, as there is no clause in the lease against sub-letting, I have arranged that a large board, indicating that the place is to be let, fully furnished and with all modern conveniences, is to go up today.'

'What's the idea?'

'Time will show, child. Possibly a mackerel will attract a couple of sprats. One never knows.'

Laura worked it out.

'Fine!' she said. 'Count on me. Meanwhile, what's the procedure?'

'I have to await a report from the Inspector. Armed with what I was able to tell him about Mr Howard's part in the affair, he is going to confront the prisoner who escaped, and find out to what extent he is prepared to amend his story of what happened between his escape and his recapture.'

'How will that help us?'

'It will not help us to identify the murderer, of course, but it may help to confirm Mr Howard's story.'

'That won't help Mr Howard himself, though, will it?'

'I fear not, but anything which tends to clarify matters may prove of general help, and nobody, I venture to think, can do Mr Howard more harm than he has already done to himself Apart from the (to me) all-important theory that he is incapable of committing murder, the idiocy of his proceedings would be enough to persuade me of his innocence.'

'You mean that he himself has seen, as he told us, that the only sensible course, once he'd spotted the body, would have been to heave it over the cliff and let the rocks and the Race do the rest?'

'Or simply to have left it where he found it and do nothing about it at all. Masterly inactivity is the keynote of successful living. Queen Elizabeth knew that.'

'So what *do* we do?'

'As I have already indicated, we shall contact the fishermen who must have winched the body from the rocky ledge up to the cliff-top and left it there.'

'But why on earth should they have done that? Left it there, without a word to a soul, I mean.'

'We will ask them. I can guess the reason, but we must get it confirmed.'

There were half-a-dozen broad, clumsy rowing-boats lying on the cliff-top, and an inspection of them, and of the gear used for launching them, showed the method employed. The derrick worked on a swivel so that the boats, when they were landed, could be placed side by side. The method of raising and lowering them involved attaching two ropes, one at each end of the centre thwart, and then using the winch which was worked from the large cogwheel which possessed a handle. Between the slight promontory (a stretch of flat, bare rock) on which the boats were kept, and the next small headland, which was partly covered by short grass, lay a tiny inlet up which the incoming tide beat viciously, and from which the outgoing tide sucked noisily. Laura stood on the verge of this and gazed down at the deep and threatening water while she waited for Dame Beatrice, who had gone to call on the cottagers.

She had less than ten minutes to wait. From the nearest cottage, some five hundred yards away, three figures came into Laura's view. Recognising the smallest of these as Dame Beatrice, she went to meet them. Her employer's companions were a bearded man in a reefer jacket and a long-haired, tough-looking youth in a fisherman's jersey. Dame Beatrice introduced them.

'Mr John Dory and his son Frank. They are fishermen, and can tell us all that we want to know.'

'As to that, it isn't unlikely,' said the long-haired boy. His father spat to leeward and grunted. 'Us don't want to be mixed up in anything.'

'Keep ourselves to ourselves,' said his father.

'There is no reason why you should be mixed up in anything,' said Dame Beatrice mildly.

'That'll come to be seen.'

'Police matter, Dad,' said the boy. 'She'm in with the Inspector. I seen 'em. Better tell her what she want to know.'

'Of course you had,' said Laura. 'Come clean. It's the only plan.'

'First,' said Dame Beatrice, 'do you go fishing every day?'

The father and son were silent, and obviously intended to remain so.

'Well, do you?' demanded Laura.

'Maybe, and maybe not,' said the boy.

'What do you know about the body which lay up here near the boats?'

'Body?'

'Yes, the body that disappeared later. The body that somebody winched up from the flat rock below.'

'Don't know nothen about it,' said the son.

'Thought he were dead,' amended the father. 'Seen him a-laying down there, like you say, spread out like, as if he'd tumbled off the top here, and us thought he'd drownd if us left him. So us lowered boat, me at wheel, Frank in boat, and dragged him aboard and winched him up, and laid him out for dead. Us needn't have troubled ourselves, for dead he were.'

'You did not think of going for help, in case a doctor could have done something for him?'

The younger man made a sound between a laugh and a snort, expressive of sardonic amusement.

'No doctor couldn't have done nothen for him assept write out the sustificate,' he said. His father nodded and spat.

'Dead and gone, and a pretty mess he were in,' he committed himself to saying. 'Wasn't no point in wasting no time on a corpus. Us had plenty to do without that.'

'What, in that mist that came up?' asked Laura.

'Mist had cleared. Us wouldn't have spotted him else. 'Sides, nobody but a fool would have lowered a boat while we was all clogged and clobbered be a dirty great bank of fog like that out there,' said the boy. ' 'Course the mist had cleared, else us wouldn't have spotted him, would us?'

'So you left the body up here and went off to your fishing,' said Dame Beatrice. 'Did you remember it when you came back? Did you look for it again?'

'It were gone. Us reckoned his friends must have missed him, and come to look for him, and found him and tookened him away.'

'So what did you do then?'

The father spat. The son asked:

'What do you think? Wasn't no business of ourn. Didn't do nothen, of course. Keep ourselves to ourselves, us do.'

'So what becomes of the Inspector's kineaesthetic theory?' demanded Laura of Dame Beatrice. 'He and his fountain pens and typewriters! Has the Inspector been to see you?' she demanded, turning again to the fishermen.

'Ah, on and off. Us didn't tell him about the body, though,' replied the son.

'Why not?'

'Might have got ourself in trouble. Best not to have no deal-
ings with the police. Too nosey by half, they be.'

'Somebody did attack Ferrars and push him over the cliff,
then,' said Laura, as she and Dame Beatrice were walking back
to the car. 'What they said confirms that much, anyhow. It
doesn't get us any further forward. It teams up with Howard's
story, that's all. How did you persuade two such reluctant
heroes to come out to the cliff-top with you?'

'I allowed them to suppose that I was Mr Ferrars' grand-
mother – although perhaps to have represented myself as his
great-grandmother might have carried the laws of probability
a stage further.' She cackled harshly.

'All I can say is that you didn't seem to receive from them
the ready sympathy which one would have expected to be
forthcoming for an aged and interested relative. What happens
next, do you suppose?'

'We go to the police station in the hope that the Inspector
has returned from his visit to the prison and will have something interesting to tell us. After that, at the right state of the
tide, (if I have read the tide-tables correctly), there should be a
yellow half-moon, large and low, which should suit our purpose and, I have little doubt, the purposes of others, unknown
to us except by inference, and, so far, nameless.'

Knowing that, when her employer talked in this facetious
vein, sensible questions were useless, Laura observed that she
had always wanted to meet a faceless fiend, and wondered how
Manoel had felt when the mist had rolled in upon the island.

The police station had the appearance of a fortress. It was
guarded by an immense gatehouse, beyond which was a broad
gravel path and then the station proper, built round a hollow
square. Most of the building, the Inspector explained, was no
longer in use, for the place had originally housed the island
garrison, and was far too large for its present purpose.

He received them in a comfortable office next door to the
charge room and gave them chairs.

'Your story first, if you please, Dame Beatrice,' he said, 'and
then we'll see how mine fits on to it.'

Dame Beatrice described her interview with the fishermen,

and added that it tallied with the story told by Howard Spalding.

'It seems to me,' she said, 'either that someone took advantage of the thick sea-mist to push Mr Ferrars over the edge of the cliff, or that, during a struggle – for, according to the medical evidence, a struggle there must have been – Ferrars got too near the edge without realising it, and took a fatal step backwards.'

'In the latter case – in fact, in either case – wouldn't he have yelled out? Nobody has reported such a cry. Still, come to think of it, those fishermen's houses – old coastguard cottages they are – are stone-built with walls so thick they'd muffle any sound of that sort, except, perhaps, a woman's high-pitched scream – and even *that* might be mistaken for a sea-gull in these parts. Then, again, the sea makes such a thundering noise coming up against those rocks and into the fissures between them, that, again, most likely, a shout wouldn't be heard.'

'And Howard Spalding, of course, would have been at the top of the lighthouse in the lamp room,' put in Laura. 'If he'd been out on the gallery he might have heard something, but not behind that storm-proof glass.'

'Oh, well, if we haven't gained much, we haven't lost anything,' said the Inspector. 'Now for the chap Marsh. I saw him in the Governor's office, and he was shaking in his shoes, I can tell you. If *he* did it, it was done in a fit of panic, I should say. I started off by taking him over the story he told us before. I warned him that I had fresh evidence, and that his only chance was to tell me the truth. Of course, he swore he had, so then I began to read his statement over to him, with plenty of pauses where I thought he'd probably lied or left out a bit.

'My chief concern, of course, was to check his statement about the clothes. He'd already told us two different stories about how he got hold of them, so I thought there might be a third version. What I got out of him this time was very interesting, and again ties up remarkably well with what you got from Mr Spalding in the Jersey hospital.

'It seems that he did see the light in a downstairs room in the living-quarters of the lighthouse, and he *did* go up to the door, hoping to steal food and perhaps clothes. He was lying doggo in the shadow of the tower when he heard Mrs Spalding call out to her husband. He realised that she was frightened and that there only seemed to be two people in the place, so he stayed in hiding and tried, in his bone-headed way, to make plans. The next thing he knew was that, after a short time – about ten minutes, he reckons – a man came out carrying a pretty big bundle. When the man reached the door in that high, white-washed wall which surrounds the bungalow, Marsh saw, by the gas lamp over the entrance, that the bundle was a bundle of clothes. The braces were dangling, he said, so he knew they were a man's things.

'Well, the man set out at a pretty fast clip, as though he knew the ground pretty well, and where he was going, but he was easy to follow because he kept switching on an electric torch and shining it on the ground. Marsh decided to go along with him and, once they were away from the lighthouse, jump on his back, put in a spot of rough work and make off with the clothes. He admits all this.

'The only trouble was that he couldn't make up his mind in a hurry – he's a dim-witted chap, at the best, and all the various times he's been inside haven't sharpened up his initiative – so on they both went. Marsh got wind up, because he realised, from a row of lights, that they were approaching some houses. However, the chap (Spalding, of course) by-passed these, and the way got rougher and rougher, and Marsh dared not get too close in case the chap should hear him and drop the clothes and swing on him. Marsh is an undersized little rat, and more than a bit of a coward, and he had no idea what was the age of the man he was following, only that he was inches taller than himself.

'Well, at last this man stopped, flashed his torch round in a semi-circle, and then chucked the bundle away. Then he shone the torch again, downwards as before. Marsh chanced it, crawled nearer, and discovered that the man was on the edge of a quarry, but before Marsh could get to him he had turned and begun to trot, flashing his torch as he went. Marsh would have given anything, I should say, for the use of that torch, but he realised that he had only to stay where he was for the rest of the night, and then, as soon as it was light, he would be able to replace some, if not all, of his prison garb.

'He was not worried, except by the cold. He guessed that the first thing the police and the warders would do would be to cordon off the island from the mainland, but he thought that, with a change of clothes, he would sooner or later get by.'

'And he got the change of clothes,' said Laura. 'Still, there's one bit in this thrice-told tale which intrigues me. According to this last version, he did not go into the lighthouse tower, but stayed in shadow at the foot of it. How, then, did he know that there were six steps leading up to the bottom room, and how did he know that the room was locked?'

'We asked him about that, of course. Obviously he saw the steps when Spalding came down from the top. Spalding had a torch. The bit about his dropping it and Marsh picking it up is poppycock. He admits that now.'

'I don't think it *was* poppycock,' said Laura. 'I can't see him risking the climb down into that quarry in the dark. I think he *did* pick up Howard's torch. Howard is certain to have had a spare one. He's that kind of man. I don't think Marsh spent the night in the quarry, either. It would have been much too cold. I think he waited until Howard had gone, then used the purloined torch to light himself down into the quarry. I don't believe, either, that, with a suit of clothes dropped to him, so to speak, from heaven, he would have wasted any time before he got himself changed into them.'

'You may be right enough there, Mrs Gavin. It doesn't make any difference. We don't think that he could have committed the murder. I don't believe we ever thought so, and, of course, Spalding and the fishermen have let him out now, quite conclusively. Mr Ferrars was dead, and still clothed, when Spalding carried the body into the lighthouse. You also think, then, that Marsh, in Mr Ferrar's clothes, got food at one of those cottages, as he said he did? Again, what's the odds? So long as we know he's in the clear regarding Mr Ferrars' death, and so long as we've got him safely locked up again, well, san fairy ann, as they used to say, so far as Marsh is concerned.'

'There's just one thing I don't understand,' said Laura, 'and I do like to get things clear. Why did he go to the trouble of putting on all Ferrars' clothes except the shirt and pullover? We know about the socks and the tie.'

'Oh, that's an easy one. We found the shirt and pullover. Nice clothes. He meant to flog 'em when he got on to the mainland to get hold of a bit of dough. Wouldn't take a minute to pull 'em off in the Gents at the back of a pub when nobody else was about, and roll 'em up and offer 'em to a back-street slop-shop. All he'd do then would be to turn up the collar of the raincoat to hide the fact that he wasn't wearing a shirt.'

'You know it all,' said Laura. 'I don't think much of the Inspector's argument about the murder, though,' she added to Dame Beatrice, when they were on their way again. 'As I see it, Marsh was as likely as anybody else to tip Ferrars over the cliff. The rest of his story could still be true. I'll tell you one thing that does intrigue me, though. What about those six steps that lead up to the room where Howard put the body?'

'What about them?' asked Dame Beatrice.

'What do you suppose is underneath them? Never mind. Which is our next port of call?'

'There are one or two questions I should like to put to Mrs Spalding, when she is available, but possibly they won't be necessary.'

'You don't think *she* pushed Ferrars over the edge?'

'I do not think she knew he was standing on the edge. I should like to find out whether she knew that he intended to visit her that afternoon. If she did not, then her visit to her acquaintances in the other lighthouse would have been natural enough. If she expected him, then that visit seems a little out of character, does it not?'

'I should say she *didn't* expect him. Either that, or else she realised that Howard had got wise to the goings-on.'

'That is a likely explanation, and one which, it would seem, she had had no opportunity of giving to Mr Ferrars. I should say that it is certain he expected to see her that day, as he did not take his car. There is one other person, however, whom I really must contact, and that is Miss Nina Beverley. I only hope she has a complete alibi for the afternoon in question.'

'Fair enough. She must have been hopping mad with Ferrars by that time. First he'd ditched her for the Keggs girl, and then he went wolfing after Fiona Spalding. But if *she* did the pushing, it wouldn't have been murder, you know, but just an impulsive shove from a righteously indignant girl-friend.'

'I would accept that theory if a vicious attack had not been made on Mr Ferrars *before* he fell, or was pushed, over the edge of the cliff.'

Laura whistled.

'Oh, dear!' she said; and was silent until they reached the school. Here they were met in the entrance hall by Peters and Chorley. They advanced coyly, with nods and becks and wreathéd smiles, as Laura put it. She looked at them sternly. 'You shouldn't be here. You know it's forbidden to boys,' she admonished them.

'Special permission, Mrs Gavin,' said Peters. 'We wanted to speak to Dame Beatrice, please, Dame Beatrice, so would you mind very much, Mrs Gavin, please?'

Correctly assessing this as a signal of dismissal, Laura went to her room, leaving Dame Beatrice with the two children.

'Am I to be held to ransom?' asked Dame Beatrice, cackling.

'Oh, no, please, of course not. It's just that we wondered whether you could get Mrs Gavin along to an Assembly as soon as prep. is over. You see, we've had a whip-round for her leaving present. The prefects dunned everybody for a bob, which, of course, they can easily afford, because we all got our travel money this morning, and we asked Mrs Eastleigh to buy us some stockings for Mrs Gavin because she got us some for Miss Beverley, so we know she likes them, and, as we got double the money, we've got the nineteen and eleven ones, four pairs. We want to give them to her tonight, because there'll be too much hoo-ha in the morning. Now you,' said Peters, breaking off his oration and addressing Chorley.

'It's the Extra English boys,' said Chorley. 'She tried to teach us to spell.' He drew a box from his pocket. 'It's only scent. Mrs Eastleigh said to give a small bottle of the good, rather than a big bottle of the not-so-good, so this is it. It doesn't really look much, but it cost ten and six, so do you think she'll know that it's really good? And could you give it her privately?'

'I am positive that she would like you to give it to her yourselves,' said Dame Beatrice, 'and I am equally certain that she will much prefer it to a large bottle of the not-so-good.'

'Her form have got something for her, too,' went on the handsome, grave-faced Chorley. 'It's handkerchiefs. To put the scent on, you know.'

'You think of everything! She will be delighted and touched,' said Dame Beatrice, knowing that the last word, at least, was true.

'de Roseda wanted to give five pounds towards the stockings,' said Peters, 'but, of course, we clumped his head and told him not to get above himself, and took his bob, like everybody else.'

CHAPTER TWENTY

The Master of *Pronax*

'What were these villains after but money? What do they care for but money? For what would they risk their rascal carcasses but money?'

Miss Beverley, whose home address had been obtained from Mr Eastleigh, was 'doing the flowers' when Dame Beatrice and Laura called. She said she was glad to see them, and introduced her mother, a gay and fashionable forty-five-year-old in bell-bottom trousers and a printed silk house-coat.

'We have come,' said Dame Beatrice, 'upon a melancholy errand, I fear.'

'Oh, about poor Ronnie Ferrars. Yes, it was terribly sad,' observed Miss Beverley insincerely. 'What do you think really happened? It couldn't have been suicide, could it?'

'What makes you think of that as a possibility, I wonder?'

'Oh, I don't – not really. I mean, I shouldn't have thought he was the type. All the same, he was sort of dating up three of us, you know, and he may have felt he'd got himself in a bit of a muddle, don't you think?'

'As I had not the pleasure of his acquaintance, I could not undertake to say. At the time of his death he appears to have been paying his addresses to a Mrs Spalding. You knew about that, I think?'

'Oh, yes, I knew about that.'

'Personally, I think Nina was well out of the whole thing,' said her mother. 'I am only too thankful that she had dropped Ronald before there was all this scandal. At least she is not mixed up in it.'

'Actually, of course, Ronnie dropped *me*, dearest. Don't let's mince our words. And all for that common little June Keggs,' said Miss Beverley, on a vindictive note which, under the circumstances, was excusable.

'Oh, come now!' said Mrs Beverley. 'June was not really common – not *really*, darling. After all, you were girls together.'

'Well, her mamma was common. You can't deny that. Anyway, she had a nice facer – both of them did – when it was found out that Ronnie was stuck on this Mrs Whatname.'

'Ah, yes,' said Dame Beatrice. 'Did you know her?'

'No. I met her son when he first came to the school. That was just before I left, you know. I looked him over, but he wasn't my cup of tea. Terribly *young*, if you know what I mean.'

'Well, he isn't twenty yet,' said Laura, 'so being terribly young wasn't really his fault.'

Miss Beverley laughed.

'Anyway, what did you come here for?' she asked, with reassuring frankness.

'To ask whether you pushed Mr Ferrars over a cliff,' replied Dame Beatrice, with equal directness.

'Good gracious! You don't mean ...? *Did* somebody?

'We are inclined to think so. I represent the Home Office in the capacity of psychiatric adviser, and am working with the police over this affair. We are at the stage of eliminating those of Mr Ferrars' acquaintances who were living on the island at the time of his decease.'

'You can certainly eliminate Nina,' said Mrs Beverley, speaking very sharply indeed, 'and I may say that I consider you have forced your way into her home under false pretences. I'm afraid I must ask you to leave. We have nothing to do with anything unpleasant which may have happened, and I really cannot think ...'

'Hold your horses, dearest,' said her daughter. 'Nothing is gained by putting on a righteous indignation act.'

'Quite so,' agreed Dame Beatrice. 'I take it, Mrs Beverley, that you would prefer this enquiry to be conducted by me rather than by the police themselves, would you not?'

'Oh? Oh, well, if that is the alternative,' said Mrs Beverley, deflated by this hit below the belt, 'very well, then. Won't you sit down? Darling, ring the bell for some coffee.'

'Well, I think it's a case of *Pass, Beverley. All's well*, don't you?' asked Laura, when the interview was over. 'It should be easy enough to check her alibi.'

'Yes, indeed. A motor-car salesman is unlikely to have forgotten the sale of a new Mercedes-Benz, and, in any case, the transaction and date will have been recorded,' said Dame Beatrice. 'Moreover, London is sufficiently far from the island for two whole days to be considered reasonable for the journey and the purchase. I certainly think we may dismiss Miss Beverley from our minds.'

'Leaves us with the Spaldings, any one of them.'

'Mr Colin, because of the time factor, is the least likely, so long as we can establish that he did not use his father's car that day.'

'What about Fiona, the *femme fatale*?'

'Oh, I really cannot believe that Mrs Spalding would make a vicious attack on her lover, push him over a cliff and then calmly go out to tea. She is a nervous, hysterical woman. It would be entirely out of character for her to behave in such a way.'

'That leaves us with poor old Howard, whose conduct, to put it mildly, has been somewhat odd all along. But do you really think he would have had a fight with a much younger and stronger man, and come off best at that?'

'I think we may accept it that what he has done was done in what he thought were the interests of his son. I do not believe for an instant, though, that he is a murderer.'

'But that leaves us with X, and there simply isn't an X on the horizon.'

'I wonder?' said Dame Beatrice. 'It seems to me that, as nobody can be found who hated Mr Ferrars enough to murder him, then he was killed for some reason other than hatred.'

'You talk in riddles, as usual. What are you going to do about Colin's car?'

'Nothing in particular. As a matter of form, I shall ask Mr Heathers whether Mr Colin came back in it at the conclusion of the games period, but, if that were so, I think Mr Heathers would have mentioned it when I questioned him before.'

'Oh, yes, I suppose he would. He couldn't say whether Colin went out that afternoon, because he was in class, but he would

G*

certainly have seen him come back. He and his babes were
playing football on the front grass and gravel, and Colin was
certainly at school in time to get his boys washed and take them
in to tea.'

'Exactly.'

'What's our next *real* move, then?'

'To the lighthouse, to take up secret residence there. Be sure
that you mention it to nobody.'

'There won't be anybody to mention it to. The boys all went
off this morning, and the Staff all go this afternoon. But what's
the big idea?'

'I quote the late Mr Asquith. In the immediate future, however, nothing remains for us to do but to call at the school,
take leave of Mr and Mrs Eastleigh, and to allow it to be in-
ferred that we, too, are going home.'

'But what *is* this cloak-and-dagger stuff? Not that I'm not
all for it. It makes me feel about the same age as Hamish. Still,
I could bear to be put in the picture.'

'I will explain later. Of course, it may lead to nothing, but
I have hopes of high adventure.'

'What put that sort of idea into your head?'

'Oh, *Moonfleet*,' said Dame Beatrice.

'I see! Do you really think so?'

'I think that by this time it will be generally known that the
Spaldings have vacated the lighthouse. Moreover, you tell me
that tonight the full moon and the full tide will be coincident.'

'Once aboard the lugger . . . ! So now for pistols, black masks,
and down with Dan Maskell and all his works! Well, I never!'
said Laura. 'To think I should live to see this day! Won't
Hamish be sick when he hears of the fun we're having!'

In front of the disused lighthouse, which Laura and Dame
Beatrice approached at just after sunset that evening, a large
bill-board had been erected. It bore the information that the
place was to let, fully furnished, and gave Howard's home
address as the tenancy was still in his hands and he was still
under contract to pay the rent.

After she and Dame Beatrice had bidden farewell to the
Eastleighs, Laura had driven herself and her employer a con-

vincing twenty-five miles towards their home in Hampshire and then had doubled back, left the car at a garage for an unnecessary check-up and testing, hired another, and driven back to the island.

Laura had obtained the keys from Colin. She unlocked the door to the living-quarters, carried in luggage and the food they had purchased on the mainland, and then she climbed to the gallery, unslung her binoculars and studied the fast-fading scene long and earnestly and from all sides, before she descended to the bungalow.

'Better have some grub while we can still see what we're doing,' she said. 'Bread and cheese and burgundy. All right?'

It had been agreed that they would use no lighting except that given by Dame Beatrice's electric torch, and as soon as the early, simple supper was over, Laura took the torch into the base of the tower and to the room in which Ferrars' body had been found. Dame Beatrice followed, and received the torch from Laura while Laura pulled back the square of cocoa-matting which covered most of the circular stone floor.'

'Here we are,' she said. 'I thought as much. It's flush with the floor, though, and there's no ring-bolt or anything by which I can lift it up.' The trap-door was of wood. It had neither hinges nor handle. 'Pity we don't possess a crow-bar.'

'We might look about in the living-quarters for a chisel. That might do it,' suggested Dame Beatrice.

'I shouldn't think Howard's the sort of man to possess a tool-box, but we may as well go and see. I can't wait to find out whether there's brandy stashed away down below. When do you think the Inspector and his men will turn up?'

'Very soon now, but they will take no action until we flash the torch from the gallery. He agrees with me that to catch these smugglers red-handed is much the best way, because then there can be no argument about their guilt. If we knew exactly where they were likely to land the cargo, the police could catch them there, but we know neither the spot they will choose nor the means they have of getting the goods ashore.'

'I know what I should do. I should lower the stuff into a ship's boat, run it in under these cliffs, and use the fishermen's davits to winch it up.'

'That might be a feasible plan if it could be done in the dark.'

'The one thing that isn't possible. Much too dangerous, on a coast like this. They may try it by moonlight, though. That's what you're hoping, isn't it?'

'It is the Inspector's idea, not mine. I put to him my theory that Mr Ferrars' death was not a murder for revenge but of convenience. I think the smugglers, taking advantage of the mist on the afternoon when Mr Ferrars last came here, realised that he had seen something they did not wish him to see, or, possibly, that he was a threat to their safety in some other way.'

'And one or more of them clobbered him and then pitched him over the cliff? I suppose they thought the sea would wash him away. They must have had a big surprise when the boatmen winched him up.'

'I should not think they saw it happen. I think they came in with the mist and went out with it, too, having surveyed the scene and, possibly, tested the tackle.'

'But that means they had a confederate based on the island itself. One of the fishermen, do you think?'

'Oh, no. I think their confederate was Mr Ferrars himself.'

'*What?*' cried Laura. 'How on earth do you make that out? And, if you're right, why on earth should they kill him?'

'That we cannot tell for certain yet, but I have no doubt that all will be made clear in time. He must have done something to prejudice their safety, I should think.'

'Wanted to protect Fiona! That would be it! But you must have something to go on, if you think Ferrars was one of the smugglers.'

'Oh, I do not go as far as that, but I have a radical objection to things which do not make sense.'

'Such as my recognising a snapshot of Ferrars which is not a snapshot of Ferrars but a snapshot of a Mr Bunting?'

'Yes, indeed,' agreed Dame Beatrice, 'and also such a young man taking a five-mile walk to meet a woman who, he must have known perfectly well, would not be there when he arrived; such as another young man consenting to run a valuable boat all round the Channel Islands at a bad time of year to please a woman he had met only once before in his life...'

'Oh, Thorvald! But I paid him for his time and trouble.'

'Was it you who was so certain that Mr Howard had taken Manoel out to Les Ecrehous?'

'Well, no, it wasn't. You mean Thorvald himself had business on Les Ecrehous?'

'And with Pierre Logard, I have little doubt. Logard's appears to have been a very convenient boat, so far as Mr Howard and Manoel were concerned.'

'Well, of course, I know Les Ecrehous used to be a half-way house for smugglers, but I thought that was a long time ago.'

'It is always possible to revive a moribund industry, I suppose. Well, let us see whether we can find some implement with which to raise the flap of that cellar.'

The slipped into the living-quarters and, with the aid of the torch, made a search, but before they could find anything useful there was a stealthy sound outside.

'Get behind me,' whispered Dame Beatrice, 'and give me the torch. I have my little friend in my pocket.' Laura did as she was told, and stood with her back to the wall on the blind side of the door which led to the small yard. Dame Beatrice stepped behind the end of a Welsh dresser and, transferring the torch to her left hand, she drew from her deep skirt pocket a small but efficient revolver. Then she and Laura waited while somebody fumbled with the catch of the living-room window.

As the intruder dropped on to the floor, Dame Beatrice stepped out and shone the powerful torch full on him and observed, in her deep and beautiful voice:

'Stand still, sir. I am armed.'

'Good Lord! It's Thorvald!' exclaimed Laura. 'What on earth are *you* doing here?'

'I might ask the same question of *you*,' replied the young man, raising both hands in response to a slight motion made by Dame Beatrice with her weapon.

'So this is Mr Thorvald?' said Dame Beatrice. 'Pray close the window and be seated. You may lower your hands. I think we may be upon the same errand, but I shall continue to keep you covered. By the way, just to satisfy my secretary, who, I am glad to say, retains the fresh, enquiring mind of a youngish child, do you know how to raise the trap-door in the floor of the lighthouse tower? She thinks there may be some kegs of brandy concealed there.'

'I thought she drank whisky,' said Thorvald, who had carried out instructions and seated himself. 'By the way, it's all right to light the gas. It can't be seen from this room because of the high wall round the back yard. I suggest it because your torch is a bit too powerful for my eyes.'

'I am sorry about that. Later on, perhaps, when Laura has satisfied her curiosity. Can you help her?'

'Oh, yes. But there's nothing in the cellar at present. We're running the stuff ashore tonight, as you seem to have guessed. All you have to do to open the trap is to tap it fairly hard in the middle of the edge which faces towards the door. The gas poker there would do it, I should think. I generally stamp on it with the back edge of the heel of my shoe, but that might throw you off balance if you don't know how the thing works. The blow releases a spring, and then the thing works on the same principle as a jack-in-the-box. The lid flies up, and Bob's your uncle. But I assure you you'll find nothing but a long, low cellar, clean, I hope, but empty.'

'I'll take your word for it, then,' said Laura. 'You're one of the gang, are you? And Bunting *was* Ferrars. I suppose you know he's dead?'

'I saw in the papers that your chap Ferrars had been killed, but that wasn't Bunting. Couldn't have been, you know, Laura. Bunting was a yachtsman, not a schoolmaster. I've known him for nearly three years. I used to base *Pronax* in Jersey. It was his suggestion that she'd be much less conspicuous among the craft here.'

'More proof, then, that your Bunting and our Ferrars are one and the same.'

'Oh, nonsense! There couldn't be any connection. Now, look here, what's the drill? My gang will turn up all right, unless somebody tips them off. Are the rozzers all round this place?'

'They are. And if anybody tips your mates off, all I can say is that it had better not be you. Dame B. is a dead shot, and a woman of blood and iron, so *Ae toot an' ye're oot*, as the elder of the kirk said to the old lady with the ear-trumpet. Understand?'

'Only too well. But look, Laura, be reasonable. You can't expect me to shop Eric and Tony and the Louse.'

'The louse?'

'Our contact on the other side, Louis by name. I call him the Louse, because that's what he is. I wish we didn't have to use him, but we can't handle the French end without him. The other two...'

'Look,' said Laura, 'I don't give a damn for the contraband side of the business. I derive from a lawless, thieving ancestry. But I *am* out to get the murderer of Ronald Ferrars, and what it all boils down to is that he must have been a member of your gang. If you yourself get caught up in the works, well, that's your problem, so, if Dame B. will keep her little rod trained on your dangerously large target of a frame, I'd better be about my business.'

'You will need the torch,' said Dame Beatrice, 'so Mr Thorvald may now light the gas, and that should make him much more comfortable.'

CHAPTER TWENTY-ONE

The Island Lives up to its Name

'First she loomed before me like a blot of something
blacker than darkness . . .'
'. . . and that was the only sound excepting the swish of
the sea . . .'

A little worried at leaving her small, elderly (although indomitable) employer alone with the large and powerful Thorvald, Laura felt, however, that she had no option but to carry out the plan previously arranged with the Inspector. He and his men, by this time, would be hidden in the quarry and amid the humps and bumps on the westward side of the lighthouse, the opposite side from that on which the smugglers would be compelled to come in from the sea.

The Inspector had argued long and earnestly against having her and Dame Beatrice mix themselves up in the affair, but had found them adamant. Their basic argument was that to deplete the force which would have to face smugglers – and nobody knew how many of these there might be – by putting even one policeman on watch from the lighthouse gallery, would be a tactical error. As Laura argued, she on the gallery and Dame Beatrice in the bungalow could be in no possible danger of getting mixed up in any fighting which might take place. She clinched the matter by reminding him that he thought the whole thing probably a mare's nest, anyway, and had only consented to bring his men on the off-chance that she might be right and that an attempt would be made to land the contraband that night.

'They've probably been cruising about with the stuff ever since Ferrars was killed,' she had said in conclusion. 'They daren't put in to port to refuel, with that sort of cargo on board. They're bound to try to land it soon, and the moon and the tide are right for the night I've picked. Besides, they've no idea how much longer the lighthouse is going to be (as they think) empty.'

Reflecting on these words, she climbed to the lamp room, then, crouching low, she went out to the gallery rail and peered into the gloom.

The wind had risen and was blowing gustily. Already it was very cold up there in the open. Lights were appearing in the fishermen's cottages and, far off, she could see the lamps which marked the promenade of the mainland watering-place. Nearly half a mile from her eyrie, its great light flashing its code signal to shipping approaching the Race, was the modern lighthouse, and somewhere over in the same direction were the Inspector and his men, crouching in the hollows and probably cursing the cold.

Laura huddled into her sheepskin jacket and continued to strain her eyes against the darkness, but there was no sign of a ship. As the moon was not yet up, she thought it was safe to retreat into the lamp room out of the wind. She perched herself on the stool which Howard had left there, and from time to time she left shelter and peered over the rail again. Then the moon rose, but the clouds were heavy, dark and low, and, more often than not, they obscured it.

'Here's fun!' thought Laura. 'I may not be able to spot them coming in.'

'So why,' asked Dame Beatrice, laying aside her revolver, 'did you decide to visit Les Ecrehous?'

'I had a thing or two to clear up there. You see, when I got the tip from Bunting that the lighthouse was inhabited, I knew I'd got to get the grape-vine working so as to give our contacts the tip-off.'

'You left it rather late to do that, did you not?'

'Yes. *Pronax* had been laid up for repairs. Anyway, Mrs Gavin's little expedition turned out to be a godsend because it gave me a cast-iron reason for going over to the Channel Islands. I had an idea, you see, that the rozzers were on the alert.'

'I see. And then?'

'Honestly, I don't know any more, except that Eric and Tony

would never have taken any hand in murder.'

'How many people would have been aboard this ship you mentioned?'

'They had to keep day and night watches, of course. I was always on board *Pronax*, so Louse had a crew of six, including Eric and Tony. The drill was to run in as close as they could to the only cove on this island, then transfer the stuff bit by bit to *Pronax*, and then I would run her round to the fishermen's derrick, put up a signal and the chaps up top would winch the kegs up in a net and trundle them round here to the lighthouse. Local chaps, of course, and I'm not going to name them.'

'And how often did this happen?'

'Oh, about every two or three weeks, I think. I couldn't tell you exactly. Then, of course, these Spaldings rented the lighthouse and that rather spiked our guns. We didn't even know about them until we got the tip-off from Bunting.'

'That means Mr Ferrars.'

'I suppose so, yes.'

'Why did somebody kill him?'

'I couldn't hazard a guess. I mean, our lot – Tony and Eric and Bunting and myself – weren't out to double-cross the others. That would have been the only motive for killing one of us, so far as I can see, and that motive didn't exist.'

'Were your friends – those you call Eric and Tony – on board the ship?'

'Oh, yes. They had a quarter share each. The other half belonged to Louse.'

'What about Mr Ferrars?'

'So far as I know, his only share was the one-tenth interest in *Pronax*.'

'Did you ever have any difficulty in receiving payment for your part in these transactions?'

'None whatever. Louse, I've no doubt, would have liked to do me down, but he couldn't do without *Pronax*. She's well-known in every creek and harbour from Falmouth to Lowestoft, as well as in the Channel Islands, so no one ever suspected (so far as I know) that she was anything but what she appeared to be, the plaything of a comfortably-off yachtsman. When I

mentioned the rozzers, it was the ship they were beginning to
be interested in, not my boat.'

'Did you make your entire living in this way?'

'Good Lord, no! I'm in films. So's *Pronax*, when required.
It all helped with the camouflage. When she wasn't available,
Louse used his ship's tender, but he wasn't too keen on that.
It's only happened that way twice, when I was laid up for
repairs, but that's when the authorities began to get a bit
suspicious.'

'And when you were filming? What happened then?'

'Oh, when I was on location, Lilian handled *Pronax* for them.
She's as handy with the helm as I am, and has a great taste
for diddling the Customs ever since they soaked her at Liver-
pool for trying to smuggle cigars in from Las Palmas. As a
matter of fact, she's at the helm tonight. That's why I'm able
to be here. She'll clear off as soon as the stuff is landed. The
fishermen will take the chaps back to the ship. The locals help, as
I said, but Louse doesn't trust a soul, so he always comes ashore
with Eric and Tony to make sure there's no double cross.'

Suddenly, under the racing clouds and the intermittent moonlight, Laura spotted the ship. She knew it was the one she was
looking for. It carried no lights. All she saw, before the black
clouds blotted out the moon, was an even blacker shape on the
dark and sullen sea. The vessel was coming in on the tide and
had rounded the Point. She wondered whether the keeper on
duty on the lighthouse proper had seen it, too, and had logged
it as carrying no lights.

'It's a damn-silly game to play,' thought Laura, 'for the sake
of saving the duty on a few dozen kegs of brandy and a few
dozen pounds of tobacco. You've got to have moonlight, and
yet that's just what lays you open to being spotted.' She
turned her back on the ship, which was swallowed up by the
darkness once more, and switched on her torch. She waved it
from side to side as the signal she had agreed on with the
Inspector, and then went down to the living-quarters to find her
employer and the master of *Pronax* in the middle of a game of
chess with the tiny pocket-set which Thorvald had brought with
him.

'Thought I might have a long wait here on my own, you see,' he explained, 'so I wanted something to do. There are always problems one can work out on one's own, but a game against a notable opponent is very much better. Does your presence down here mean that the ship has been sighted?'

'It does,' said Laura, 'and I've given the police the signal. What, exactly, did you come here to do?'

'I thought we'd agreed that I came here to make certain the place was empty and to warn the gang if it was not.'

'Well, it isn't empty, and, if you attempt any signals, Dame B. will plug you.'

'There will be no need for anybody to plug me – not that I'd risk it, mind you. I'm sorry for Tony and Eric, if they get dropped on, but I suppose it will only mean a fine. But if Louse killed Bunting – Ferrars, I suppose I should say – then I'm as keen as you are to get him.'

'How many of the ship's company are likely to land and come here?' asked Dame Beatrice.

'Oh, as I said (I thought), Louse, Tony and Eric. We don't let the deckhands know where the hide-out is. It wouldn't do. They must know we're running contraband, but they get good pay and are willing to take the risks for the extra money.'

Laura said, 'There's somebody outside. In case it's the police, Thorvald, you'd better scram. Go into one of the bedrooms. They won't search the bungalow, but they may look in on Dame Beatrice and me. They know we're here.'

Thorvald, aware that the cargo could not possibly have been landed in so short a time after Laura's report that she had seen the ship, apparently decided that her advice was good. He tiptoed along the dark passage with one hand stretched out in front of him (to warn him of any obstacles which might be in his way) and the other groping along the wall to find a door-handle. Dame Beatrice parleyed in the entrance hall. He flattened himself against the wall to listen.

'Who is it?'

'Me. The sergeant, madam. We thought we saw a signal.'

'You did.' Dame Beatrice, who had picked up her revolver, let him in. 'The ship is standing off the island.'

'I see you've lit the gas, madam. Better have it out if they're close to hand. Perhaps, when you've turned it off, you and the other lady had better lock yourselves in. There's bound to be some unpleasantness with these customers when they realise we've caught 'em redhanded.'

'Is the Inspector with you?'

'No, madam. He's detained over the other side of the bridge.'

'What bridge?'

'Why, the road that's been built on the shingle to join us here to the mainland. Visitors call it a causeway, but on the island it's known as The Bridge. Being as we *are* an island, that's the rights of it.'

'Well, come in, sergeant.'

'No, thank you, madam. I only wanted to let you know we were on hand. I've got half-a-dozen men outside surrounding the place. The Inspector's plan is to let 'em bring the stuff right inside the tower. We'll take 'em with the goods actually on 'em, that way, and make sure, too, as they don't run off in the dark.'

'What has detained the Inspector? Not that he was at all convinced that they would be certain to land the contraband tonight.'

'A couple of bodies has detained him, madam. Murdered bodies, so the call came through. Bashed on the back of the head and chucked into the sea on the ebb, so the local police officer thinks. Of course, you can't rely on what our tides'll do. That's a chancy coast, that is. Matter of luck where anything might fetch up what's chucked in the sea off the island. There's double tides, you see, and a nasty swell all along our great old pebble bank. Why, the sea even sizes up the pebbles theirselves, let alone chucking out a couple of bodies as it don't fancy stowing away in Davy Jones' locker. You can't rely on the tides off that old bank of ours. Treacherous as a jealous woman, her be. Well, with your permission, I'll get my men in position. You won't forget to turn the gas out, will you? We mustn't risk it giving them a chance to smell a rat.'

'Let alone a rabbit,' said Laura. The sergeant caught his breath, and then spoke sternly.

'Us don't care to have they things mentioned on the island,' he said. 'That's very bad luck, that is. Best not forget that while you're here.'

Laura apologised, but was mystified. When the sergeant had gone, she said:

'What an odd superstition! By the way, it's a nuisance Thorvald had to be here when the sergeant came. Even if he's gone to earth in one of the bedrooms, he could have heard what was said. The sergeant has a fine, loud, carrying voice.'

'I can make certain that Thorvald does not go out by the door,' said Dame Beatrice, 'but if he decides to get out of the window . . .'

'He can't, except for this one. He's far too big. Have you got your little gat handy?'

'Yes, and my torch, too. You remain here. I will go and guard the outer door.'

'No need,' said Thorvald, from the doorway. 'I wasn't supposed to contact Louse. I shall be very glad to see him, all the same.' His tone was quiet and grim.

'Stay where you are,' said Dame Beatrice. She shone her torch on him. 'I have you covered. What is more . . .' she switched off the torch – 'my hearing is acute, and I share just one attribute with Mr Sherlock Holmes. I can see pretty well in the dark.'

'May I talk?' asked Thorvald.

'Yes, if you keep your voice down. But I know what you are going to ask me.'

'About those two chaps washed up on the ridge? You don't think, do you . . .?'

'That they may be your friends Eric and Tony? There are answers less likely, I fear.'

'They tipped me off Louse wanted to change the cargo. Dope, they thought. That's why I'm here – to see fair play.'

'So that's it,' said Laura. She pulled back the curtains which she had drawn. The moon, which, for the moment, had swum quite clear of the clouds, was high in the sky. Laura picked up a chair and placed it so that Dame Beatrice could be seated. She herself perched on the table. Thorvald reached out a long leg and hitched a small chair forward and seated himself composedly on it.

'Mind if I smoke?' he asked. Laura glanced at him, but could see little of his face, even as the match spurted.

'It will assist my aim when clouds cover the moon again,' said Dame Beatrice amiably. Laura also took out a cigarette. The time passed very slowly. The room became very cold. Because of the racing clouds, much lighter now, the moon appeared to be swimming in the sky and was seldom obscured.

'I'm going to light the gas fire. It will never be noticed,' said Laura, 'and it's getting dashed chilly in here.'

'A good idea,' said Dame Beatrice. 'Mr Thorvald, you may move away from that draughty doorway, but mind you continue to behave yourself.'

'I'll behave myself until Louse turns up,' said Thorvald, through his teeth. 'After that, I shan't behave myself at all.'

'And you may lay to that!' quoted Laura. The door was opened very quietly and the sergeant put his head in.

'All right, ladies?' he murmured. A cloud was passing over the moon. He missed Thorvald, who was in the shadows, away from the glow of the fire. 'I'd turn the key of this door, if I was you. I've just had the tip from one of my men. We're off!'

Dame Beatrice went over to the gas fire and turned it out, and they sat on, in the alternating moonlight and blackness, straining their ears. At first there was nothing to interpret. The silence, except for the slight sounds occasioned by their own breathing, seemed absolute. Then they heard the smugglers. There were hushed voices and then a creaking noise. Thorvald left his chair and crept to the door. Dame Beatrice fingered her revolver. Laura watched the moonlight on the wall above Thorvald's head. The sounds became louder, but were indeterminate. They ceased, and the voices took up again in the form of a low murmuring.

Thorvald crept up to Laura.

'Any moment now,' he whispered. 'As soon as the police take over, I shall nip out and do my stuff. I wonder how many journeys they'll have to make?'

'This one will be enough for the police,' Laura whispered back. 'Don't do anything stupid. You're in the clear, so far, and I'm not going to shop you.'

All sounds of activity from the smugglers ceased. It was clear that they had entered the base of the tower. Thorvald opened the door, peered out and listened. Then he stepped into the moonlight. Laura followed him and Dame Beatrice followed Laura. The next moment the dark figures of the sergeant and his men came in by the door in the wall which surrounded the yard.

'The big moment,' said Laura, writing the rest of the story to her friend Alice Boorman, 'came when the gendarmes had rounded up Louis and the two men with him just as they were in the act of opening up the cellar. There was no end of a kerfuffle and a lot of bad language, and then the police, two of them to each of the gang, came marching into the yard. That was when Thorvald stepped forward and did his stuff. Melodrama was no word for it.

' "Stop!" he shouts. "I want a word with that man!" '

'Well, you can imagine the effect. There was the moon, sailing along like the ghostly galleon Alfred Noyes compared it to, and there were the blaspheming captives, and there was Thorvald, standing up like one of his Viking ancestors, or a priestess of Isis, or someone, denouncing the whole lot of them and calling on heaven to witness that Louis the Louse had murdered three of his friends.

' "Where's Bunting?" he demands. "Where's Tony? Where's Eric? Why aren't Tony and Eric with you? I'll tell you why, you murdering runt of a half-breed!" ' (That's my polite interpretation of what he actually said.) ' "They're dead and cold, with the salt in their hair and their faces all nibbled by the fishes! They're lying out there on the shingle, with their eyes, that can't see any more, turned up to the sky and the moon. They're..." ' At this dramatic juncture the sergeant interrupts him. "I don't know who you are, sir," he says, "or what you're doing here, but it seems you might be in a position to help the Inspector identify a couple of corpses he's found on the beach."

'Well, that was the end of it, except for the explanation. It seems that this Louis had decided that to run brandy and tobacco was chicken-feed to the rake-off he could get by running dope and diamonds. Tony and Eric (identified without trouble by Thorvald – the fishes hadn't had time to nibble them, thank goodness) didn't object to the diamonds, but had jibbed at the dope, I fancy, so clumping them over the head and ditching them over the side had been cheaper than buying them out.

'As for Ferrars, he'd had a message to meet Louis on that cliff by the lighthouse. Apparently they'd found he visited there, and it came out (for the two deckhands turned Queen's Evidence on Louis) that suspicions had been aroused by the sight of Howard up on the lighthouse gallery with his field-glasses. They weren't to know that he was only looking for birds.

PS 'Mrs Croc. says her son will get poor old Howard off with a ten-pound fine for "failing to report a death". Knowing, as I do, the Machiavellian mind of Sir Ferdinand Lestrange, Q.C., I bet she's right. I hope so, anyway.'